Other books by this author

DISGRACED IN ALL OF KOALA BAY

By: Mark Lawson

But few could ride beside him when his blood was fairly up

-The Man from Snowy River,
Banjo Patterson, 1890

BALBOA
PRESS
A DIVISION OF HAY HOUSE

Balboa Press books may be ordered through booksellers or by contacting:

Balboa Press
A Division of Hay House
1663 Liberty Drive
Bloomington, IN 47403
www.balboapress.com.au
1 (877) 407-4847

Print information available on the last page.

ISBN: 978-1-5043-0611-9 (sc)
ISBN: 978-1-5043-0612-6 (e)

Balboa Press rev. date: 12/30/2016

Having left journalism after 38 years, I would like to dedicate this book to all those I shared the fun, and frustration, of journalism with over all that time.

Mark Lawson

I have added a few notes on various references that may puzzle non-Australian readers at the end of the book.

CHAPTER ONE

Miles Black walked several paces from his battered utility before he realised he had absent mindedly put on his hat when getting out of the vehicle. It was a broad-brimmed akubra scarred by work on his parents' stud in Victoria's high country. Back home he would have kept on walking, but he was wearing his dark, pin-striped suit, white shirt and red tie and he was in Sydney for an interview. A hat did not fit the picture. He went back and dropped it in the utility, and then had the usual trouble closing the passenger side door. Rust had eaten into the door catch which meant that the door had to be lifted and slammed at the same time to close properly. Apart from a second-hand computer and a few clothes left at a hostel, it was all Miles owned. He locked the door again and walked around to his interview.

The headquarters of the Bugle Newspaper Group was a long, two-storey brick building set back from a main road – a busy one – in one of Sydney's far northern suburbs. The building was built beside a natural, sharp drop in the ground, so that visitors could walk along a short footpath, past the modest sign saying 'Bugle Group', through double glass doors into the reception area at one end of the building without realising that they were on the first floor, which was reserved for administration and sales. The reporters were kept on the ground floor, well away from any visitors.

Having seen plenty of young reporters came and go the receptionist barely glanced at Miles. If she had looked a little longer she would have seen a well-built man in his early twenties of medium height, with sun tanned face and clear eyes. She might also have noticed a firm jaw and dark eyes and judged him "passable": and an even closer inspection would have revealed a hint of bow leg in his stance. He had, in fact, been brought up working with horses. As it was she checked her list and told him to wait, pointing to one of the green vinyl chairs by the wall. There was a stairway to the lower level on the other side of the entrance hall, which Miles thought led to both the reporters and the printing presses, for he knew the Bugle Group still did its own printing.

He killed time by inspecting a series of framed front pages of various Bugle Group newspapers set on the wall above the receptionist's head. He was too far away to read the stories on the pages but on one, for the *McCarrs Regional Bugle*, he could see the headline 'Residents flee' with a dramatic picture of burning forest beside it. Another for the *South Forest Bugle*, which serviced the suburb in which the Bugle Group headquarters stood, had the headline 'Local musos win through' with a picture of a school band with their instruments poised. There were plenty of front pages. For alone among the local newspaper groups the Bugle had refused to amalgamate its papers when the local councils were merged in Sydney many years previously.

Instead of the informal industry rule of one paper per local council, there were four for the City of McCarrs – the *McCarrs Regional Bugle*, the *South Forest Bugle*, the *Smith's Creek Bugle* and the *Brown Beach Bugle*. Instead of having one local paper for the City of Lovett Bay, the Bugle group had three and so on. This meant Bugle papers were tiny with two or perhaps even one, lone reporter, instead of the teams of reporters found elsewhere in Sydney.

Miles was aware of this history, having surfed through several web sites before making the long trip to the South Forest building, and was vaguely aware that a job with the Bugle group did not rate highly in journalism. However, his knowledge of the group's history, such as it was, did not solve the problem of the framed front pages he saw. A few were important stories but mostly they were routine. A life saved here, a new shopping centre opened there; and the local MP making a fuss about something else on another page. But why had those pages been framed? Much later he learned that they had all received awards for printing.

As Miles scanned the framed headlines he saw, out of the corner of his eye, a woman appear at the top of the stairs. She was a stern-looking woman perhaps in her 40s, wearing dark-rimmed glasses, and a dark blue dress. Her hair was swept up in a bun at the back that made her look older. This was Mrs. Bronwyn Forester.

"Miles Black?" she asked, in a tone suggesting she was about to make an arrest. Miles nodded. She gestured for him to follow, then walked back down the stairs without saying a word. The interviewee hesitated for a moment, wondering if he had actually been summoned – the women had been very abrupt – then trailed after her down the steps and through a set of double doors into what seemed to be the editorial room.

The building's architect had obviously been venting his feelings about journalism when he designed the room. It had no windows. One side was well below street level, thanks to the drop in the ground. On the other side was the main access corridor for the building with no windows in the internal wall between the corridor and the newsroom. It was possible to sit in the newsroom, and not know whether it was day or night, cloudy or bright outside. The interior designers played their part by installing green carpet and wood paneling which must have looked dated the moment it was installed, and gave it a pallid hue by fluorescent lighting.

To the left was a series of offices and meeting rooms, mostly unused. On the right the room had been divided into two sections by a panel and half glass partition. In the smaller area, closest to Miles, sat reporters, each behind a PC mounted on a narrow adjustable desk. They also had vinyl-topped desks which they mostly seemed to use to stack piles of papers and reports. As he walked in they were laughing over a shared joke.

On the other side of the partition were the sub-editors who set the stories into the paper and wrote the headlines. They were mostly a lot older than the reporters, more female and considerably more harassed. Keeping track of all the different stories - some stories ran across all titles, some in a sub group and some in just one - was a production nightmare, which should have been handed over to News Ltd or Fairfax long ago to be straightened out. However, the nightmare was kept going by the *Bugle Property News*, with pages and pages of glossy, expensive ads. Several web sites competed with it, but *BPN* still ruled because it got packaged with the local newspapers that were thrust through all the mailboxes find once a week.

On that visit all Miles saw was a group of sub-editors staring into battered PCs on desks scattered at random through their side of the room, with connecting data cables taped to the floor. No one looked up. The printers, who tended giant presses through a set of double doors at the far end of the room, wrestled with production problems as bad as those of the subs.

Miles was led to the far corner of this editorial cavern to the office of Justin Brock, editor-in-chief of the unholy mess. Bronwyn rapped on the door, looked in briefly then gestured for Miles to enter. Without a word she returned to her desk, a few paces from Brock's office, to brood on how life could be better.

Miles pushed the door open to find a man in his late fifties, of robust physique albeit with the beginnings of a pot belly despite frequent golf that gave him a healthy tan. His hair had long fallen away to silver side fringes, framing a round, youthful face that featured a long nose and two small, brown eyes. Those eyes could turn hard, but sparkled with charm when he chose, which was not often with staff members. Potential recruits were a different matter. Dressed in an open-necked business shirt and casual slacks, he looked like an executive who had come into the office on the weekend. His BMW was the only journalist's car allowed in the company car park at the back

"Miles is it?" said Justin getting out of chair to shake

hands, and gesturing at the chair in front of his desk. "Bronwyn's not great at announcing people. We're not formal around here." Miles glanced around the office. The main wall decoration was framed awards, one from the Law Society of Victoria for the best story on law for the year, another from a financial institution and another which appeared to be a legal document.

"It's a writ," said Justin noticing Miles gazing at the decoration. "Only one I got in my hand from twenty-five years on the metros. Guy who issued it went to jail just after, but it makes a nice memento."

"It does at that." replied Miles thinking that the mementoes and the book case, on which stood a cricket trophy of long ago, could do with a good dusting – and he was not one to notice dust.

"So you want to join our crew, do you Miles?" said the editor in chief leaning back in his leather chair.

"Yes, I do."

Justin took a sheaf of papers, which Miles recognised as his CV sent in by email, from the top of a stack on one corner of his desk. At the other corner was an identical tray which contained two envelopes. He wondered briefly about the two trays.

"From the bush, I see. You're from down south - Curriwong."

"Corryong."

"Yeah, right. Where is Corryong?"

"On the Murray Valley Highway, just short of the Kosciuszko National Park on the Vic side."

"Snowy River country! You're a real bushie!" Miles never saw why anyone from the city became so enthusiastic when he said where he was from. If they felt that way, why didn't they go out and live there?

"Can you muster cattle?'

"Matter o' fact, I can." Miles could well have added that Corryong was the home of Jack Riley, the stockman generally accepted as the original for Banjo Patterson's poem *The Man From Snowy River*, but did not. If he mentioned the poem city folk were likely to start loudly reciting what they remembered of it.

Justin smiled. "You talk like a bushie. Got a drawl there."

"So do your reporters have to talk fast?"

Justin dropped back in his chair, opened his mouth and shook his shook his head as his way of expressing mock astonishment. "Mate, I wish most of 'em w'd shut up and get out there and get stories. Never mind how fast they talk... Well, let's see," he glanced at the CV, "An ag science degree at a college in Albury. Ag science? Never had one of those before. Then you did two years on the *High Country Gazette*, part-time. Why didn't you get busy on a farm like every other bastard with an ag science degree?"

"I was. Had to help out with the family stud."

"A stud? Racehorses?"

Miles shook his head. "Not that sort of stud. We do stock and quarter horses for farms, mustering cattle; a few of what they call warmbloods for dressage and show events." The stud had briefly tried to breed racehorses with the only result being a big financial loss, which was part of the reason Miles had to help out. The other part was that his father had fallen ill.

"I see," Justin put the CV down and folded his hands

across his small pot belly. "So tell us Miles, what brings you to the Bugle Group?"

"The stud was in a bit o' trouble. Took the job on the *Gazette* to bring money in, any money, 'n liked it."

"Bitten by the newspaper bug, eh?"

"You could say that."

"Not a good bug to be bitten by Miles. Newspapers are dying. They don't pull in the readers like they use to and the advertisers are going elsewhere. Even the celebrity magazines who still have readers, are finding it tough. All that also comes with a complete lack of community respect. Every now and then some bunch of clowns or other run polls of community attitudes to the professions. In those journalists typically rate somewhere between used car salesmen and sex workers and, Miles mate, last poll like that I saw the sex workers were gaining. You're jumping onto a sinking, disregarded ship, Miles."

The high countryman shrugged. "So I get my feet wet."

Justin laughed. "Fortunately, a few bastards still read us because we get shoved through their mailboxes every week, along with a whacking great chunk of real estate ads for which the Dixon family," - the Bugle Group's owners who refused to sell to the big publishing houses - "curse every one of 'em, charge like wounded bulls. But we're a newspaper group just like the big ones are and that means the journos don't take orders from sales guys. We decide what's best for our readers. Gotit?"

"Sure."

"But you didn't have to come this far to get a

newspaper fix. There's a daily in Albury, right? Border Mail?"

"Yeah. Getting a junior spot there can be tough."

"Suppose. Or what about cross the state and try the Bendigo paper, or any one of the regionals. Must be a couple on this side of the border not so far from home. Let's see – there'd be a paper at Wagga or *The Canberra Times* maybe. That'd be tough too but worth a try and easier to step up into the metros if that's where you're aiming."

Miles shrugged. In fact, he had gone for interviews at the *Daily Advertiser* at Wagga Wagga, *The Goulburn Post* in Goulburn and the *Illawarra Mercury* at Wollongong, before winding up in Sydney. The editors of those papers had been good natured enough to see the blow-in from the bush at short notice but had no openings.

"Tight at the moment," was all he said.

Justin nodded. "It's tight all over, mate. Same on the wires and on newspapers and online, what there is of it that pays."

A disastrous turn in his private life had driven Miles away from high country with its clear skies and sweeping views, and forced him to fall back on his skills as a journalist - such as they were after a short time on a bush paper. But he had not fully realised, until he started his trip, just how difficult it was to get a job as a reporter without the editor owing his family a favor.

"See Miles," said Justin, "we do usually hire reporters from the bush or other suburbans. If we take anyone from metros or radio or anything like that they don't do the job. We deal in local stories, local personalities. Sometimes we might do courts or get a local robbery, or expose local councils for the thieving, corrupt bullshit artists that they are, but a lot of it is arranging pics for the school's Easter hat parade, and writing about car parking near the town mall. The metro guys don't want to do that stuff. You follow me, Miles?"

Miles did follow him. Among other things he had written about were the Corryong sewer system; a man who collected beer bottles; a shop keeper who had retired after 40 years on the job; and an interesting rubbish tip. He also knew all about arranging pics for the school Easter Hat Parade. In that respect, at least, The Bugle Group could have few terrors for him.

"If you're aiming high they can be pretty shitty jobs, but they can be what you make of it. Survive here for a while and you can do anything. I see the stuff you've been doing is the sort'a stuff we do around here." Jason picked up the resume and flipped through the copies of stories Miles had included. One story was of the man who collected bottles. Jason paused at it, snorted in an amused way and flipped on. "And you have a referee, who I remember from state rounds on *The Age* 20 years ago. I wondered where Rod had got to." Miles was interested to hear this. He had gotten on very well with Rod – a journalist of the old school who had insisted on lecturing his junior staff at length on reporting – but he had left so quickly that the parting had not been amicable. "Rod says you're an operator."

"Nah, not me."

"I wouldn't admit to it either, but he says you should be given a go and if he says so then I'll give you what you wish for – a job here - but it's a tough one. You know Koala Bay?"

"Suburb around here."

Justin nodded. "Most remote office we've got, about half an hour's drive north of here. Mate, it's almost in bloody Newcastle. Some of our reporters work out of this office, but if the paper's area is too far away the reporters work out of satellite offices. Koala Bay is a satellite office. It'll be you and another reporter, Angela, and some admin people and such but you won't have much to do with them. You'll like the office – just a couple of streets down from the beach."

"So Angela is the editor?"

"No, she's a junior – less experience than you - but she doesn't report to you."

Miles had never expected to be made editor, but he was naturally curious. "Then who's editor?"

"I'm the closest you've got. Listen, if you want the job I'll take you through to Evelyn who'll be your sub and she'll explain how our system works. The money is poor – you get J3 at our rate." (Miles was not quite sure what that meant, but suspected he would not be paid very much. His suspicions were later confirmed.) "We pay a car allowance but we don't pay for mobile phones." He put particular emphasis on the word don't. "But I gotta rush this. If you want it the job is yours from Monday."

"Happy to be aboard."

"Good, good! And I expect some stories from up there. The woman you're replacing, Jan, was hopeless." He said the last word with force. "She's been there a month and she's getting out before I can sack her. What

we do is not all dull stuff, but Jan didn't get anything."
He handed Miles the latest issue of the Koala Bay Bugle, the first issue he had ever set eyes on. The front cover featured a group of school girls who had done a walk against hunger, and a lead story about the local MP having planted trees on the foreshore. Miles blinked and read the story again. Even the High Country Gazette had never been reduced to that sort of desperation. He flicked through the rest of the paper. There were no news stories worthy of the name.

"Did you speak to Jan?"

"Tried a couple of times but she always called back after I was gone."

Somewhere in the back of Miles' mind a warning bell sounded, but when you want a job warning bells are easy to ignore.

CHAPTER TWO

The local media organ that spoke with a voice like thunder to the inhabitants of Koala Bay, the *Koala Bay Bugle*, was in a cramped set of rooms in a nondescript, red-brick building above a bargain shoe store a few steps away from the commercial centre's main drag. A block east was Surf Road, the beach car park and a large surf lifesaving club of crumbling concrete. The club looked out on a fine white surf beach and small bay, Koala Bay, skirted with trees and guarded by two rocky promontories. The first settlers had found the bay area covered by trees which provided food for a substantial community of koalas, but now the only koala to be found in the area was in the name.

Going the other way, west, from the thriving commercial centre was several kilometres of suburbia where the news-hungry readers of the *Bugle* lived. Mostly isolated from the general sweep of Sydney suburbia by tracts of bush that had been spared from the developers, Koala Bay was a quiet and prosperous community.

Any visitor to the community's newspaper who opened the street door, as Miles did on that first day, found a set of narrow and steep wooden stairs which went up to a shared corridor. On one side of the corridor was an insurance broker, and on the other was the *Bugle's* grim offices. There was more of the Bugle Group's trade mark green carpet and wood paneling, but the chairs were several steps closer to a junk yard and the desks looked like old-fashioned, half-sized kitchen tables badly painted a light brown.

On that first day Miles entered from the front door, rather than via the rear stairs which led to the building car park (not that he was allowed to use the car park, but it also led to a back street where parking was free). On the front desk in the first room was Kelly, a very young girl who was good looking in a washed-out sort of way, with red-streaked blonde hair. Her main topic of conversation, as Miles soon found out, was her boyfriend. Kelly introduced him to the office manager, Ros (short for Rosalind), who grinned inanely at him. She was a short, plump, plain women with a mop of curly, reddish-brown hair and flat, brown eyes. In season and out she wore tweed-pattern dresses and a succession of plain shirts of varying shades.

"Hope you're better than the last one," she said, without any preliminaries. "Other one was a real pain. A real whinger."

"Um, right!" said Miles, remembering Justin saying he would not have much to do with the admin staff. Ros led him off on a tour of the office. She gestured at one very large room indicating that it was her private office, then showed him a cramped room adjacent to the reception room, in which sat Kate, who sold the advertising. She had greying hair and a permanently worried look but flashed Miles a nice smile. Then he was led to an ex-storeroom into which, in defiance of fire regulations, had been crammed two elderly desks for the reporters, separated by an equally old filing cabinet. The cabinet was topped by a printer which printed from the bog-standard PCs on each desk. The right-hand desk, furthest from the room's single, tiny window had obviously been vacated, bar a couple of anonymous stacks of documents, a computer, and a stained off-white phone with a headset.

The room already had an occupant. At the left-hand desk, nearest the window, sat a blonde girl wearing earphones attached to a music player on her desk. She had been typing away but as they came in, she stopped typing to wave her hands around in the air, apparently in time with the music. Ros tapped her on the shoulder. She turned, taking off her headphones and flicking her long, blonde hair in a way that Miles found distracting. Her long hair framed a narrow, oval face with high cheek bones and dazzling blue eyes.

"This is Angela who you'll be working with," said Ros, "She's a real treasure."

"I'm Miles," said Miles, putting on his best winning smile and holding out his hand.

Her blue eyes rested on him for a split second, her lips twitched in what may have been a smile and she touched the proffered hand. Then she turned away and started to put her earphones back on. Miles was taken aback.

"You have any stories for me?" said Ros. Reluctantly Angela let her earphones drop and even went so far as stopping her player, before handing over two sheets of paper, with tiny stories on them. Ros read both items with apparent concentration, and handed them back. "They seem alright."

Miles wondered what was going on.

"I see all stories, Miles."

"You do?" Miles was astonished by this.

"I do," said Ros in a decided voice. "And keep the door open, and I don't want anything hung up on the walls in here."

Miles had wondered why the room had looked bare. The directive was so ridiculous that it even distracted him from the question of Ros seeing stories. "Why not?"

"It'll spoil the look of the place."

Miles laughed out loud, to Ros's obvious puzzlement.

"In this hole? Ros, this is a store room in need of paint. Couple of posters might lift the place."

"Excuse me, I've seen the Mayor sit in that chair," she pointed indignantly to the one other item of furniture in the room, besides the reporter's desks, chairs and the filing cabinet – an orange plastic chair wedged under the narrow window beside Angela. Anyone who wanted to use it would have to squeeze by Angela and then move a stack of past issues of the *Koala Beach Bugle* onto the floor. "I won't have him staring at pictures of rock stars and half-naked women."

"Ros if he's in that chair he's already in a store room down the back. Why don't we use that big office up the front for interviews. We'll have more room and we can put posters up here."

"That's my office, thank you very much," snapped Ros. "I can't have reporters cluttering it up. Important business is done in there." She turned and left muttering about whingers.

"Nice people in the city," said Miles half to himself and half to Angela who had condescended to listen, hoping that Ros might allow posters to be hung on the wall. He turned and realised that she was reaching out to start her player again. "Just before you start the music again…"

"I have a boyfriend."

"Don't doubt it, but I wanted to find out stuff about the newspaper on which we both work," he emphasised the last few words, "if you have time". She half shrugged and quarter-smiled, as if to imply that she really knew what Miles was up to but did not start the player. "Like, when is deadline day?"

"What day?"

"When do we have to get our stories in to Eve?" Justin had introduced him to the sub editor, who also happened to be chief sub editor, but she had been in a hurry to finish work on another paper and there had been no time to ask about basic production details.

"Who? – oh – um, dunno. I just write 'em and send 'em."

"I see," said Miles. "Well, what sort'a stories do you write?"

Another half shrug. "Stuff that comes in. Stuff from council. Go to the cops on Monday."

"As in today?"

"Uh huh!"

"Did you get anything?"

"Anything what?"

"Stories. Stuff to write for the paper."

"Go in about half an hour. Never get anything much. They take me into their tea room and have coffee – all the cops and detectives sometimes too, 'cept the woman detective."

Miles was sure this was the case. "So if you get anything from this cosy talk with the cops, when do you have to put it into the system?"

"Before lunch."

"So I guess the deadline's Monday lunchtime. A lot of stories have to be done by Friday to keep the subs quiet about copy flow."

"Guess so!"

She was plainly tiring of this conversation. Being the shrewd country lad that he was Miles had already made a fair estimate of Angela's worth as a reporter. He had also come to the regretful conclusion that they were unlikely to ever be soul mates, but he still wanted a few snippets of information from her.

"Before you get back to your music; the stuff you showed Ros, do you mind if I have a look too?"

She handed them over.

"These are community notices," said Miles. "Why did Ros want to see them? Justin never said anything about someone up here vetting stories?"

"She's office manager."

"So – does that mean she gets to vet community notices, or anything else? Does she write anything?"

Another half shrug and another puzzled look. "Don't think she writes."

"So how do ya reckon the Bears will do?"

"The who?"

"The local football team. In this community notice you've printed out for Ros you've said they've got a pre-season match Saturday week against a Newcastle team." Miles turned the notice in question around to show her. "It says 'Koala Beach Bears' and 'Match', and since the football season's starting soon I guess it's a football team."

Angela looked at him blankly, both hands on her ear phones ready to put them back on. "I don't follow football."

Miles sighed and put the notices back on her desk, then turned to his own. He switched on his computer to find that there was nothing to find out about it. He looked at the paper's website, which allowed users to look at that week's front page stories. That was about all the group had in the way of a library system. His first call was to the South Forest head office to ask about Ros. He got to Bronwyn.

"Yes Miles," said Bronwyn, in a resigned voice.

"Is Justin there?"

"He's in a meeting, what do you want?"

On his first day in a new job, Miles bit back a sharp reply.

"Well, I need to talk to him. The office manager here is saying she has to vet stories."

"That's right. She does."

"She does?"

"You heard me."

"Look, I really need to hear this from Justin."

"Well, I'm telling you that's the procedure there. Ros has a position of authority. She's trying to build the place up so she needs to check the stories."

"How can checking the stories help her to do that?"

"That's not for you to ask. That's the way it is."

"Justin never mentioned any of this to me. I was told I report to him and my stories are to go to Eve."

"She's the sub editor."

"I know that! And I know Justin's the editor in chief, but he never said anything about Ros."

"I just told you who she is, she's your boss. You have to do what she says."

"Look, I need to hear this from Justin. He said I wouldn't have anything to do with admin here. Have him call me."

"It's not going to change."

"Then he'll tell me that. Have him call me."

Miles then called Eve.

"Listen, what's the deal with Ros up here?"

"Oh, she and Jan were always arguing. Ros was always telling her not to run stories."

"And did she run them or not?"

"Sorry, I dunno.. all I know is that the stories she sent were weak. We always had to use stuff from the other papers as leads. Never had anything good. Every time I said something she complained about Ros, but I didn't take it very far. You don't get time to talk much with the reporters in this job. One paper after another, you know how it is. But I don't think she was very good."

"What does Justin say about this?"

"Umm.. I don't see Justin much. We handle a lot of papers here. Why don't you try Ellen at Lovett Bay? I think she and Jan use to talk a lot."

The *Lovett Bay Bugle* served the patch of suburb adjacent to Koala Beach and also had its own editorial office. As it was a much bigger paper and its area included the Lovett City council chambers – the headquarters of the local government area that also included Koala Bay - it had three journalists, including a trainee. Ellen took about half an hour to return the call and proved to be a cheerful person with an obvious Kiwi accent.

"So you've found out about Ros have you?" she said when Miles explained the problem.

"I dunno if I've found out anything yet. How come she's looking at stories."

"She use to drive Jan mad the way she was always checking her stories. She'd even get into her system at night and Jan'd come in, in the morning and find comments on her stories. She only stayed a few weeks because of Ros."

"So is Ros entitled to look at the stories? What does Justin say about this?"

"Justin agrees, so Jan said."

"He does? It's a strange arrangement?"

"It certainly is?"

"Does your office manager look at stories?"

"No way – we don't really have one anyway, the sales manager and receptionist split that job between them."

"Then why here?"

"I don't know, but I do know that Ros is the managing director's sister."

"WHAT!"

"Have you spoken to Justin?"

"Left a message. He hasn't gotten back to me. All I got was Bronwyn insisting that Ros has authority over stories."

"Jan tried for weeks to speak to Justin I know that. She was almost going to try the union."

"But she didn't?"

"Her boyfriend got a job in Perth and she decided it was easier to move with him than keep arguing with Ros."

"So she never got to speak directly to Justin?"

"Don't think so."

"Hmm, okay. Do you speak to him?"

"Try to avoid it. The only time you ever hear from him it's trouble and if I want something like more staff, even replacement staff, resources, pay rises, I don't get them so I've given up asking. I was told it use to take a full union strike to get a pay rise at the group but no-one's a member of the union now so no strikes."

"Just what a boy from the bush wants to here."

They talked on for a time, then Jan said, "Why don't you come up here for the usual few drinks afterwards on a Friday. That's just after deadline for us; we go half a day earlier than you. A few of the journos from South Forest come up, so you can talk about this stuff."

"Sounds good, see you then."

In short order Miles called the other two group titles adjacent to his own, including the *South Forest Bugle,* where he encountered Tom. All the other reporters he had spoken to where roughly in his age group but Tom, to judge from the timbre of his voice, was closer to retirement age than Miles was to his 21st birthday. He was also a well-educated man with a keen eye for the ridiculous.

"I've never heard of that one," said Tom. "The Bugle Group do some strange things, and hire some strange people – there was a reporter years ago who use to expose himself out of the back window of one of the offices."

"WHAT!" Miles was not sure he wanted to be told that.

"The other reporter on the paper only found out about it when the police came. He was a Baptist too."

"The one exposing himself or the other one?"

"The flasher. Anyway, I've never heard of an office manager looking at stories. But then the Bugle Group is such an odd place because no one checks on what's happening in the branch offices, least of all Justin. So people out there can do anything."

"'cept expose themselves."

Tom chuckled. "Except expose themselves out the back window."

After speaking to Tom, Miles sat for a few moments looking out of the tiny window for a few moments, wondering what he had got himself into. Angela still had her ear phones on and was still typing heaven knew what – Miles suspected email. He turned back to his computer and phone.

CHAPTER THREE

Miles' main task in the next few days to come, his main task of every week, was to find a story which could be used as a lead story for the *Koala Bay Bugle*. While Miles was looking for a lead, he also needed a few more stories plus pictures for inside, although that was much less of a problem. Interviews with returned exchange students; a high–spirited lady who had been 60 years with the Red Cross; a man with a genuinely interesting collection of antique cars and residents complaining about a noisy air conditioner in a nearby supermarket, were all grist for the local media mill. But none of those relatively small doings would be acceptable for the lead story itself.

In his first calls Miles made contact with Lovett council. The council itself was covered by the Lovett Bay journalists but the council press officer occasionally dealt directly with the *Koala Bay Bugle*. He was happy to hear from Miles, but could not point to much that week apart from a few events which belonged in community notices. There was an ambulance station and a fire station in Koala Bay, but all their recent calls had been outside the area. What about the surf lifesaving club on the foreshore? They had nothing and, in any case, summer was over, but they would keep Miles in mind. The local chamber of commerce had little to say, while the Rotary Club president had a great deal to say but none of it was worth repeating. The local branch of the State Emergency Service was involved in a fundraising, as was a drop-in youth coffee shop in the main mall down the road. Miles thought he could throw a little publicity their way, but the stories were not going to be candidates for the front.

Unusually, there were two state Members of Parliament for his area, as the boundary between the two electorates neatly bisected the Koala Bay Bugle's circulation area. The southern-most of these two electorates was a Liberal but the northern-most was held for Labor by a strong local member, David Lindley. His electorate was shown in the maps printed in newspapers around election time as an island of red amongst a sea of blue north of Sydney Habour. The press secretaries of both of these MPs wanted to be Miles new best friends. Lindley took the trouble to call him personally to spruik a press release about housing for the elderly in the area. The release said there should be more accommodation for the elderly, and that inspired Miles sufficiently to ring two nursing homes in the area. Both said their waiting lists were always long but their length had not changed in years; in fact, if anything, they had shortened; but there could always be more accommodation for the elderly. Hmm! All that could be stretched to a "crisis" in housing for the elderly, but he instinctively recognised the story as 'a bit thin', and went on looking.

At one point Miles got up to look in the filing

cabinet, earning a glare from Angela. She had finally taken off her music earphones, only to replace them with a phone headset to make what were obviously personal calls. Miles found these calls wearing. Angela had a penetrating voice, the tiny office had a tendency to echo and the conversations were inane.

"Well, that's what I told him," she would say. "He didn't! He didn't! That arsehole! Tell him where to get off! … New person's a guy." (This was said in a particularly scornful voice.) "… You guys coming out with us? Dunno…. Maybe we c'd go into town – that new place. No, I see him tomorrow…" And so on, and on. Miles suspected it would be even more mind numbing to hear both sides of the conversation but at least Angela's phone chats drove him to put his own phone headset back on to make more calls.

Before going back to his phone that time, Miles found that the filing cabinet was full of reports. There were several Lovett Council annual reports; a state government drainage report of two years ago and a Federal Government report on the development of north-eastern Sydney of five years ago, which had a useful map. He found some blutack in a drawer and put it up, earning another glare from Angela.

"We're not supposed to put anything on the walls," she said, after finishing her call.

"Uh huh," said Miles without moving or looking at the offending map, "so you've got any stories on this week?"

"How do you mean?"

"Well, you know, things you can write up to put in the paper. The stories that keep the ads apart. Any interviews lined up; anything happening you know about?"

"I told you," she said, after an exasperated pause. "I just do the stuff that comes in."

"Okay, then," said Miles patiently, "how does the stuff come in? Where do you get it?"

Angela gave him the look she reserved for total idiot-loser, drop kicks who tried to pick her up in pubs and gestured vaguely at the screen. "There's an inbox with stuff that comes in."

"Do I have access to it?"

"Guess - Jan did.. I got on really well with Jan."

"Glad to hear it." He was soon flicking down a list of not very interesting statements, notices, releases and occasional letters to the editor. One was about the beautiful trees in the park, another was commenting on a story of two weeks ago. There were several reports from sports clubs on games they had played. It was the job of the secretary of the local clubs to write a report about the club's latest game. Sometimes they did.

"What do we do with the sports reports?"

"Send to the subs."

"Just send it back out again as an email?"

"Uh huh!"

"What about this item on hiring an extra parking officer?"

"What about it?"

"Its not worth much at the mo – they're just hiring an extra parking officer. But it c'd be worth more. Everyone hates parking fines, so maybe they're hiring an extra officer because they're getting lots of fines, or maybe they're not getting enough? How many officers have they got for this area?"

"Didn't it just say they're hiring someone," said Angela.

"So we ring 'em up. Why are they hiring the extra person? It may be worth something.'

Angela shrugged, evidently unconvinced. "Maybe."

"I'll do it if you want."

"I'll do it!" she said quickly, shooting Miles another look of withering contempt. She never did anything about the parking attendants story. He discovered it later in a corner of the paper, almost unchanged except for Eve having rewriten the lead paragraph. He later rang up himself to discover that a story about a general increase in controlled parking areas requiring an additional inspector had been prominent a month previously in the other two papers for the City of Lovett – the *Lovett Bay Bugle* and *Cowan Creek Bugle* - but not in the *Koala Bay Bugle*. Well, it had been worth a shot.

At lunch time he walked to the mall and bought lunch; a hot dog and chips. His tastes were not refined, but on his salary lunch would be sandwiches made up at home, when he found a place to live. He was living in a hostel but the room rate even for that down market establishment was eating into his savings at an alarming rate. On an impulse he walked the two blocks to the park behind the beach and sat on a bench to eat.

Although it was almost winter the sky was clear and blue and the sun bright enough on the broad, rolling Tasman to make Miles squint against the glare. He wished that he had brought sunglasses. A stiff, cold, offshore wind forced him to wrestle with the sheets of the *Sydney Morning Herald* he had saved for lunchtime reading, after eating he watched a container ship float south on its way to the Botany terminals. As a high country man born and bred he had not often seen white beaches and the sea, but he thought he could get used to them. On the way back he lingered for a moment in the mall, which had a distinct colonial feel of sandstone combined with wide verandahs and big shop windows. There were a few, more modern buildings down side streets. In all, it was a nice beachside suburb.

"Not such a bad place to work," thought Miles, "if it wasn't for Angela and Ros." That thought reminded him that Justin had not called him back.

Back at the office there was no message from Justin but there was a young women sitting in his chair, legs crossed. She had long, dark hair, wore tight jeans and T-shirt and carried a camera. She raised one eyebrow when she saw Miles, eyeing him speculatively, then smiled. Miles thought that he liked the legs.

"Hi, I'm the photographer, got any pictures for me?" she said, cheerily, lifting her camera as proof that she was the paper's photographer.

"Emma, is it?"

"That's the one."

Emma was shared between the three Lovet papers, which meant that she maintained a work schedule that would make metro paper photographers call their union. She moved around a lot, dropping into the Bugle offices as the mood took her and digitally processing her pictures at the South Forest building. Miles sat on the corner of the desk. Angela had her earphones on and was firing off email messages; ignoring them.

"Just down from the country, someone said."

"That's right."

"From Orange myself."

"That's big smoke where I come from."

"Round here it counts as country, let me tell you. So you've already met Angela," she waved her hand slightly to indicate Angela - Miles got the impression that the wave also indicated what she thought of his fellow reporter.

"I've met you, now I've met all the important people."

"Of course! First time in a big city?"

"Been to Melbourne a few times."

"Sydney's different."

"Oh I dunno. Bit faster. Weather's nicer, so far anyway."

"Bring your family up here?"

"Just me. Got a horse back home with my folks, if that's any help."

"Miles – I'm going to ask you this - did you and the horse split up?"

Miles considered this for a second, nodding his head sagely. "We'd grown apart and I think she understood that. My sister's riding her."

"Well, listen Miles, when you get over this horse breakup thing, I'm engaged myself, but I've got single girlfriends who are always telling me there are no single men around."

"Sounds good. Interesting women have interesting friends."

She slapped his leg playfully. "Ooooh! Country charm. Okay, I'll see what I can arrange."

"Do I have to tell 'em about the horse?"

She looked at him seriously for a moment. "Miles, these are city girls, they may not understand about the horse. But listen, have you got any piccies for me?"

"Been on the phone a bit; got a couple. Do I just tell you?"

"I'd really like the form filled out." She indicated a pad of photographer request forms in the corner of his desk. "Or you can just do it on the form on the system and email me. I c'n check my messages on the road."

"Sure. How many pics do they usually want?"

"Four or five keeps 'em happy. Get below that and you have to start thinking of something. Ring around the schools to see if they're doing stuff.. you know."

"I know," said Miles. As it was more convenient at that time to write out the requests, he wrote on the request pad while Emma waited.

"That SES guy again," she said of the second request, "I could open an exhibition with the pics I've taken of that man."

"Umm, well, you don't have to have him; it's just a fund raising thing. Get 'em to get someone else."

"Think I will."

"I dunno if Angela's got anything. You could ask her?"

Emma rolled her eyes to indicate what she thought of that idea. Angela, for her part, had continued to listen on her ear phones and type emails the entire time the photographer had been there. "I won't worry, I think," said Emma, "she's more important things on her mind. Getting on well with her are we?"

"No."

"What about Ros?" she said lowering her voice to a whisper. "Get on with her do you?"

"Nope!"

"Miles, those are just the right answers to give to me," she said. "We're going to be great friends." She took a business card out of the small purse she wore on a long strap around her shoulder and handed it to him. "My mobile number and email address is there."

"How long have you been working for Bugle group?" Emma was the first colleague he had met who had not been frantically busy or plainly contemptuous of him.

"'Bout a year. I was a junior accountant in a suburban practice before that."

Miles looked at her with renewed interest. He was not sure he had met an accountant before. For that matter he had not met a full-time photographer before. The editor of his previous paper had also doubled as the photographer.

"Thought there'd be more money in accountancy."

"At a price, Miley. I was bored solid. I did a course and pushed my way in here."

After a few minutes she looked at her watch, squeezed past him with a "Ciao", leaving a hint of perfume, and left Miles alone with Angela. With a sigh he went back to the phone.

Although he had some experience as a reporter, this was Miles' first time alone with a newspaper, and that meant he had to find a lead by himself - Angela did not count - in a place he had never been before. He made calls. One local councillor who represented the Koala

Bay area in Lovett City council was overseas, the other did not return Miles' calls. The local community radio station had little to say for itself, and a community health centre could offer only a picture story. And so it went on. There were a few more glitches than might be found in any other editorial office. Miles came in on Tuesday to find the map he had stuck on the wall ripped down and a note from Ros.

"Miles – don't put things on the wall. Your files are password protected. I can't get in. See me with the password.'

He had no intention of giving out passwords to anyone. He put the map back up and called Justin to ask why he had not returned his call of yesterday, to have an almost identical exchange with Bronwyn. On Wednesday morning, the same thing happened, except that the map was beginning to look a bit tattered. By this time Miles knew a bit more about the community on which he had to report and went out to meet people twice. But he still had only the housing for the aged story, at a stretch, for the front. He was beginning to worry. Also, Justin still had not called him back.

He rang Bronwyn. "So is he in?"

"Who's in Miles?"

"Who do you think I mean! Justin. He still hasn't called me back."

"Don't take that tone with me. I told you what the message was."

"Look, I need to speak to him about it. No other office manager in the group has authority like that."

"Yes they do."

"No they don't."

"They do."

"They don't! I rang up the other offices. No one else does it. All the copy goes straight to the subs. Ask Justin to call me back."

The result of that exchange was not to make Bronwyn realise that she could be wrong, but to make her furious that she had been contradicted by a mere journalist – a junior who obviously knew nothing! A few moments later Miles received an email from Justin which had been copied to Ros.

Miles – Ros has complete authority there, including over editorial staff. Please do exactly as she says.

Miles sent back his own email.

Justin – very odd arrangement. I have left messages to call me, please call back one of your own reporters to discuss this.

Now exceedingly puzzled, Miles went back to the phone. In succeeding weeks, when he got into the rhythm of his weekly round, the first part of the week would be for features and the second part for news, but for that first week he was all over the place and still without a lead. Angela, for her part, never seemed to finish her irritating phone conversations.

"That drop kick! … Well, whadda you expect…. I told her, see a doctor.. Bullshit! .. No, bullshit! She just doesn't listen… So, you doing anything tonight?"

On Thursday, after leaving him another message about being unable to see his stories on his PC Ros poked her head in the door to ask, with a smile, whether he had any stories for her to look at. Miles had heard her laughing on the phone a few times during the week, but otherwise had not spoken to her. Despite her office being a few paces away from his desk, she had not troubled herself to visit someone she saw as a highly unimportant junior.

"Justin still hasn't called me back about that," said Miles, taking off his phone headset and swiveling around to look at her.

"Call you back about what?"

"About letting you look at stories."

Ros gaped at him with a look between stunned bewilderment and horror.

"But I'm the office manager."

"So?"

"But.. that's what office managers do in newspapers."

"What is it around here! Bonwyn also had this idea and its wrong. If the group allowed office managers to look at stories they would be alone, but they don't... I rang up the other offices." He added the last part hurriedly as her mouth opened to contradict him. She shut it with a snap and glared at him. "It's unusual anywhere."

This was not strictly accurate. In small magazines anything can happen. But it was certainly true for the Bugle Group. In any case, as the Bugle Group management could add little value to stories about aged care and foreshore regulations in Koala Bay, it was better that they be able to plead ignorance. Miles knew something of this; Ros knew nothing.

"Now look you!" said Ros, her voice rising. Miles felt his own anger rise to match Ros's own. "You've been told. You got an email."

"It's gonna take more than email. If they do things differently here then Justin should tell me about it, personally. When I took this job he said I wouldn't have anything to do with admin."

"Do you know who my brother is?"

"Sure I do, but if you've got such influence round here then don't argue with me, get – Justin – to – pick – up – a – phone – and – tell – me – what's - happening." He emphasised those last few words by pausing between each word and pointing downwards with his forefinger.

She crossed her arms. "It's not going to change."

"You mean the copy still goes through to the subs."

"No, I get control – that's not going to change."

"Ros – mate - have – him – call – me." With that, he swung back to his desk. Ros glared at his back for a moment then stalked off.

Angela, who had taken off her ear phones, for once, to listen to his exchange with Ros, with a hint of bewilderment in her clear blue eyes, made one of her few remarks to him.

"You know, I don't think she likes you."

"Nah! You think? Ros and I are the best o'mates. We're gunna be going out soon."

She puzzled over this for a moment, shook her head and went back to her music.

Later in the day, after Angela had gone and just as Miles was about to steal away the phone rang. The voice on the other end was deep, educated and assured.

"It's Jim Charles here."

"Yes? What can I do for you?"

"I'm the managing director."

"Right! You are too." Mr Charles – the only person

in the group that rated a mister - ran the place for the Dixon family.

"Glad you agree."

"It's my first week."

"So I understand. Up from the country I believe?" Miles told Mr Charles where he was from. "Yes.. ummm, Rosalind.."

"Your sister."

".. My sister has called to ask me to ask you to let her see stories."

"Ask me or tell me?"

Mr. Charles hesitated. "Well, I am asking you. You see, I give Ros some leeway up there in forming the strategic direction of the paper and, to be honest, I never saw the reason why management couldn't have some say in stories."

Miles was not going to argue that point with the managing director, on his first week, but he had thought of a way to side step the whole issue. "That's a big issue Mr. Charles, but it's not up to me to argue it. I'm not even really editor of the paper. Justin's editor in chief and he should tell me these things. I've been trying to get him on the phone since Ros told me of this arrangement and it's still no show. You don't happen to know where he is? I'd like to talk to him."

"Well no, I don't know where he is right now."

Miles thought that at the mention of Justin's name some of Mr. Charles's assurance melted away.

"I need to talk to him. Is that too much to ask to get your own editor in chief on the phone?"

"No, I suppose not. Look, all I'm asking is that Ros look at the stories."

"Look?" said Miles, scenting a loophole. "Just look? I mean, it's not as if she adds value She just blocks stories – made some of the past issues flat and tame. Hurt the paper if anything."

"All I'm saying is let her look."

Miles sighed. "Is it just a question of letting her see what's in the paper before it comes out?"

"That's right, and she can always make suggestions."

"Suggestions?"

"Yes, suggestions. Managers should always be able to make suggestions about the direction and tone of newspapers."

Miles did not agree or, at least, he might have been more agreeable, if the manager concerned had shown that she was knew what she was doing. Rather than try to explore this with the managing director he contented himself with a non-committal "hmm!"

"So we are agreed?"

"I've really got to talk to Justin about this."

"Well.. any assistance you can give me in this matter would be greatly appreciated."

Miles thought there was a faint note of pleading in the voice.

"Sure," he said, hesitantly.

"Good, very good, well I must go now."

After Mr. Charles had hung up Miles sat staring at the screen saving pattern on his PC for a few seconds then printed out the stories he had written so far from the copies in his sent items file, walked through to Ros's spacious office, slapped them on her desk without looking at her or saying a word and then left. Walking out to the car he wondered if the wire services were now hiring.

CHAPTER FOUR

When Miles came in the next morning he found, on his PC keyboard, the pile of story print outs he had dropped on Ros's desk last night, with a note attached. It read -

Miles – you must be more polite! I won't have papers thrown on my desk like that. It is disrespectful. See my comments. One story banned. Also need two stories done.

Miles glanced through the small pile. On a few of the pages, Ros had attempted copy editing. The one she had banned was an innocuous story about a new president for the community radio station – the previous one had died in office, mourned by all – which might get above page five on such a slow news week. She had scrawled "no - not an advertiser" across the front, and slashed two lines down it. A few paragraphs in two other stories had been inexplicably crossed out. Ros's suggested stories were a feature on a panel beater, and another on a planned council industrial park. Miles was sure that sending the subs a story on a panel beater without some sort of justification for it would quickly earn him a call enquiring what on God's green earth he thought he was doing up there. The industrial park was a possibility. What was happening with that? After noting all this with mild interest, Miles dropped the pile in his waste paper bin. He looked at the discarded pile for a moment, thinking that act had been satisfying, then he picked up the papers up and stuck them in one of his desk drawers. There was a chance Ros might see it and call her brother, before the paper came out. After all, he had done exactly as the managing director asked and shown the stories to Ros for her comments. Those comments he had given as much consideration as he thought they deserved. Instinctively he had chosen a strategy of passive resistance – unkind people might call it obstruction - to bizarre directives from higher management.

There was another item on his desk. The map had been ripped down again and another note scrawled across it, in red texta.

This has become annoying. Stop it!

He might have to concede defeat on that issue. He rolled the map up and threw it so that it lodged behind the printer on the filing cabinet, earning Miles his first glare for the day from Angela, who was in the middle of one of her irritating conversations.

"Nah, just someone chucking things around," she told the other party.

The phone rang. Was this a lead? No, it was from the sub, Eve. She had begun to look through the copy. Most of the paper was sub-edited and laid out on Friday afternoon, with a few details to be sorted out on

Monday. It was waiting in the resident's mailbox when they arrived home from work on Tuesday.

"Stories seem better Miles, so you got rid of that woman you were talking about?"

"Ros. Nope! She's still around, causing me misery. Has Justin been in this week?"

"Yeah, he's been around. I've seen him on the floor."

"I've called him every day this week about Ros. He never gets back to me."

"Yeah?... He's not the hardest worker I've seen. Never does anything for you," there was a certain bitter edge in that last remark, "but he doesn't ignore calls".

"I've even had Jim Charles ring me up, asking me to let her see copy."

"What?" Eve was silent for one shocked moment. "What does Justin have to say about that?"

"I've been trying to talk to him all week. He just doesn't return my calls. If you see him around, can you ask him why he hasn't returned my calls."

"Sure Miles, I can do that. You usually have to leave a message with Bronwyn, you know, if you just leave a message with her..."

"I've been leaving messages all week," snapped Miles, "it doesn't work. Grab him when you see him and ask him what the problem is about returning calls. Don't leave messages and expect anything to happen."

"All right – all right, don't get testy with me. As soon as I see him, I'll grab him. In the mean-time what do you want to lead – anything I've seen so far?"

"Nope. I'm keeping back one in case I have to stretch it, but I'm still hoping."

"Okay, so what about the sports star? I haven't seen that yet."

"The what?"

"The sports star. Each paper has some sports star; just some local who's doing well at sports. You let it run for about eight pars, if you can get that far. Longer is okay. Weren't you told about this?"

"Not a word." Miles had wondered about the sports coverage, but he had assumed, incorrectly, that someone would tell him what he had to do before the matter became urgent.

"No one's told you anything?"

"Seems not."

"Well, I suppose this week we can make do with the Lovett Bay star. She's pretty good. Just remember it for next week."

"Sure."

Miles had barely hung up when Ros poked her head through the door. "You saw the stuff I left last night?"

"Uh huh."

Her face was neutral, expressionless, but in her eyes there was a glint of battle. She was expecting a fight.

"You have any questions for me?"

"Nope!"

"Any comments on the stuff I left?" Her eyes flicked over the desk, looking for the pile of stories she had left there.

"Nope!"

"Humph! Always had to put my foot down with Jan. You're not going to argue about my decisions?"

"Nope!"

Ros was baffled over this. She had figured Miles

for a fighter. Then her eyes flicked to where the map had been, but where there were now only faint blu tack marks, and smiled slightly. "Well, that's a pleasant change. Makes my job a lot easier. If I can help you with any of the stories, let me know."

"Sure!"

With any luck Ros would not work out she was being ignored until Tuesday morning when the paper reached the Koala Bay office. Then he would point out that her brother had said nothing about her having control, just the right to make comments. If that did not work then even Justin might get involved. Miles was an 'operator', as his first editor had told Justin. He turned back to his phone and PC.

Later that day, just before lunch, someone rang up to tell Miles where he could find what he had been searching for all that week – angry residents. In one of its committee meetings, Lovett Council had declared that it would transform Mudlark Ave, on which the angry residents lived, from a cul-de-sac into a through road. As matters stood Mudlark Ave, on the outskirts of suburban Koala Bay, ran from a feeder road for several hundred metres before petering out in scrub. A few hundred metres further on, through the scrub, was a housing development which could only be reached by a circuitous tour through narrow side streets to the North and West. Council wanted to extend the broader Mudlark Ave to make a simple, direct route to the development. The builders would be happy and, much more importantly, the consumers who took up residence in the new development would be happy to have a direct route out to the Koala Beach shopping centre. Those consumers would also be Lovett City voters. Everybody was happy with the change, except for the residents of Mudlark Ave. They did not want their quiet cul-de-sac changed into a through road. A soulless council was destroying their way of life. They wanted their say. Miles would give it to them.

The president of the recently formed Mudlark Ave Action Group (MAAG), one Kenny Grover, who had rung Miles, agreed to meet him on the street to explain. A beefy, red-faced man he greeted the reporter dressed in an open necked shirt, green jumper and slacks, looking as if he had just stepped out from behind a store counter. In fact, he had - a hardware store down in the shopping centre. His wife, Alison, a hefty blonde women popped out of her house early in the interview, curious about why her husband was standing in the street in mid-afternoon, and stayed to add her authority to the interview. That meant she echoed everything her husband said.

"Look at this, I ask you, look at this," Grover said, pointing to Mudlark Ave. Miles saw a street like any other in the area - except that it was not a through road - lined with modest but solid brick houses with above ground swimming pools in the back gardens. The one difference was that there were rather more trees in the distance. It was a nice, quiet if not particularly affluent neighborhood, at some risk of bushfire during summer. But if council was to have its way, so Miles was given to understand, this nice life would be ruined; the aged and children would be subject to extreme risk. All because the road could be used by through traffic.

"We'll have trucks running down here all hours…," said Mr. Grover

"Trucks at all hours..," said Mrs. Grover.

"Children play on this street all the time," said Mr. Grover.

"Children out here all the time," said Mrs. Grover.

"Then there'll be cars always going through... there'll be traffic all the time."

"Traffic all the time.."

"And the fumes. There's Mrs. Simpson at number 16 – she's quite elderly.."

"Quite elderly poor thing."

"And all the families along here with children."

"Lots of children…"

"Sure," said Miles, "but don't all the other streets in the area have through traffic with those problems."

"Not with trucks going to this development," said Mr. Grover.

"Yes, there're the trucks.."

"And the fumes."

"The fumes.."

"We've found studies connecting truck fumes to cancer.."

"Ooh, they cause cancer.."

"But when the development goes ahead, won't the trucks have to come in some how?" asked Miles. "Won't they then have to come in from the North?"

Grover shrugged. "Don't have the development.

"We don't want the development.."

"We're here, we don't need other new houses here. Turn the place into a park and a wildlife sanctuary."

"Yes, a park and a sanctuary."

"But won't the park and sanctuary need an access point? Your street seems like an obvious access point. Won't you have plenty of traffic then, and people parking in the street all day?"

Miles remembered reading about an American editor of an aliens ate my baby-style tabloid who had warned his reporters against asking too many questions of sources. But he could not help occasionally picking at a story. Fortunately, the Grovers had a ready answer.

"They can come in from the north like they do now."

"Yes, the north.."

"They've already got the cars coming in there."

"You've spoken to council about this?"

"They won't do anything for us. The councilor Nick Gouter" (this was the councilor overseas) "told us the approvals were all done before any of us even came here. Well, we didn't know about any approvals."

"We didn't know.."

"And someone's making real money selling the development."

"Yes, selling the development.."

"Here we are, our lifestyle's been adversely affected; our risk of disease has been increased and there's people out there making money.."

"Yes, money.."

Miles dutifully wrote this down. Residents could be relied on to object to anything new - roads being opened, roads being closed, toilet blocks, infant welfare centers (too much traffic), council depots or half way houses for the mentally handicapped, or anything else at all. Sometimes the complaints were justified; sometimes not; but angry residents always made for a story.

Excusing himself from the exhausting statement-chorus double act that was the Grovers, Miles drove back to the office. He had a lead. It was not much of a lead, but it was better than many of the stories he had done in the country. Now he had to ring council for its response and organise a picture. As it happened, Emma dropped by just after he had returned.

"Got anything for me, Miley," she said from the door of the news cubby hole (it was not big enough to be called a news 'room').

"Got angry residents."

"Oh okay – what are they angry about, Miley?" He told her. "So I have to get this Grover guy on the street, looking angry."

"Yep. Ya know. Grrr!" Miles barred his teeth as if he was snarling. He was not the type of reporter that took his own stories very seriously.

Emma giggled. "I see. Grrr!" She barred her own teeth in a pretend snarl. "So I get Grover and his missus to go Grrrr!"

"Yep, they're angry."

She giggled again. "Housewarming at my place in a few weeks Miley. Lots of girls."

"I'm there - just gimme a date."

"Just don't mention this horse break-up thing, Miley."

"Don't mention horses romantically. Gottit!"

"Be charming and suave."

"Where I come from, it's all suave."

"That's what the guys round my way use to say, Miley, and I'm marrying a Sydney guy." With that she departed, leaving Miles alone with Angela in the midst of one of her lengthy, inane telephone conversations.

Two minutes after 4pm the next day, Friday, Miles was waiting by Justin's car in the car park at the South Forest office. An attempt to get in to see Justin unannounced had been angrily rebuffed by Bronwyn so, after glad handing the subs, he had posted himself by Justin's BMW. Just to be sure, he was standing by the driver's side front door. Justin soon came out in no very good mood, carrying his keys in one hand and a small, tattered brown leather briefcase in the other. He stopped short when he saw one of his reporters standing by his car.

"Miles?" The charm of the interview had been replaced by a hard tone. He was not used to finding one of his reporters standing by his car. "What are you doing here?" He walked forward until he was standing in front of Miles. The car beside Justin's had gone so they had space for confrontation.

"I've been trying to catch up with you," said Miles. "I've been leaving messages all this week. You've trouble picking up the phone?"

"I didn't get any messages," he said, exasperated. "Eve was telling me earlier that you'd been trying to call. I haven't seen anything. Just leave the messages with Bronwyn."

"I've left every message with Bronwyn."

"Yeah?" He shrugged. "I'll speak to her on Monday. Miles, mate, you're in my way. I'm done with this shit heap for the weekend."

Miles did not move but he was taken aback.

"You didn't say anything about the place being a shit heap in the interview."

"Miles, mate, it was an interview. I wanted you to go up to that smaller pile of shit up the road. You think I like nurse-maiding a crowd of wannabes and metro rejects? You think that listening to them whine about not having stuff, and getting paid fuck-all to write about fiftieth wedding anniversaries makes me want to stay here?"

"Thanks very much. I love you, too."

"Yeah, right. So whadda ya want anyway? Can't it wait until Monday."

"It's about Ros wanting to see stories."

Justin's mouth gaped open. "Is that what this is about? That fucking women is up to her old tricks. I told Jimmy to shift her somewhere, anywhere she can't get in the way. I don't give a shit who's sister she is. She doesn't get her nose into editorial and that's flat."

"I even had Jim Charles ring me about her."

"Shit! Jim's up to his old tricks too. Whaddid he say?"

"He asked me to let her look; to consult."

The editor in chief shook his head emphatically. "She doesn't consult about anything. She writes reports on the titles which I just chuck away. If Jim rings again, just tell him to ring me. His sister doesn't exist as far as you're concerned. Now get outta the way, I'm late for the weekend."

Having got what he wanted, Miles moved away from the car door and Justin got in.

"I even had Bronwyn tell me that I had to take orders from Ros," he said quickly, just before Justin slammed the car door. "I GOT AN EMAIL FROM YOU," he yelled through the glass.

Justin rolled down the window. "If it's not one thing it's another," he muttered. In fact, it was the only crisis he had been handed all day. "Ohhh, she's a mate of Ros, and she has access to the editor's inbox. I'll talk to her too - on Monday. Watch your toes Miles!"

The editor in chief drove off, tyres crunching on stones, leaving Miles shaking his head over his first, strange week at the Bugle group. But the week was not over yet, he was due for end of week drinks at the offices of the Lovett Bay Bugle.

CHAPTER FIVE

The Lovett Bay Bugle had a larger office than its Koala Bay counterpart and was a shop front on the busy main drag, instead of a one-floor walk-up down a side street. Otherwise the basic layout was the same - a receptionist at the front, two sales people and an office manager behind her and then, in a cramped area beyond, the newspaper's three reporters, who were still there filing their last stories to meet deadline.

There was Ellen - cheerful, personable blonde - who sounded even more like a Kiwi in person than on the phone. She was getting rid of some emails from the subs at South Forest, where the Lovett Bay Bugle was being bedded down. The other reporter was Karen, a thin, intense women who wore no makeup, had her brown hair cut short, and wore round framed glasses. She had aboriginal artifacts on her desk and her first act on meeting Miles was to hand him a pamphlet about an aboriginal rights group weekend workshop. Her boyfriend, a young, bearded activist with an environmental group, came in just after Miles to perch on the edge of Karen's desk. Being a little earlier, Miles had taken the newsroom's single free chair.

"Are there any aboriginal groups near here?" asked

Miles after glancing at the pamphlet, more in hope of a story than through any political interest.

"All massacred and driven away long ago, mate," said the boyfriend.

Miles put the pamphlet in his pocket. "What about a group for oppressed journalists?"

Karen smiled slightly. "Union, I suppose. Are you a member?"

As a matter of fact, Miles was; he had thought it advisable to join when he was looking for work. At that point the third reporter, a dark complexioned, dark-eyed trainee called Nathan got off the phone.

"Pleased to meet you," said Nathan, "getting lots of stories here. Lots of hot stories."

"Glad to hear it! You must've had a better news week than I did."

"Lots of hot stories… Speaking of things hot, how's Angela?"

Karen made a sound that was somewhere between a sniff and a click of her tongue. Her boyfriend just grinned.

"Good, I guess."

"She coming tonight?"

"Don't reckon."

"She was here a few weeks back with some guy. Oh man, is she hot!"

"Uh huh!" Having no wish to talk about his colleague Miles changed the subject. "What are these hot stories you've got?"

"Hot stories mate, real hot."

"Like what?"

Before Nathan could answer the receptionist called

from the front, "inspectors, Nate". The trainee shot out from behind the desk with, as the old police reports put it, the speed of a thousand gazelles, and sprinted across the carpet scattering bits of paper. He came back a few minutes later.

"Damn!" he said. "those bastards! Eighty bucks for parking out there. I could have gone to dinner on that." He sat down behind his desk and slammed his biro down on a stack of council proceedings on his desk, to demonstrate his feelings.

"You park out the front?" said Miles, "when it's a clearway after four? Why don't you just make it a rule to park out the back, or round the side street like I did. Almost the same distance to walk."

"You just walk through the laneway," said Karen.

"I'm not walking through a laneway," said Nathan, obviously disgusted at the suggestion.

This last statement was so ridiculous that Miles looked at Karen for an explanation. That reporter caught his glance and, by way of explanation, lifted her shoulders slightly and flicked her eyes upwards.

"The rest of us have to. If I'd known I could walk through the back lane way I'd have done it when I parked," said Miles. "What makes you so different?"

"I'm not putting up with any shit!" said Nathan indignantly, "they shouldn't make us walk through a laneway. We should have car spaces."

"Sure! But you haven't got a car space. You've lost the argument by eighty bucks."

"Humph!"

As Miles later discovered, that sort of arrogance, which extended to petty issues such as refusing to put together the community notices because it was not the work of a "real" journalist – and that from a trainee on the Bugle Group, the journalistic definition of humble - was the bane of Ellen's life.

"Car spaces out the back!" said Ellen, who had finished her emails. "Why not ask for bar service and a separate interview room while you're at it."

"Yeah, interview room," said Karen.

"We need car spaces. Why do we have to walk through a back alley?" said Nathan.

"I could always ask again," said Ellen, "the office guys need a laugh. Why don't you ask? Time for you to be laughed at."

"Humph! They should give us spaces," muttered Nathan.

They adjourned to a seedy pub a few doors down the road. A television installed in a bracket high on the wall showed racing, for the benefit of a mix of the local businessmen and labourers around the bar. There were few women. They pulled two tables together in one corner of the green carpet and ordered - mainly beers.

"Not many for Friday," observed Miles.

"Place down the road shows music videos," said Karen's boyfriend, "trendies go there. We stay here."

"Wise move," said Miles, but thinking he might look in on that place later. Then he told them about his battles with Ros, Bronwyn and his encounter with Justin. His listeners made sympathetic noises, but otherwise showed no surprise.

"Jan complained so much about Ros, but it was a put up all along," said Ellen.

"Bronwyn's a mate of hers. Justin says he never got

any of my messages. She must've blocked them both ways with Jan."

"Bronwyn think's she deputy editor-in-chief," said Karen, "'n we're all scum. But the reason she's in editorial is because she stuffed up so much in admin."

"Why doesn't Justin heave her?"

"He doesn't care," said Ellen. "Did he give you that line at the interview about preferring journos from the country because they'll do the work?"

"Yeah he did."

"It's bull dust. Did you come on as contract or one of the union grades."

"Grading."

"The grade you're hired at, that's what you're stuck with."

"No changes," added Karen.

"You mean the money I got now, that's what I'm stuck with?" Miles had been hoping that after a few months he could get his fortnightly pay packet pushed up from pathetic to being merely inadequate.

"You been on any of the metros or the wire services or anything like that?" asked Ellen.

"Course not. Just up from the country."

"Then you're stuck with what you've got."

"And they wonder why we leave, " added Karen, bitterly.

Actually, Mr Charles had a good idea why his journalist turnover rates were well above the industry average, but he also knew that better pay and conditions would make little difference as young journalists were always looking for jobs in more exciting places.

"They may be hiring at the *Sunday Telegraph*," said Ellen.

"I've still got my guy at the ABC," said Karen wistfully.

"*Herald* for me, no question," said Nathan.

"Maybe you c'd try the Economist?" suggested Miles.

"You mean the Brit magazine?"

"That's the one."

"That where you're going?"

"Sure mate, they hire from the Bugle Group all the time."

The others laughed; Nathan looked exasperated. "Don't you think about moving onto something bigger."

"After my first week? The reason I'm here is that the metros and wire services wouldn't look at me – just up from the country. Now that I've sorted out some issues, it doesn't seem such a bad place to get my time up."

"You gotta wait," said Ellen. "Maybe a wire service after 18 months?"

"Maybe – if I want to follow the Treasurer around, phoning in anything the man says."

"They watch to see which service gets in first, I hear," said Ellen.

"That sort of thing worries me," said Bronwyn's boyfriend, "the sort of mentality it creates."

Before Miles could retort that the service was used by markets that traded billions in seconds the party was joined by Jake and Ethan, two of the reporters from the papers based at South Forest. Miles had met them earlier in the day, but had only exchanged greetings.

Like Miles they were, at the most, two or so years out of university.

Ethan was a small, dark, quiet man and an arts graduate who also happened to be gay. Far more importantly he was known to be a poor reporter who Justin wanted to force out. Jake was tall and heavily built, with angular features, a clean shaven head and a small ear ring in one ear. He looked more like a gang enforcer than a journalist – an air of menace reinforced by his habitual uniform of brown leather jacket, T shirt and jeans, supplemented with a roll neck jumper in winter. His deep, booming voice, Miles was later told, could be heard all over the South Forest building, and that was when the owner of the voice was trying to be quiet. But Jake's looks were deceiving. He had recently gained an honours degree in philosophy, along with a gold medal for a distinguished essay, but had turned aside from the academic path to explore journalism. That eccentric whim had landed him a job on the South Forest Bugle with the old hand Tom, writing about garden festivals and problems with sewage outflows. Justin had hoped that Jake might frighten the much older reporter into checking his facts. For despite all his years of experience Tom had a problem with facts. Instead they had become good friends, with Tom taking on the hard task of making Jake's stories less like philosophical essays and more like news reports. Jake was also aiming for higher things, perhaps an overseas posting via Canberra.

"Refills anyone?" said Jake. Miles held up his schooner and it was taken away. The conversation wandered on. Ethan played the flute seriously, Miles discovered, and wanted to turn professional. Then he would shake the dust of the Bugle Group from his feet. Miles got up to buy and, after downing that one, he found that he had mellowed towards humanity in general and the Bugle Group in particular. Another round arrived. He began to feel silly. It had been a hard, strange week and he was beginning to discover the best part about the Bugle Group – the other journalists in it.

"Have you ever wondered what was beyond beer?" he asked Jake, after hearing of the other reporter's training in philosophy. He pointed, a little unsteadily, at the glass in front of him. He noted that it now had only a little beer in it. He could have sworn there was more a moment ago.

"Never really had beer in front of me long enough to consider the issue, mate," said Jake. "Anyway, I generally take a solipsistic view – the only verifiable fact is the existence of self. Everything else is debatable."

"So you can't be sure that the beer in front of you exists?"

"As a verifiable fact, no."

"Then why not give it to me?"

"Cause I want to drink it."

"But if it doesn't exist, what's the problem?" Miles had read well beyond his agricultural college studies. He also became more talkative when drunk. "If you don't reckon it exists, why do you wanna drink it."

"If I let that unverified beer mingle with my verified self, then maybe it would gain some measure of verification – only I'd have to drink a lot more before I work out what I mean by verification."

"So what you're saying is that this beer will become more real to you, when you've stuck it in your gob."

"In my reality."

"So if I took the beer off you, you would react."

"Correct. I'm reacting to my universe as I experience it. Two young guys decided to intrude on my reality in the street around here a couple of nights ago. They must've been debating the existence of alcohol earlier, but I don't think they wanted to discuss metaphysics with me."

"What's metaphysics for god's sake?"

"Investigating the question of existence, as such."

"Alright, but they weren't philosophy students?"

"Reckon not."

"So what happened?"

"One of them had a brief experience of non-existence, when the fist on my physical self as I experience it, interacted with his unverified self. The other buggered off."

The conversation became more disjointed. The ladies slipped away, more people joined and they all adjourned to a nearby pizza place for food. Ethan left and Jake and Miles went on alone to a second, even seedier pub. Miles found that his jaw had gone numb and that he might have fallen off his chair had he not been leaning against Jake. By that time the bartender was visibly wondering if he could serve them without risking the pub's licence. Driving home was out of the question - Miles was not even sure he could find his car – but fortunately Jake's place was within long staggering distance. So they wandered off to it singing as much as they could remember of the Monty Python philosopher's drinking song.

Immanuel Kant was a real pissant
And very rarely bable

"Stable, mate," said Jake, who was much less the worse for drink than Miles. "The line is 'And very rarely stable'"

"Right! Right! Who was Kant again?"

"German loony who said our senses define everything and we can't know anything outside our senses. He hung around his home town in Germany and did bugger all for decades except write about philosophy. I gotta gold medal and I get to write about sewerage in South Forest."

"Kant should've been a journalist, mate," said Miles, who thought it advisable to lean on a power pole which, with great civic foresight, had been placed just where he happened to need support. "Would've learnt about real stuff.."

"Mate, he could never've handled it. The sewerage system in South Forest is in a shocking state. Where were we?"

"We did Kant."

"Yeah, yeah! Next is Heidegger."

"Heidegger, Heidegger was a boozy beggar
Who could think you under the table
David Hume could out-consume
Schopenhauer and Hegel,
And Wittgenstein was a beery swine
Who was just as sloshed as Schlegel"....

"Mate, mate! Do you know we create hyper reality?" said Jake suddenly.

"We do?.. what's hyper reality when it's at home?"

"The way people experience an event involves lots of different types of reality, right?"

"Uh yeah, right. Ooops!" Miles had cannoned into Jake. He righted himself and kept going.

"So when we report stuff it fuses those different realities into one, see. 'n that's hyper reality."

Miles thought about having to search Koala Bay for a story to put on page one and the reality of the Grovers. Then he had a flash of insight of the kind that is sometimes granted to the seriously drunk.

"Mate, I've never heard so much bulldust in all my life. I'm from the bush; I know bulldust 'n that's it."

"I don't get to invent the stuff. I gotta get a few more years up messing around in libraries before I get to invent. I just gotta try and understand the stuff. Hyper reality it is."

"Then there are some people in Koala Bay," said Miles, thinking of Mrs Grover, "on a different fucking plane of existence altogether."

"Mate, you are an eloquent drunk."

Later he recalled vaguely getting to the flat and Jake producing a bottle of what he insisted was vintage Port. Miles thought it was the best stuff he had ever tasted. He also remembered looking up to see two women. He thought they were angels, and even said so. The evening ended abruptly.

Miles awoke thinking that a blacksmith had mistaken his head for an anvil, to see a women's face looking down at him - a narrow face, with delicate features, set with bright, gray eyes. The hair on top of the face was light brown and cut short, with the business-like look softened by two small ear rings. She wore a skivvy and jeans which were both tight enough to prove a point.

"It's alive!" said the face, and put something down close to him.

Miles realised that he was lying on a lumpy couch in a flat that he recognised vaguely from the night before. Someone had taken his shoes off and thrown a spare doona over him. The face had put a cup of coffee on a small table beside him. He sipped it and the hammering slowed. He took a long sip, almost burning his tongue, but he now felt that he would live. He sat up and almost yelped in anguish. His brain was about to hemorrhage! He took another sip of the coffee. Okay, maybe his brain would not hemorrhage, yet. His saviour was sitting at the nearby dining table sipping a mug of her own coffee, glancing through one of the Saturday papers. It was a small flat.

"You're an angel," he croaked.

"You said that last night," she said matter-of-factly, without looking up.

"I did? Okay.. so, you've proved it."

"Thank you." Miles was rewarded with a glance in his direction and a slight smile which, even hung over as he was, he found interesting. "You also asked me to marry you."

"I DID?" He clutched at his head and went back to croaking. "I did? That's embarrassing. What did you answer?"

"I said you're drunk."

"True. Good answer. What would you say if I asked you for a date now?"

As he was unshaven, blurry-eyed, in rumpled clothes and had an enormous hangover, the question was ill-advised. But he had already drunkenly proposed he could not make matters worse.

She looked up sharply. "I'd say you're hungover. Drink lots of fluids."

"Is that a maybe for when I sober up?"

"No."

He took another sip of coffee. "I'm Miles," he croaked.

"I know. You said so last night along with a lot of other things. You also told me you recently had a fiancée, back in where ever it was you came from."

"Corryong." I said all that!"

"You did." The girl flicked over another page of the newspaper.

"I don't know your name."

"I'm Anne – I'm a friend of Jake's friend, Tomasina."

"The second angel from last night. There were two of you… a lot of light shining around both of you."

"Your eyes weren't focusing."

"It was a moment of spiritual insight; happens to journalists sometimes."

"Then they sober up, I suppose."

Despite his hangover, Miles chuckled. "But no date?"

"No date. Recovering from a bad break-up myself."

"What's this about dates?" said Jake, arriving suddenly in the living room dressed in an old bath robe and looking rumpled but otherwise none the worse for last night's binge.

"I'm being naturally selected out," said Miles. His head was splitting, and now that he thought about his stomach he dare not move suddenly for fear of events becoming messy, but he still managed to make a joke of it. "It's Darwin in action."

He noted that Anne half-smiled again.

"That Darwin guy is to blame for so much shit," said Jake, disgusted. His booming voice made Miles' head throb. "He needs a real kick up the bum."

"Who needs a kick up the bum?" said an attractive Asian girl, with an all-Australian accent and manner, coming out of the same door from which Jake had emerged. Miles guessed she must be Tomasina. "So Miles, have you apologised to Anne for last night?" She smiled at him.

"I can't believe I proposed."

"You did. You slurred. What every girl wants in a proposal, for the guy to be dead drunk."

"You proposed to Anne?" said Jake from the kitchen alcove.

"You got me drunk."

"That's right!" said Tomasina, rounding on Jake, "you got our visitor drunk, arsehole. He didn't know what he was doing."

"Mate, you're so country," said Jake. "This is the city; you don't propose to girls."

"Oh, you don't?" said Tomasina folding her arms.

"You tell 'em they're beautiful, tell 'em you're working on a doctorate in philosophy and your unfinished thesis is back at your flat; and do they want to look at it?"

"Huh!" said Tomasina.

"Wait! Wait!" croaked Miles. He was thinking hard about his stomach, but he also thought he might need to remember this point for later. "What happens if the girls don't care about philosophy?"

"Dunno about philosophy, mate, but a lot of 'em seem to know about Darwin – they do a lotta shit in his name."

"But is the rejection part Darwin's fault?" asked Anne. "Maybe it's the guy's fault for asking the wrong way."

Miles wondered if that last statement meant he had chance with Anne if he asked again, when he cleaned up.

"Mate, we work on local papers," said Jake. "We listen to residents complaining all the time. It's all someone else's fault. I know natural selection is not us guys' fault, so it must be Darwin's. Before I met Tommo, natural selection was the bane of my life. But now I'm doing muffins. Anyone for muffins and OJ?"

When they had all gone, Miles looking the worse for wear, Tomasina was left alone with Anne.

"Miles seemed nice," said Tomasina.

Anne shrugged. "He seemed okay. Better when he's not drunk or hungover."

"He thinks we're angels."

"More fool him but now that I think about it, I'm not interested."

"Why not? You've had worse offers."

"Sure, but am I really going to tell people I'm going out with a reporter on the – what was it?"

"He's Koala Bay, so the *Koala Bay Bugle*."

"Yes – tell people I'm going out with a reporter from the *Koala Bay Bugle*."

"Who do you think I'm living with?"

"Jake has the gold medal and all that – Miles is just a local reporter from somewhere in the bush – Karrajong – now stuck in a corner of Sydney. My men have to do something more. I can't take .. losers."

"I don't think Miles is a loser."

Anne shrugged but did not reply.

CHAPTER SIX

On Monday of his second week at the Bugle Group, having spent most of the weekend recovering from Friday night, Miles came in to find a young police constable sitting in the visitor's chair worshipping Angela. Men occasionally dropped in to see Angela on various pretexts. She soon sent them on their way, but this visitor had stayed more than the usual few seconds because he had actual news to convey - namely inside information about the robbing of a local service station by a knife-wielding bandit. Miles became interested.

"... so we get there and the attendant is flipped out."

"Uh huh," said Angela. She was dimly aware that a service station robbery counted as news in quiet Koala Bay and scribbled a note on a pad. It was the first time Miles had seen her take notes.

The constable realised that Miles was also listening and nodded at him. "So we went through the deal – we took a description and all that."

"Uh huh!"

The constable paused as if expecting another question.

"What was the description?" asked Miles.

Angela clicked her tongue in exasperation.

"Youth, 172 centimeters tall, heavily built, red-haired. Jeans, black skivvy, old gray jumper."

"Stands out a bit more than the usual descriptions."

"Yeah," the constable, a decent sort, smiled, "he matches a description of an offender in Lovett Bay."

"If you don't mind!" said Angela, without looking around.

"Okay. Sorry." It was her story.

Miles sat down and logged on, but could still hear the cop say "service station" and "knife" and, unusually, which service station had been robbed. The police did not usually give out the names of the victims or businesses robbed.

"So you're going to write that up?" Miles asked after the cop had gone with a big wave and a smile to Angela, who answered with a half smile and tiny wave.

"Yes."

"Um, well, I was wondering weather it was worth ringing up the service station."

"What for?"

"They might have something to say. They might hate being held up."

"Mightn't be the same guy there," she muttered after a moment's thought.

"Might be, might not. It happened Sunday right? Might be."

"Gotta go to the cops."

"This is the biggest story you'll get there. But tell you what, why not let me ring up and we can have a joint byline. Yours 'd be the first name."

She thought for a few moments, probably searching for an excuse to refuse such a sensible suggestion. "You can ring if you want, I'll send my stuff. Subs can work it out," she muttered.

"Sure." Miles knew that he could fix things with Eve in a few moments on the phone. "You, er, going to write up that stuff with the cop now."

"Now!" She was outraged. "I've got to go to the cop station now. Waddya think I am, made of time." Miles thought he could hear her mother talking

"Shouldn't take you too long. Its just a few pars.."

"Give it a rest!" she snapped and stormed out, note book in hand, outraged that the newcomer trespassing on her turf should dare to suggest that she stretch herself for a few moments.

Miles waited until she was gone, found the number of the service station and reached for his phone headset. Ros chose that moment to stick her head in the door.

"Miles, I heard about that service station. You can't run it."

Now that he knew Ros had no say in what he did, Miles found her less irritating. In any case he was busy, but he was curious about the latest directive.

"Why not run the story?"

"Because it'll give people the wrong impression about Koala Beach."

"That service stations don't get robbed here?"

"That it's a crime area. Decent people have businesses here and we can't have stories like that. It's bad for business. Okay?"

"I listen to everything you say," said Miles turning around and putting his headphones on. Ros went away puzzled.

As it happened the same attendant was on duty then

as had been robbed on Sunday and he was willing to speak about his ordeal.

"I was terrified, mate," he said. "When that guy stuck a knife almost in my face, I thought I was a goner."

After a few minutes Miles had all he needed and hung up. He did not need Angela's contribution and would not wait for it. As the story had come through her sources and he was still trying to placate her, he give her first spot in their joint byline credit. But after a week of writing about the problems of the residents of Koala Bay, it was a pleasure to write a story with a little meat.

Koala Bay resident Carl Yosif was terrified when a bandit waved a knife in his face in a hold-up in the Brunten Ave service station on Sunday.
"When that guy stuck a knife.."

By the time Angela came back from police rounds, almost as huffy as when she left, the story was done and gone. The attendant had given all the details that would have come from the police, except for the official description and the fact that the offender might have pulled other jobs, which Miles knew already. He had a long way to go but his journalistic skills were developing fast. Angela, on the other hand, had learnt nothing during her few months as a journalist. Without bothering to speak to Miles she hashed out her police notes exactly as the police had given them to her, over the table in the coffee room at the back of the station. He later asked for a copy, which Angela very grudgingly gave to him. Sans the service station story they read:

Koala Bay police are looking for a man exposing

himself to young girls in the district. He is tall with gray hair and a long, black leather coat. Anyone with information should call the Koala Bay station.

A 22-year old women has been charged with high range drink driving. The charge arose when police were called to an incident in Tolhurst Street, central Koala Bay. An early model green Holden car was discovered inserted in the front fence of a house. The engine was still running. The women was sitting in the driver's seat, laughing. She stopped laughing when police approached. She made remarks to them of an offensive nature. She attempted to exit the vehicle and elude police. She had to be restrained. A preliminary breath test indicated that she was over the limit. A blood test found that she was 0.15. It transpired that she had just left a party in Tolhurst Street.

A 19-year old man driving a late model, white Ford was stopped by police in Lochlan Drive, Koala Bay, last week for a traffic violation. A quantity of household goods were found to be in the car. These goods were later discovered to be stolen. Detectives accompanied the man to his home and recovered more property. A number of the recovered items have been returned to their owners. The man is now assisting police with their inquiries into other matters. He was charged with a number of offences of breaking and entering in a court in Downing Street in Sydney, and was refused bail.

Miles felt some bitterness when he read those items. When added to the service station hold-up they amounted to an exciting week for the local police. He had misjudged Koala Bay. Instead of being a quiet, unexciting slab of suburbia there were flashers and drunk drivers, not to mention thieves in white Fords, on every street corner. But Angela had managed to write those three items while putting what should have been her lead sentence right at the bottom, or without doing a stroke of real journalist work. He knew it could be dangerous to stray too far from the details given by the police, but the stories could easily have been made more exciting. Also, some details could be explored further.

"Why did that guy in the white Ford they caught with stolen goods get charged in Downing Street down in the city? Why didn't they charge him up here?"

"Dunno."

"Maybe you could ask next time? You seem pally with some of 'em."

"I'll think about it, alright! The police stuff is my job." Her voice was rich with contempt.

After lunch Miles answered a couple of questions from the subs and cleared up the mess on his desk. One week's paper had gone, now it was time to start thinking about next week, which naturally led to the question of a lead. Perhaps the God – or was it the devil? - of journalists would provide, but in the absence of any supernatural intervention the journalists at Lovett Bay might come good. Ellen had mentioned on Friday that a major decision about a transport plan for all of the Lovett Bay Council area was to be released. He could tailor the story for his paper or perhaps simply add a side story. Both stories would then take out his front page. He lived in hope. Then there was the rest of the paper to fill.

Mid-afternoon Emma dropped in for the usual list of pictures to take and, of course, to gossip.

"So you had a fiancée back in Corryong?" she said without preamble, arms folded and leaning on the news room door frame. As on her previous visit she ignored Angela, who had her ear phones back on. "You said you just had a horse."

"You asked about family. The horse is closer to being family than an ex-fiancée."

"Ex is it? Did she know about the horse?"

"She was broadminded. You've been talking to Jake?"

"Tomasina. She's a mate. I know Anne too, but not as well. Nice girl, but Miley," she took on the air of a teacher explaining something to a backward pupil, "in Sydney first you ask the girl out then you get to know her, then you propose. Just a word to the wise my friend."

Miles sighed. "I thought that in Sydney a bloke could get drunk and do stupid stuff, and not have the whole town know by breakfast."

"Uh uh," she said, shaking her head, "not in front of work mates, anyway. The Bugle Group is a different sort of village. You got blind I hear."

"Totally off my face. Jake is a dangerous man to be around. I was just ordinary dunk until he brought out the Port."

"Port on top of beer! Lucky you didn't end up in an ambulance."

"It seemed a good idea at the time."

"Jake is a lunatic."

"I spent all of Saturday next to the dunny or using it."

"I forgot to ask Miley, where are you staying."

"Hostel, but it's not cheap. Its eating into my savings. Gotta look for a place."

"Hmmm! May be able to help, I'll let you know. Now what piccies have you got for me?"

Tuesday afternoon saw the inevitable confrontation with Ros. Miles came up the stairs after lunch and saw a stack of the newly printed copies of that week's Koala Bay Bugle. On the front was Miles' story about the residents of Mudlark Ave with a large picture of several residents, including the Kennys, underneath the Mudlark Ave street sign looking sour as the next best thing to looking angry. Below that main story was the service station story. Miles thought that it all looked well, and there was of course that nice feeling of seeing one's own byline on a story, even on one about angry Mudlark Ave residents. The service station story was much better but Angela's byline was first. Then Ros saw him.

"EXPLAIN THIS TO ME!" she screamed coming to the door of her office, and pointing to a copy of the paper in her hands. "I TOLD YOU NOT TO RUN THOSE STORIES. AND THE OTHERS. LOOK AT THIS! THIS!" Ros flicked open the paper pointing at the stories she had banned.

The receptionist and the sales lady, Kate, sitting in her small office, stared at Miles in alarm. The reporter, for his part, flicked through the other pages, ignoring Ros. The subs at South Forest had done a good job in laying out the pages.

"Looks good doesn't it," he said to no-one in particular.

"IT'S SHOCKING. THIS IS GOING TO RUIN US. I'VE BEEN BUILDING UP A REPUTATION AND NOW LOOK AT IT. ITS JUST A SCANDAL SHEET! MISTER YOU'RE IN BIG TROUBLE."

"Oh no, I'm not…"

"YOU WAIT UNTIL JIMMY HEARS ABOUT THIS."

The noise was such that the receptionist from the adjacent insurance broker looked curiously through her office door.

"Ros…"

"DON'T THINK YOU CAN CRAWL OUT OF THIS ONE."

"Ros…"

"YOU DIDN'T DO ANYTHING I SAID. YOU BASTARD!"

"Ros…"

"I'M GOING TO SEE YOU GET TRANSFERRED – NO I'M GUNNA GET YOU SACKED."

"Ros.."

"YOU'LL GET WHAT'S COMING TO YOU.."

"Ros.. I WAS TOLD TO IGNORE YOU!"

"What?"

"Justin told me you had no say in editorial."

"When did he say this?"

"Friday. I confronted him in the car park as he was leaving work. Your mate Bronwyn never passed on any of my messages, so I went down there." Ros's mouth gaped open, as did that of Kelly, the receptionist. "He was surprised to find you were still here. He thought you'd been moved on."

"Why did he think that?" she snapped.

"He also said that you have nothing to do with editorial, and that he'd have a word with Jim Charles about it. Now I answer to Justin, and he answers to Jim Charles."

"Jimmy told you I control editorial here."

"Beg to differ. His exact words were I should listen to your suggestions. Well I listened to your suggestions and none of 'em were worth a rat's rear end. You want to block all the stories worth running and you want me to write about panel beaters and real estate agents."

"I promised them.."

"Don't care! I report to Justin. I'm not even the editor, I'm the reporter who's here. If you wanna get stuff in the paper that's got no news value then he's your man. I'd have to say I don't think he's going to care about panel beaters in Koala Bay."

"We'll see about this, mister!"

"You couldn't have kept it up much longer, anyway. They were beginning to notice at South Forest that there was no news in the newspaper."

"I'm going to call Jimmy."

"Whatever! Why don't you tell him, while you're at it, that I said you should never have been allowed anywhere near editorial," Miles turned away from her and grabbed a handful of papers. The receptionist was still staring at him open mouthed. "Hello Kelly!"

"Oh, hello Miles."

"Hello, Kate, have a nice lunch?"

"Hello, Miles," said Kate from her tiny office. She

had to put up with a lot of nonsense from Ros for the sake of providing for her two teenage daughters, and had vastly enjoyed the confrontation.

"You haven't heard the last of this, mister!" spat Ros.

Not bothering to reply, Miles sat at his desk. Angela was also starting at him open mouthed.

"Hello Angela."

"Hmph!"

He put a newspaper on her desk out of courtesy and she glanced at it, meaning to toss it unread with the others on the orange interview chair beside her, when she caught sight of her byline. She read read the story without recognising a single sentence in it, then folded the newspaper and put it on her desk without comment. Later, when Miles was not there she looked at it again, with the thrill that even the dullest of journalists knows of seeing their own byline. When her mother called to say she had seen the story and to say how she was developing into a "real" journalist, Angela never mentioned that she had not touched it. Over time she even came to believe she had written it. But somewhere, deep down, she knew she was unable even to begin to do what Miles had done in the short time she had been out having coffee at the police. That was Miles' crime in her eyes. He knew stuff.

Just as Ros started shouting on the phone, Jake called.

"How's the hyper reality going over there?"

"Mate, we are knee-deep in hyper reality," said Miles, half listening to Ros shouting on the phone. He was surprised to find that his confrontation with Ros had made him shaky inside, and a little apprehensive that Justin might buckle under the pressure. All of what he had said was common sense, but Miles suspected that common sense was not valued highly in the Bugle group. He was glad of someone to talk to.

"Told you're looking for a place in which to bound your infinite spirit nightly?"

"A flat to live in. Yes."

"Mate of a mate from uni looking for a house mate cum house minder. Cheap but you gotta keep the garden under control."

"The cheap part sounds good, but where is it?"

"Up your way somewhere. Call ya back. We gonna have another debate about alcohol on Friday?"

"I reckon I've tasted port enough to take its existence as read. I'm with Kant on that one."

"Maybe it does exist 'n maybe it doesn't. Mere sensory stimulii alone cannot decide the issue."

"Yeah? The sensory issues are real hard to escape the next morning."

"Details my friend. Drink a shit load of water before reality sets in. But listen, you're a Mexican."

"Victorian. Last time I looked."

"You're from South of the border and came up here to take jobs away from us hard working New South Welshman. Anyway, another mate o' mine is looking around for a few guys to play that weird aerial ping pong game you've got down there."

"You mean the grand game of Australian Rules Football?"

"That's the one. This mate is also a refugee and a few of us other guys have decided we've gotta show southerners how to play the game. In fact, there's whole leagues of that weird game around here."

As there were leagues of teams for almost any sport that does not require snow in Sydney Miles should not have been surprised by the news, but he was. It had not occurred to him that AFL would be played much except by the Sydney Swans. As it happened back home he had been selected to represent his district – an honor - and had been wondering about playing the sport in Sydney.

"I see. I would've picked you for league."

"Mate, rugby has nothing more to offer me and how hard can AFL be?"

"Dunno about that, but if a Victorian turns up – a guy who might know the rules – will he get a run?"

"Rules are for Victorians mate, but as I understand it they're desperate. A heap of players are moving to Queensland."

"Sounds grim. I'll be there. But at the mo' the mate of a mate's place sounds more interesting."

"Get right back."

Jake called back within a few minutes and, as it happened, the house in question was about 15 minutes drive away – very close by Sydney standards. As it also happened the owner was home and wanted to see Miles right away. Muttering to Kelly that he would be about an hour, and leaving Ros still shouting down the phone in her office, Miles drove off. Reporters have considerable freedom of movement and Miles was freer than most as he was the only reporter in the office - or, at least, the only one who mattered.

His hopeful landlord, Joshua, was not much older than Miles but very much better dressed in a business suit and armed with a laptop, briefcase, luggage that went on wheels and a suit bag, all piled neatly by the front entrance when the reporter arrived. He was one of those high-powered computer system consultants who flew around the world sorting out computer problems in exotic locations for an immense salary. Miles felt a twinge of envy. He had been called to journalism, but his calling seemed to have a vow of poverty attached. Later he discovered that many consultants wanted to become journalists, that is, provided they could keep their vast salaries.

One part of Joshua's life that Miles did not envy was the house. It was a two bedroom timber bungalow on wooden blocks, covered in peeling paint. There was an equally dilapidated shed on one side which turned out to be the garage, and a tiny back garden with a circular clothes hoist.

"I thought I should buy something in Sydney – the way house prices keep going up," said Josh, almost apologetically. "And I got this block. The house came with it, but I couldn't help that."

"It's more than I've got."

"As soon as I get the money this place is history, but I'm not here much."

"Spend a lot of time overseas. Hard life."

"Not all it's cracked up to be," said Josh warming to the reporter. He had decided that Miles would be acceptable. "Um, I've got a taxi coming for me and you come highly recommended. Jake says you're a man who knows a lot about philosophy."

"Certain subjects, I guess," said Miles cautiously. "We've talked about metaphysics."

"That's - that's good." Joshua tried to look as if he knew what metaphysics meant. "You can take the keys and move into the spare room. I've cleaned it out. You can use whatever in the house. Someone got in when I was away last time and took the lot. I've replaced it with second hand stuff."

"They took everything?"

"No one here, see, and not much to take but they took it anyway. There are some real desperate people in Sydney, Miles."

"Seems so."

Josh told him the rent.

"That sound do-able"

"But you gotta mow the lawn. There's a lawnmower in the garage. And keep the front looking reasonable. I don't give a shit what you do with it, just keep it so the neighbours don't point, which they've been doing."

"Got it!"

"Here's the key for the door, and the windows. That's the key for the garage but prefer you didn't use it; my car is in there. Park yours in the driveway. Is that it outside?"

There was a mild note of disbelief in Joshua's voice, seeing his new house mate's battered orange utility in the street. A near neighbour back home had given the vehicle to Miles in exchange for some farm work and, after being notified of the amount he could expect each fortnight by the Bugle Group pay office, Miles knew the utility would remain with him for some time yet.

"It got me to Sydney," he said.

A taxi pulled into the driveway and beeped its horn. Josh looked at his watch, and forgot about Miles' vehicle. "Gotta run. Take care. I'll call you with my numbers 'n stuff tonight. You'll be here?"

"I think after seven, after I grab my stuff."

When he got back to the office, there were no urgent message from South Forest. Kelly looked tense but otherwise, after her initial eruption, volcano Ros had subsided and was now only giving off clouds of muttered curses and threats.

Ignoring Ros, Miles went back to his desk and decided that life at the Bugle Group might be bearable after all.

CHAPTER SEVEN

No one at the Bugle Group ever spoke to Miles about his confrontation with Ros, not even Mr. Charles. The Bugle Group had not forgotten its reporting traditions. If panel beaters or real estate agents wanted to get their message in the paper then they could always buy an ad. However, Ros also did not move. Instead she tried to make his life difficult, no doubt hoping that he would leave. Unfortunately for her, Miles was not the sort of man to wilt from a few harsh words.

"And where have you been?" she would say to Miles from her office door when he returned from an interview.

"Out Ros," he said, without stopping, his mind on other things.

"What have you been doing?"

"Stuff for the paper, Ros."

"I demand to know what you've been doing."

"'Been having fun Ros," said Miles almost as his desk.

Later, Kelly said: "she really hates you, you know. I've heard her on the phone and some of the things she says about you."

"Nah, she really loves me," said Miles, not

particularly worried that bad words from Ros would affect his career, "talking with her reminds me of talking with me mum as a kid."

The occasional exchange of views with Ros aside there was the paper to produce and the reactions of readers to deal with, including a piece of official reaction to the front page story about Mudlark Ave which unexpectedly filled up the news room door the day after publication. Detecting a darkening in the room, Miles turned to see a tall, heavily built, middle-aged man, with receding black hair and spreading midriff. He had squeezed himself into jeans, topped with open-necked, coloured shirt and a gold chain. In the cooler months he wore a light, black leather coat. His hawk-like face, hook nose and dark-complexion spoke of a Mediterranean heritage but his mouth was all Australian.

"Bastards in Mudlark Ave," he said, without introducing himself. "Told 'em it was no-go, already. Council says the road's gotta go through and they gotta go to court – not much hope there – or forget it. Bastards, dropping me in it! Already rung up that deadshit Kenny 'n gave 'im a serve."

"Um.. Councilor Gouter, I presume."

"Yeah, that's me." He and Miles shook hands, the latter thinking that the Lovett City councilor whose ward was one of two wards in the circulation area of the Koala Bay Bugle, looked like a cross between a used car salesman, a gangster and a fruit stall owner. Having seen the size of him – Gouter had played prop forward for the Koala Bears for 10 years, making up

84

for a lack of skill by charging hard in the scrums - and the way he had walked into the office as if he owned the place, he was glad he had only mentioned Kenny's complaints about the councilor in passing and had made every effort to contact him. For reporters on the local papers community, or official, reaction is likely to take the form of gigantic councilors who walk right in of the streets and make their thoughts on a story involving them known in good, round terms.

"I rang you twice."

"Know you did.. overseas. So, alright, not worried about a serve or two. Serve it straight back. 'specially to the likes of Kenny. So where did ya come from?"

Miles told him but the information did not mean much to him. The councilor's eyes flicked once or twice to Angela who had her earphones on, but did not try to speak to her.

"Where did you go overseas?"

"Um, New York for a bit, then Bangkok - business, ya know."

Miles wondered briefly what business a Lovet City councilor who ran a plumbing supplies wholesaler might have in Bangkok but let it slide for the moment.

"Tried ringing the other councilor for the area. Theo.."

"..Georgiou. Half ya luck if you can get him. Never seen him anywhere or do any bloody thing since he got on last election. Council can't even get hold of him half the time. I didn't say that by the way. You do your own shit work."

"Fair 'nough."

Councilor Gouter then put one elbow on the filing

cabinet, waving away Miles' suggestion that they try and lift the newsroom's one visitor's chair over Angela.

"Never see you fellas right down here, do they?" he said, looking around. "That lunatic Ros" – Miles opinion of the councillor lifted a few notches – "takes the good office to do bugger all, at least that's what Jan always said. She wasn't here long. What happened to her?"

"Ros got to her. She kept claiming she had to see stories.."

"'Cause she's Charles' sister?"

"Yeah. And Ros had her mate fend off any queries down at South Forest, so Jan could never get through to the editor in chief to find out otherwise."

"Ha! That's why the paper was shit. People were thinking nothing happened in Koala Bay. Nothing much does o' course, but the paper's gotta say something."

After a few more minutes of this the reporter asked again about the missing councilor Georgiou.

"Off the record, right? Don't want you quoting me on this. He got on last year on a Labor-greenies ticket. He was sorta known through the surf club and his wife'd done a few charity things. Dunno why he agreed, 'cause he's been invisible since. He had one interview in the paper when he was running, and I saw him at one council thing after the election. Since then he's not been seen. Been overseas a couple of times they reckon but even when he's here he just has the answering machine on. If they do catch him, he's always got some excuse for not doing things – kids are sick, or wife needs help, or some bloody thing. Even the Labor guys 'd reckon ram it up 'im. Been completely useless."

Miles nodded. He had never rammed it up anyone in a newspaper before but he was certainly prepared to try.

"Where would I go to get confirmation of the fact that he doesn't attend meetings? There has to be a record."

"Ah dunno – give the city manager, Barry Michaels, a call. Come ta think of it, try the Mayor first, but you might end with Michaels. He's got a stud up in the back blocks somewhere, so you and he should get on fine. Maybe he can give a statement about attendance. No one's gonna say more on the record, I reckon. Anyway gotta go. See ya"

The gigantic councillor moved away, turning his head to look at Angela's glorious, golden mop on the way out but not saying anything.

Miles rang the mayor, a women who ran a fast printing and delivery franchise. The mayor rang Michaels who promptly invited Miles, via an assistant, to his office. Miles drove down to find the city manager to be white-haired and close to retirement, but still with the dark active eyes and ruddy complexion of someone who worked on the land. He soon detected Miles' accent and, when he found out that he grew up on a stud, became quite animated. He owned a tiny, thoroughbred stud with which he expected to occupy his retiring years. With good management, and luck, it might not cost too much to run.

"So what's brought you down here. Why not breed horses?"

"Its like everything else in the country, Mr. Michaels…"

"Barry.."

"Barry. You've gotta get big, get specialised or get out. My dad can't do the finance to get big, he likes working with different types of horses and he doesn't want to get out."

"But you're in newspapers," he protested. "Aren't they going the way of small studs too? Who reads newspapers these days?"

"I'm a content provider. I provide content, some other poor sod decides what media its going in. Maybe they'll bring out an electronic version of the Bugle that'll run stories about Lovett Councilors no one can find, but the stories won't be there unless some stupid bastard like me goes 'n asks stupid questions."

The older man smiled, and shrugged. "I spoke to the mayor about the, um, issue you raised. This is the best we can do by way of creating content." He passed to Miles a bland, extremely brief statement saying that councilor Georgiou had been recorded as absent from all council meetings, as well as absent from meetings of the works committee of which he was also a member. Apologies had been recorded on two occasions. "Neither myself nor the mayor have any further comment. That's the line."

Miles nodded. He still had to make every effort to contact Georgiou, but he could make something of this.

WHERE IS CR GEORGIOU?

Elected last year on a Green-left ticket in the Koala Bay North ward Cr Theo Georgiou has yet to attend a single council meeting, or a meeting of the council works committee of which he is also a member.

The City Manager, Barry Michaels and Mayor Joyce McKinley, made a formal statement, in response to a query by the Koala Bay Bugle *that Cr Georgiou had not attended any meeting of the council or the committee. They had received apologies on two occasions. Neither Mr. Michaels nor Mayor McKinley would make any further comment.*

The Bugle has attempted to contact Cr Georgiou on a number of occasions....

By necessity it was a brief story. Miles could not step outside the facts and there were not many facts. With a little searching he found years of back copies of the Bugle burned on DVDs which were kept under Kelly's desk, and had managed to unearth Georgiou's one and, as far as he knew, only interview. That stretched the story for two more paragraphs. He added exactly one adjective - "spectacular", as in "spectacular non-attendance" – but Eve insisted on showing the story to a lawyer, who crossed out the "spectacular". Miles would find out more about lawyers later. Finally, it ran in the paper and resulted in a phone call.

"Its Councilor Georgiou here." To judge from the voice, the councilor was in his mid-30s.

"Hello Mr. Georgiou. I've been trying to get a hold of you for some time."

"Yes, I heard you left messages. You never said what it was about."

"Now hold on. I left a message saying the council was asking where you were."

"You never said you were going to write a story."

"Well, what did you expect me to do? I'm a reporter."

"I've had so much grief over that story. My friends have seen it, my neighbours, my colleagues. My kids got grief at school over it."

"Stories in the paper are like that, I'm told. People read them."

"I want you to print a retraction tomorrow."

"The paper's weekly, Mr. Georgiou, and here we come to the point – are you saying you have been to council meetings or not?"

"I'm not making any comment."

"Okay, then it's no comment."

"I don't want you to say anything."

"As far as I'm concerned this whole conversation is on the record."

"What!"

"You knew who I was when you rang. You didn't say anything about going off the record."

"I didn't know I was supposed to. All I want is for you to take the story back."

"You haven't denied it."

"Well, no.. its just, I've been overseas..."

"Since being elected?"

"Well, yes… look forget it. I would have expected more co-operation from the local press!"

"So how long were you overseas for?"

Georgiou hung up. Next thing Miles heard he had resigned from Council and a by-election had been called. He used two sentences from the interview in the subsequent story, but never heard from Georgiou again.

CHAPTER EIGHT

Miles moved into his new residence - a box-like room with an old fashioned lino floor and a single, small window - unpacked his stuff, which had been several weeks in boxes, and spread it around. It was a poor collection. He also had no furniture. His PC he put on the dining room table; his socks and underwear in a cardboard box. His bed would be an air bed he had borrowed from his parents, which he put along one wall.

He rang Jake from work the next day. "Seems like I owe you one, but this Friday we should debate the existence of one type of alcohol at a time – no port."

"'Spose we can do that. Port is way too expensive to be real anyway."

A few calls came in. The community center wanted to publicise its activities and would the Bugle feature a person involved in one of the activities at the centre? The perennial question of residential zoning reared its head. Developers wanted more apartment blocks, residents did not; nor did they want units. One child in kindergarten had his aunt in year six at the same primary school, and the younger child's mother thought to ring the Bugle. A youth outreach program about to run through its grant also called. And so it went on.

Then there were the personal calls. In fact, there was one personal call and Miles did not want to take it but, like all his calls, came directly to him. At Miles' request Kelly never asked who was calling, she just put them through.

"Hey Miles, it's Jas."

He had known Jasper Willis from the year dot.

"What is it?" said Miles, in what he hoped was a truculent voice.

"I'm in Sydney for a few days, mate, for some high times. What's say we hit the Cross?"

"You're too late; it's become civilised. They're closing the strip joints and opening restaurants. Try the places out west, that's where all the low lifes go." Miles kept his voice flat but he felt anger rise within him.

"Whaddya mean low lifes?" said Jas, passing off the remark with a laugh. "Haven't had a chance to do anything yet, but just show us where a boy from the bush can get into trouble."

"Just go out west somewheres," said Miles. "There's places out that way with girls used to guys like you. They'll give you things you can't spell."

"Then let's go!" whooped Jas, thinking the conversation was back on track.

"'Ave a good time."

Jazz stopped whooping. "You're not showing me?"
"Nope!"

"Awww! This is the one time I'm gunna get off the farm all year. You gotta come with me. I don't know anybody else up here."

"It's Sydney. Wave money around. Someone 'll be your friend."

"Why won't you come with me, mate."

"'Cause you're a fuckwit. I suspected it in school, I knew it in college and now I'm telling you to your face you're a flat out fuckwit."

Jas had finally realised that Miles was serious and he had to search his shadowed mind for a few moments to work out what was biting his long standing friend.

"Aw mate, why are you taking it out on me for. I didn't do anything."

"'Cept didn't say anything. And laughed when I found out."

"Oh yeah, well.." Jas was sufficiently tactless to laugh again. Miles could not believe he had ever had anything to do with the man. "Mate ya gotta admit it was funny."

"Glad you're amused, mate. I wasn't."

"Aw com'n mate, it's been months."

"Jas!"

"Yeah?"

"Don't bother with the girls here, mate. Go back to yer farm, 'n fuck a few cows. It'll make 'em milk better." He slammed the phone down. Lots of journalists slammed phones down but not Miles, at least, not much. Kelly looked up from her desk, surprised at this uncharacteristic gesture.

"Miles, I hope that wasn't a girlfriend?"

He tried to smile and shrugged, but did not answer.

That had done it. Now that he had shown he had been hurt and was upset, he would never be allowed to forget. Well, so what! After a taste of the city and beaches, he was no hurry to move back. But was he doomed to write about residential zoning and the over-50s exercise groups until he died? Then Ros poked her head in the news cubbyhole to tell him not to bang phones down, and Miles cheered himself with the thought that if he was going to die there he could at least spend a lifetime making Ros miserable.

Another almost as unwelcome piece of business occurred later in the week in a call from Eve, just before Miles was about to head off for the day and look in second hand shops for tatty furniture to put in his tatty, rented room.

"About this story from Angela."

"She's written a story?"

"Um, yeah. It's something to do with a panel beaters."

"Oh right. I guess it's that thing Ros was trying to get me to do." He looked through the stuff Ros had given him, which was still in his drawer, and found that Angela's story involved the same independent business that had been promised editorial. Ros must have spoken to Angela quietly after Miles had rebelled.

"So its advertorial," said Eve.

"Guess so. She's gone for the day. Why don't you drop her an email?"

"It's completely unusable in its present form. It doesn't even make sense. Listen, 'the business on Grey street, standing in for 10 years, has gone from strength to strength on its present form'."

"That's her first par?"

"Its her first par. The next sentence is 'Greg Robard says he knows heaps about the business and says he will take on anyone, for a free quote'."

Miles laughed. "Okay, its bad but leave her a

message. I'd take it for you but she'd just chuck it at me. Anything else you wanted?"

"Actually Miles, I want you to have a word with her about this."

"Me! But I'm not the editor here." This was true to a point. Miles nominated a rough order of importance of the stories he submitted, but Eve could move them around as she saw fit. Justin made decisions about the shared content but had no interest in individual news stories. It was a decentralised system which mostly worked but there was no editor to deal with reporters who lacked certain skills - such as being able to write stories that made sense. Justin should really handle those problems but no-one seemed to consider the editor-in-chief fit for the role. "Angela doesn't report to me and there's no point in me talking to the woman, she seriously hates my guts."

"Why, what have you been doing to Angela?"

"I haven't been doing anything to Angela," squawked Miles. "I never even got a chance to even think about doing anything. She just hated me from the moment I walked in the door, and won't listen to a word I say. Anyway, you're chief sub you should do it. She may even listen to you."

"We just don't have time and you need to start from the beginning with something like this. You've got a good style, Miles, and you get stories."

"You're trying to charm me into this aren't you? Well, where I'm from we invented charm, and it's no good. We sit here for the whole day, I swear, and don't exchange a single word. And we're the length of a desk apart. I don't even know what she does apart from community notes and police stuff, which she takes verbatim from the cops."

"What about the service station story last week? That was good."

"I did it. I gave her the lead byline because one of her police contacts told us where it was and gave us the story. I spoke to you about dropping her police note on the same story."

Eve sighed. "So you did."

"Anyway, she reports to Justin. I was told that at the first interview. We just co-operate. So Justin is the guy to speak to, if anyone. Maybe he can switch her somewhere where she can be taught. Here she's learnt nothing but won't forget anything."

Miles was proud of the last remark, an adaptation of a famous jibe about the old French kings restored after the revolution, but it passed right over Eve's head.

"I've tried Justin on this before, he just says things like 'give her time, or give her feedback'. This is not feedback material, this requires major work."

"I told you she won't listen to me. Show the story to Justin and ask him to give her feedback about it."

"Why don't you try first. Then I can tell him you tried raising it with her; then maybe he'll listen."

"Why don't you tell him that now?"

"You can use your charm. You remember you just said they invented charm where you come from."

"We only use it on special occasions. It's too dangerous otherwise… Against the Geneva Convention."

Eve did not reply. Miles sighed. He did not understand why Angela's training had suddenly become his problem, when he had been in the office just weeks and she had been there months, doing heaven only knew what, without the subs taking such an interest in her. This was training in the Bugle Group – random and messy. In fact, it was not unlike the training system for special forces in the military. The weak were selected out.

"Okay, if I raise this with her and she bites my head off, you join with me in pushing her off somewhere where she might learn something."

"Fair enough."

"I still can't see why you can't just spike it and forget it. If I served up a story like that about a panel beater, you'd scream at me and spike it without a second thought."

"You're not Angela, are you?"

"It's discrimination that's what it is. All hands to save Angela, but if the country boy falls overboard you laugh at him from the deck. This is a big, evil city."

"Oh please! I don't have my violin. You know some of the guy subs here still talk about the time she was down here three months ago. They'd kill to be in the same room with her."

"If they were in the same room with her for a month, they'd kill to get out."

That Friday Miles and Jake had a drink or two with the journalists from the *Lovett Bay Bugle*. When he walked in, Ellen was having one of her regular fights with Nathan over the trainee refusing to do stories that he considered beneath him.

"I'm not doing that," Nathan said disgustedly as Miles walked in, through the back entrance.

"What's wrong with doing a story on the local fair for heaven sake," said Ellen, "Hello Miles."

"Hi!"

"Hello Miles," said Nathan, without looking away from Ellen. "It's such a boring story. Who gives a fart about the local fair."

"The residents that's who?"

"Then they can write about the fair," he said laughing. Ellen did not get the joke.

"It's our job to write this stuff, and you're the junior."

"So what's happening," said Miles to Karen, who seemed to have added to the aboriginal artifacts on her desk.

"One of the councilors covering our district is going to marry his boyfriend," she said happily. "He's making a stand for gays." Miles was amused to see Karen so delighted over this act of defiance. "It's Saturday week. We're hoping the police will break up the ceremony."

"Great story but, hang on, it's not illegal to have the ceremony is it?" Miles had a legal turn of mind. He did not know where he got it from, but it was occasionally useful.

"Oh but gays can't marry."

"That's right, but there's no reason for the cops to break up a ceremony, unless they have a riot or something. I think you'll find that the ceremony's not recognised – that's it, they just won't be legally married. You can have a ceremony if you want – nothing against that – it's just not recognised as a marriage by the act."

"Oh!" Karen's smile failed. Facts had an unfortunate tendency to mess up good stories. "Well, it's still a symbol, isn't it."

"Not a bad story," said Miles, wishing one of his councilors would be revealed as having a gay lover, "but timing's a bit off for the next issue. You've got a preview in the one just gone but the big story is the ceremony itself, right? 'N that's just after your deadline."

"Ellen and I were talking about this before. What do we do if something happens – you know, the police bust it up."

"Well they won't, so why not do the usual. Get Emma to take a picture of councilor and intended – I dunno, with the wedding cake; and one of 'em wearing a veil or whatever.. and splash it on the front."

"This about this gay councilor," said Jake, walking in through the back door. "He wants to get arrested, I hear."

"We're going to run him big, 'n see if the cops do anything. We can really help gays," said Karen, her grin back.

"Use the paper as a social weapon, you mean?" said Jake.

Her smile faded again. "Isn't that what the paper's there for?"

"I thought it was there for readers to read, not serve minority causes. However worthy the minority," he added seeing her open her mouth to defend gays. "Do readers care whether one of their councilors is gay? Do they want it thrust down their throats?"

"They should be made to care," said Karen.

"Why's that?" Jake had his philosophy hat on. "Doesn't that mean we're trying to tell them what to think?"

"When they read about the gay councilor and his

lover," said Miles, heading off what promised to be a tiresome argument, "they'll want to know where they go for the honeymoon."

"They will at that," admitted Jake.

In the round of drinks that followed at the Bugle local the gay councilor was forgotten in favour of the stand-by topic of general bitching about the Bugle Group, and wondering if they could get jobs somewhere – anywhere - else. Ellen was in a foul mood over Nathan who flatly refused to do the basic work of a trainee – that is, the unpopular jobs that no one else wanted to do - and simply did not care what Ellen thought. He went off grinning. Ellen could do little short of complaining to Justin, which she was considering. Miles thought of Angela and wondered again why the chief sub simply did not throw her copy onto the editor in chief's desk.

Karen also had some news. "I'm in line for the ABC radio job in Karratha," she told Miles in confidence.

"Karratha? That's WA isn't it?"

"Up the coast; two hours flying time from Perth."

"Ye Gods! 'N people think that Corroyong's in the sticks. That's outback, that is."

"There are aboriginal communities, and if I stay long enough I get transferred."

"You could work your way up to television at Broome. If a cyclone hits, you'll be person on the spot."

She gave him one of those puzzled-reproachful looks that, Miles noticed, he occasionally received from women. "There'll be aboriginal communities with problems and that's all that matters."

The ladies departed to their respective boyfriends

leaving Jake and Miles to grab a hamburger and then, at a whim while passing a video game parlour a few doors from the pub, to play video games. After a couple of rounds on a shooting game, with the local youths busy all around them, they switched to the Daytona car racing game, racing against each other on the intermediate track. Miles beat Jake easily.

"Where did you get so good at this stuff?" asked Jake.

"I'm from the bush. It's all we do."

"Yeah, country boy. Let's see if yer can do it again."

They were part way through the race on the beginner's track – they had decided the beginners circuit would make for a fairer competition - when Miles was aware that someone had tapped Jake on the shoulder, just as the philosopher's video car had pushed past Miles' vehicle.

"Hang on," said Jake and promptly crashed. He started again.

"Listen man!" someone slurred. The owner of the voice, the same person hassling Jake, was drunk. Jake elbowed whoever was pestering him to one side and tried to continue with the game, but the other man came back and shook his shoulder. He abandoned the game, got out of his seat and turned to face his tormentor. Miles followed, leaving his car to be counted out by the game.

"What was the big idea?" said Jake. "We're playing."

The two reporters found themselves facing off with a group of four young boys who brought the headline 'Youth gang terrorises city' to mind. All four were in jeans and T-shirts with denim jackets. Two were sandy haired, pimpled and looked as if they should be doing their homework. They hung back. The other two looked more serious. The one facing off Jake was lanky, of the physical type Miles knew well from up his way, with arms long enough to worry any boxer. The second, who was eyeing Miles, was shorter and much darker, perhaps of Italian extraction. He was wearing a bandana and sunglasses, despite the gloom in the video parlor, as if he was a black from South Central Los Angeles instead of a second generation Italian in a video parlor deep in suburban Sydney. The bandana in particular made the youth so ridiculous – he was too obviously copying style from American films – that Miles would have laughed but for the fact that the youth was also heavily built, and sneering at him.

For their part the youths were surprised by the size of Jake, when he unfolded from the video game, but they had been drinking. And they were stupid.

"These are our machines, man," said the lanky youth.

"I don't see your name on 'em," said Jake.

"We own these machines man."

As far as Miles was concerned they could have them but the lanky youth then pushed Jake to emphasise his point. Jake shoved back, hard, throwing the youth into the users of a street fighting machine, scattering them. The youth sprang back, moving as he imagined someone who knew karate might move. As Miles watched all this, stunned, the bandana youth belted the high country man shrewdly in the eye, throwing him back against the chairs of the Daytona machine, then stepped back with a stupid grin on his face, as if he had achieved something. Miles was not really one for fights but where he came from blows to the eye were not taken lightly. More surprised than hurt he sprang back and charged, head down – his favorite tactic (his father had often remarked that his son's head was the hardest thing about him). More by good luck than skill his skull thumped his opponents nose. Bandana-youth threw his arms around Miles, trying to get him in a head lock, and the pair smashed into another machines. Bandana gave the high country man another whack to the head. Miles kneed him in the groin and heard the youth yell, but he still hung on like grim death while they crashed into another machine. He was aware of Jake wresting with his opponent and the other youths standing around in awe. Then he heard sirens.

"Cops," said someone.

Jake was suddenly there, trying to drag bandana-youth off Miles. The youth hung on until Jake stomped hard on his foot, then he yelped and let go. The lanky youth had vanished.

"Cm'n mate, time to leave."

Miles glanced briefly at his opponent who, he noticed with grim satisfaction, had a bloody nose and was rolling on the floor holding his foot, then followed Jake to the rear door. It was alarmed. Jake pushed through the double doors setting off the alarm, and closed it just as quickly stopping the electronic shriek. The sudden rush of cold air stung Miles' rapidly closing left eye. They weaved through a back alley, walking but trying not to run – they had retained enough sense for that precaution - and into a nearby pub through its back entrance. The toilet was just by the back door.

"Tuck in your shirt mate," hissed Jake.

Miles duly tucked in his shirt and straightened his clothes, badly disarranged in the fight, as did Jake. One of the pub's patrons came in, glanced at them curiously but went about his business. Both reporters walked calmly out into the street. A police car had stopped at the video parlor but the police were inside and no one was looking their way, so they walked slowly in the opposite direction.

"We'd better duck into that other pub," said Jake. "Just in case the police get enthusiastic and look around the streets."

The fight had not really been either man's fault but both knew from their reporting work that it would be the police's job to sort out exactly what happened - who had hit whom and at what point. Perhaps their conduct did not bear strict examination, as they say in the law courts. In all it was best to shoot through and leave the paperwork to someone else.

They reached the second and seedier pub, which was full, and ducked into the toilets where Miles saw that his eye had swollen up badly in the previous few minutes. Together with a big bruise on the side of his face where bandana youth had hit him a second time, it was not a pretty sight.

"Oh great," he said, "what type of philosophy did you say you followed?"

"Greek philosophers, mate," said Jake, unabashed at having just got them into a brawl in a video parlor. "Socrates was a soldier; could handle himself in a fight. He was even in pitched battles. Now the Chinese philosophers, they believed in harmony and in finding the way forward."

"Maybe you should try a bit more Chinese."

"Maybe." He grinned.

Jake bought drinks and they wedged themselves in well down the back with Miles facing the wall. The police may have looked in, but neither man noticed. A couple of the other pub patrons observed Miles' bruises, and one made a remark to his mates about the night being "lively" but otherwise they ignored the two reporters.

Miles and Jake discussed the fight over several rounds, in fact until closing time when Miles realised his chin had gone numb again. There was nothing for it but to accept Jake's offer of a couch and stagger through Lovett Bay back streets. At the flat, chatting amiably was Tomasina and Anne.

"What have you been doing!" squealed Anne, on seeing Miles.

Tomasina clapped her hands to her mouth. "Oh migod!"

"Um, well… we were just playing Daytona, the racing game at the video parlor," said Miles lamely.

"How did you get a black eye doing that?" asked Tomasina.

"Some other guys wanted to play it while we were playing it," said Jake, casually.

"You're supposed to be a top philosophy student and you still get involved in fights in video parlors," said Tomasina.

"Hey, look, the other guys didn't know much about philosophy – except maybe they knew about Darwin, except he was a scientist not a philosopher, and we're always flunking Darwin."

"So I see," said Tomasina, folding her arms.

By that time Anne had found an ice pack in the fridge and handed it to Miles who put it to his eye.

"Thank you," he said, wincing as he applied the ice pack to his eye, "you're an angel."

She sighed. "Drunk again."

CHAPTER NINE

Miles laid low that weekend which was not difficult as he did not have many friends in Sydney and was, in any case, hung over for most of Saturday. But on Monday, when he had to face the world again, his bruised eye had turned an interesting shade of yellow and purple. That area had also merged neatly with the bruising on side of his head so that, in Miles' imagination, it seemed as if half his face was one big bruise. He wore sunglasses in the street but there was no point in maintaining a disguise while in the office.

"Miles, what have you been doing?" Kelly shrieked.

"It was an argument on philosophy. You know, Locke versus Nietzsche. Individual rights versus the deeds of the great."

"Huh?"

"Nietzsche guy didn't like losing."

"Who is Nietz.. whatisit.?"

"German philosopher."

"So did he hit you?"

"Not him," said Miles ducking away to the tiny newsroom.

Unfortunately, the sales lady Kate had emerged

from her own cubbyhole to speak to Kelly and accosted him before he could walk that vital few steps.

"Miles, have you been a bad boy this weekend?"

The reporter liked Kate and had recently opted to split the cost of a jar of coffee with her – as far as Ros was concerned the Bugle Group did not provide coffee – so he felt that he should say something. There was no need to stick to the same story, however.

"I was asking women for dates. No one told me Sydney women were so tough."

She inspected his injuries critically. "A date, Miles? Is that ALL you were asking for?"

"As God is my witness."

"I've heard that, before. It usually means you started it."

"I never start anything."

She sighed. "I see I'm not going to get a straight answer. I'm glad I had girls. Boys are too hard."

He finally escaped into the news cupboard. Angela looked up briefly, raised one eyebrow over his injuries and then went back to doing nothing, without deigning to comment.

Emma also clucked over his eye, during her usual Monday afternoon visit.

"My sources say you got into a fight."

"They started it."

"Maybe. Tomasina has been giving Jake all kinds of hell."

"Good!" Miles felt that Jake should be given a hard time, on principle. "They shouldn't teach philosophy at uni, gives city folk big ideas."

"Spare us the country crap, just be presentable for

my house warming, so no fights in the next few weeks please. Anne – the girl you're keen on – she's coming."

"I'm keen on Anne?"

"You are," said Emma, firmly. "You know, she works around here."

"She does?" Miles was interested in this information.

"She's an administrator or an executive in one of the offices around here. Her family's mega-rich. I think she works for her dad."

"Oh! Okay." Miles thought of his rented room and not-very-flash job as a journalist on the Koala Bay Bugle, and his heart sank. He thought of taking her out in his battered, orange Ford utility, and his heart sank further. He did not know much about mega-rich girls but he did not think that they went out with guys who drove rusty, orange utilities.

"I wouldn't get your hopes up. Some guy called Allen has been sniffing around."

"Glad to see you're keeping an eye out for me, Ms Hawthorne."

"Someone has to, especially with the way you're looking now. Anyway Miley, there'll be lots of girls at the party. No need to worry about Anne. You'll be there?"

"Try to keep me away."

She told him the address and left with a "bye bye Miley," and wave, leaving a whiff of perfume and Miles alone with Angela. In the silence he could again hear his colleague's irritating phone conversation.

"Yeah, yeah, right! … So she said to him; if you go, kid, then you're gone… Yep! Oh no, now she's off with some other guy…"

For the next few days, while his bruises faded, Miles did his work by phone. Another issue emerged from the printers and into the letter boxes of the thriving community of Koala Beach. He was relaxing into the job; catching the rhythm of it. But there was still a major internal issue to be dealt with, before he truly settled in, namely the sub editor's seemingly irrational demands that he help his colleague. Late on Thursday when Miles was writing up his lead for the following week – community anger over a new no-leads policy for dogs being walked in one of the local parks – Eve rang again.

"Miles can you talk?"

Angela was always in the office earlier than Miles, and always left earlier. She never said either good morning or goodbye.

"Yes."

"Angela's filed another story."

"Good as the last one?"

"Worse. I think it's about a music store."

"Music store? That's new. Ros never said anything about a music store."

"Did you remember to talk to her about that story?"

"Oh yeah, sorry, I forgot." (Actually he had been hoping that Eve would forget about the matter.) "Just hold it over. I'll have to do it next week. Did you talk to Justin? He really is the guy to do this. She's gotta listen to him. Maybe she and Nathan over in Lovett Bay can go to South Forest."

"Um, it's that problem with Nathan that's got me worried about Angela."

"What's Nathan got to do with this?"

"Ellen complained to Justin about Nathan, earlier this week," Eve said.

"And?"

"He's demanded Ellen write out reports and set progress goals which have to be met, or else."

"Did he speak to Nathan?'

"Not a word, Ellen says. She was just told to lift her game.'

"So it's all her fault, basically. Going to Jason just added to her troubles."

"Seems so."

"So this is why you want me to become boy trainer from the bush. But you're chief sub, aren't you? Do what chief subs do - yell at her that's terrible copy, slam the phone down in her ear, then spike it. It's just advertorial anyway. No-one else in the group is doing it – unless you count that stuff in the fashion and beauty section."

"Don't talk to me about the fashion and beauty section," said Eve in an exasperated tone. "It's just that we can't be too negative about this."

"Don't want to be negative?" exclaimed Miles. "Eve, mate, from what I've seen of this group, a lot of it's negative. The technical term we use in the bush is 'fucked'. We're very wise in the bush."

"Exactly," said Jenny. "You're a real wise, homespun type, just the sort of guy we need to help trainees with copy."

Miles had suddenly become very tired of this argument. "Look, I said I'd try once and I will but it's a complete, total waste of time. Counter-productive if anything. She should be switched somewhere else – anywhere else."

"Okay, just talk to her, and we'll see. And have a word to her about her police stuff. It's terrible and we don't have time to rewrite it here."

"I'd love to talk to her about her police copy, but it's a waste of time."

"Whatever."

"Sure."

Miles attempt at being an editorial counsellor was, as he had predicted, disastrous.

On Monday afternoon of the following week, just before he plunged back into the maelstrom of news generated by the community of Koala Park, Miles printed out Angela's two stories, sent on by Eve, as well as the last set of police notes. Mustering what courage he had, stood up to speak to his colleague.

"Look, ah, Angela, have you got a moment?"

Angela's look could have cut diamonds but she condescended to take off her earphones.

"It's about your two stories. The panel beater one and the – um - music store piece, is it?" He made a half gesture of showing the copies to her, as if to prove that he had some authority. "Um, Eve sent these things back to me, saying that they needed more work and, well, perhaps if we.."

"WHAT!" Angela slapped the desk in front of her. "WHAT'S SHE DOING SNEAKING AROUND BEHIND MY BACK!"

"It's hardly sneaking. She doesn't have time to work with you on these things. I got nominated because I'm here."

"WHAT'S THAT GOTTA DO WITH IT.. I DON'T REPORT TO YOU."

Kelly was now looking around curiously from her desk to see what all the noise was about.

"It's not a matter of who reports to who. I'm just trying to help. Eve wanted to try this before taking the stories to Justin..." Miles words of reason were wasted. Angela was beside herself with rage.

"WHY DIDN'T SHE TELL ME HERSELF THEY WOULDN'T GO IN THIS WEEK?"

"um, well,..." Miles suddenly realised that Eve had not bothered to tell Angela that he would speak to her about the stories. She could have at least sent an email. What a mess.

"NOW SOME FUCKING AMATEUR FROM UP WOP WOP WAY WANTS TO TELL ME WHAT TO DO!"

The reference to being from the bush nettled him for a moment, then he realised that the attempt was over and dropped the print outs on her desk.

"Fine! If that's the way you feel, I'll just tell that to Eve. You and she want to take it up with Justin."

"DON'T WORRY I WILL!"

"Okay, you talk to Eve. I'm out. I tried."

Angela dropped the volume from extremely loud to plain loud, but with overtones of seething hatred. "Why doesn't Eve talk to me, huh? What's wrong with that."

"That's what I told her, but she says she doesn't have the time, and this stuff requires a lot of work."

"There was never a problem when Jan was around."

"That's 'cause no stories were getting through. Ros blocked anything interesting."

"Jan was good at her job! Not like you!" she spat.

"Well, thanks for that, but you want to take it up with the people at South Forest. I'm out."

"You sure are out."

"Fine!"

"Fine!"

Angela plainly wanted to hurl a few insults but Miles was not biting. He turned back to his computer and phone. So she turned back to hers, putting on her ear phones and humming elaborating to show that she did not care. Miles did not care that she did not care. The sooner Justin got off his rear end and did something about the problem the better for everyone, and he wrote an email to Eve to that effect. While he was at it he pointed out, diplomatically, that Angela should have been given some warning he would speak to her. That should end the matter, he thought.

Later in the week, Justin walked into the office. It was the first time Miles had seen him in the Koala Bay office, and he only realised the editor-in-chief was there when a shadow was cast across his desk. He was just finishing an interview.

"Justin! Hi!," he said, turning around. "I.." It was the first time he had spoken to his boss since confronting him in the car park, which made it their third meeting. He did not get to finish the sentence.

"So you think you're better than everyone," snarled Justin.

"No I don't." Miles was both puzzled and stung by the accusation

"Shuddup and listen! You don't have any say in Angela here."

So that's what all this was about.

"No I don't, all I was doing.."

"SHUDDUP! I'm not interested. You're just here to report. You leave her alone, with your unreasonable demands.."

"WHAT!"

"And nitpicking on copy.."

"You're joking, I haven't.."

"I SAID TO SAVE IT." Justin yelled so hard that Miles, stung, stood up sharply, staring fixedly at his editor in chief and slowly turning red – a warning sign to those that knew him. Justin was forced to take a step back but kept yelling. "SHE REPORTS TO ME, NOT YOU. ANY STORIES SHE WRITES GOES TO ME. I'M NOT HAVING A JUMPED UP NOBODY WHO'S FARTED AROUND ON A COUNTRY RAG FOR A FEW MONTHS TRYING TO TELL PEOPLE HOW TO WRITE."

"SO DOES THAT MEAN YOU'RE GOING TO DO YOUR JOB!"

The editor-in-chief thought exactly nothing of yelling at any of his journalists, but if they yelled back at him at least he did not despise them.

"I DON'T NEED WANKERS LIKE YOU TELLING ME TO DO MY JOB. WHAT I WANT IS FOR REPORTERS TO GET DOWN AND REPORT, AND LEAVE MANAGEMENT TO ME."

"FINE. SO THAT'S WHAT I TELL EVE!"

"SHE ALREADY KNOWS."

"NO SHE DOESN'T. WHY DON'T YOU TELL HER."

"SHE KNOWS - I DON'T WANT TO HEAR OF THIS AGAIN."

"SHE DOES NOT!"

Justin did not bother to reply, he abruptly turned from Miles to Angela and said, in a sweet voice, as if Miles did not exist and he had not been yelling, "I'll call later". She smiled at him, and Miles bit back another insult. He was suddenly suspicious that the visit had a lot to do with Angela's charms.

Justin left as abruptly as he came. Outside Miles heard Kelly say, "Oh Mr. Brock, I just came back. Didn't see you come in. Ros isn't here at the moment."

"Thank Christ for that!"

With Kelly stunned into silence, Miles could hear his editor in chief stomp down the steep stairs and out into the street. He turned his gaze back to Angela who had put her earphones back on but, aware of his gaze, stuck her index finger in the air. She started humming elaborately, looking triumphant but ignoring her colleague. Miles for his part felt the hatred welling up within him. For a moment he became almost dangerous thinking wildly of overturning Angela's desk and shaking her. Then he took a deep breath, and the red changed to pink. Assaulting Angela would get him fired on the spot. Yelling at her was also useless; as she was immune to reason and had the backing of the editor in chief. It was intolerable.

Miles cleared his throat and stomped out of the office; Kelly looked up curiously. He got as far as the back door to the car park, then he stopped, backed up against the door jamb and hit the back of his head against it, hard. Somehow that seemed to help. He did it again. THUD! That was better. Maybe if he did it again. THUD! Ouch! Okay that was enough.

He rubbed the back of his head then walked to the beach, where a stiff wind was whipping big rollers from the sea. The Koala Beach surf never reached the heights of the surf at Bell Beach, or the beaches to the south. It was too sheltered but it had its moments. Miles stared at the rollers for a time until his own inner sea had calmed. Perhaps there were newsrooms in the city where he would not bang his head against a door jamb? Maybe he should make more of an effort to find one. A stint on the Bugle Group carried little weight in the journalistic world, he had now realised, but a stint cut short by a protest resignation would carry even less weight. So he would stay. After all, he hardly ever saw Justin, and he cared not a jot what Angela thought. He was later assured by the other reporters that his screaming match with Justin had not damaged his career prospects at the group, as he never had any in the first place.

Miles trailed into work the next morning, doing his best to ignore Angela who elaborately ignored him. Situation normal. At that point in his train of thought, Eve rang up to find out whether he had spoken with Angela.

"What is it with this place?" asked Miles, after checking out of the corner of eye, that Angela still had her ear phones on. "Don't you guys look at your emails? Don't you talk to one another at all down there?"

"How do you mean?"

"Yesterday, I had Justin up screaming at me because I dared to say anything to Angela about her work."

"Oh!"

"That's right, 'Oh!', and you didn't even send her a message saying you'd told me to speak to her, so now I'm out of the mentoring business. You have to speak to Justin. He made that very clear. He also seemed to think you already understood that."

"But what am I going to do about the stories?"

If Justin was interested in a jumble of words on panel beaters and music shops in Koala Bay they should be handed to him.

"Put them somewhere everyone can access in the system," said Miles, patiently, "print 'em out, write 'Angela's copy for attention editor in chief' on the top, along with where they are in the system, then drop them on Bronwyn's desk. Bronwyn only has to move the bits of paper to Justin's desk without losing 'em. She may be able to do that but then again, on past performance, she may not. Either way, you're covered. If he gets them you can say that from me you understood that he was handling those stories. If he doesn't you say you left the stuff on Bronwyn's desk."

"Oh okay," said Eve brightening with the thought that she could shuffled the problem to one side. Miles hung up shaking his head.

The next call was from Jake. "You sound down in the mouth. What's been happening?"

"Tell you when I see you but I found out what a really right bastard our beloved boss can be."

"Tell me about it. There is a form of philosophical analysis that can be used on guys like that."

"Yeah? What is it?"

"A boot up the bum. But listen, have you seen the latest Lovett Bay Bugle?"

"Can't say as I have."

"Look up the front page online, I'll hang on."

The front pages of all the Bugle papers were put online in the week they came out, as a further service to the community. A story at the bottom of Lovett Bay's front page read;

YOUTH GANGS FIGHT

Two Lovett Bay youths were taken to hospital following a fierce gang fight in a video parlor in Sampson Road. The fight that has left police deeply concerned over gang violence in the area.

Police arrested two youths, both from Lovett Bay, after being called to the video parlour around 9PM in response to an 000 emergency call from the parlor on-duty manager. The youths were taken to Koala Bay hospital for treatment.

Two others, described as "older youths" by terrified witnesses, escaped despite a search of the streets and near-by businesses by police.

"Older youths!" spluttered Miles. He read to the bottom of the story. The arrested youths had been treated and released from hospital, then released from custody with a warning. As the "older youths" had not been found or identified, there was not much of a case against the pair in custody. The manager of the video store was quoted as being "terrified", and the local police senior sergeant commented that youth violence was an increasing problem. Police investigations into the matter where continuing.

"Seems like we're a real problem to society, mate," said Jake.

"Seems so! We'd better give that games place a miss for a while."

"Been thinking that. There's a better one around here, anyway. What I can't understand though is why take 'em to hospital. I'm pretty sure we didn't do much damage."

"Procedure," said Miles, after a moment's thought. "You can't have injured people in police custody without doing something to treat them, so they got taken to hospital. The guy whose foot you trod on w'd have to have a scan just so the cops are covered if he tries to sue."

"Sounds if we've been laying into 'em with iron bars.."

"Whatever. But mate, we've gotta agree on one thing."

"Just one thing?"

"Our future social outings are to be respectable. No messing with the local wild life. If someone wants a seat on the Daytona machines, let 'em have it."

"Sounds fair," said Jake. "This weird Aussie-rules code game on Saturday is a good bet for the philosophically inclined." Jake and Miles had been to a practice and, thanks to a number of team members moving on, had managed to get spots in the side. "I'll indulge my natural masculine instincts for aggression then."

CHAPTER TEN

Rain pelted down. Standing in his assigned position around the half forward flank, Miles could only see the other players as shapes in the rain, scrambling in an undignified way over the ball in the mud on his team's half back line. It did not rain often in Sydney but when it did, as he had discovered, the heavens opened for hours, even days, turning the playing ovals into mud puddles and drenching players. He was just as wet as if he had been swimming. He moved towards the center, mud squelching under his boots, more to keep the opposing half back flanker occupied than through any real hope the ball might come his way. It was late in the final quarter, his team was five goals behind and the scramble that passed as the game action in that muck and rain had been mostly confined to the opposition's half. As well as being wet through, mud splattered and tired, despite the comparative lack of action – he was not as fit as he thought he was – Miles faced a long drive home. Sydney, he had discovered, was a gigantic wilderness of houses, roads, shopping complexes, blocks of flats, more houses, roads, reserves, sporting fields, more houses, traffic lights, shops, golf courses, schools, more houses, parks, more houses and, well, more houses.

Another and comparatively minor problem was his opponent – a hefty Western suburbs thug who had been sent to cover Miles for the second half, after the reporter had run rings around his previous opponent, in the few times the ball had come his way. He suspected that this beefy Western suburbs gentleman had been told to "knuckle" the upstart flanker whenever the umpire was not looking. Thugs had tried to knuckle Miles on a football field before. The thug was now trying to provoke Miles, but he was not very inventive, and after weeks of Ros and Angela for company Miles was well use to hostility. He hardly even heard the man.

"Bush fuckwit," said the opponent, trailing behind him. "Your dad fucks sheep mate."

Miles almost said "uh huh" by reflex but stopped himself in time. Then he saw the play turn. One player wearing his side's colors booted the ball off the ground, in a spray of mud, and miraculously it went to the Lovett Bay center. That player turned and, half blinded by the rain, looked for a lead down field. The center half forward ran forward but was well marked by his opponent.

"Ya mum.." Miles never heard the gross insult against his mother. He had heard it earlier anyway. He swerved and dashed across the field. "Ohhh!" said his opponent and splashed ponderously through the mud after him. The center, an accountant who had gone with his wife's career to Sydney, saw the flash of Lovett colors, opted for the big kick, and had the sense to kick where Miles was going to be. It worked. Miles sensed rather than saw the ball in the rain, and it thudded onto his chest as he ran. The umpire blew his whistle for the mark then yelled "play on". Glancing behind to see that his opponent was still wallowing through the mud behind him, Miles charged down field. He touched the ball once on the ground – bouncing it was out of the question in those conditions. The full forward was too well marked for a pass. He touched the ball on the ground again. His opponent was sending mud flying in an effort to catch up. Another Westie back was closing on him from the front. No one to hand pass to. Then, abruptly, the rain stopped; an open goal beckoned and he kicked. The ball sailed through, well above the outstretched fingertips of the full back. The goal umpire, a Lovett player's girlfriend, ducked out of the way with a squeal when the ball went through the goals, then jumped back to signal two thumbs up, all without letting go of her umbrella. His second goal for the game.

Miles watched the ball go through then jumped in the air, hands raised, half turning. Whump! His frustrated and still charging opponent barged straight into him, the Westie's shoulder colliding with Miles' nose. The reporter sailed through the air. For a moment he felt almost a sense of peace. So he had to put up with Ros and Angela. So he had no date this evening. What did it all matter? Somewhere far off, almost in another world, the umpire blew his whistle. Then he landed with a distinct splat in the ground's biggest mud puddle. Before he could pull himself out, players were involved in what sports writers call an "on-field incident". Enraged Lovett players converged on the tough. A few of the other side decided to help their team mate. Miles' only role in this was to be stomped further into the mud by three struggling players falling on top of him. When he hauled himself to his feet, Jake, as the substitute ruck, was in the middle of a pushing and shoving match with Miles' opponent and assorted players from both sides.

The umpire raced up and blew his whistle so hard that players held their ears – that official's own way of breaking up the occasional brawl.

"Quit it you blokes!" he yelled, "Or I'm gonna send names to the league." Jake was pulled away by team mates. "You!" The umpire pointed at Miles' opponent. "It's a goal, it goes back to the center and a free kick from there against you!"

The Westie spread his arms, his mouth open in astonishment, to suggest total innocence. "Whaddit I do, ref?"

"I'm an umpire not a referee. You flattened him clean after he'd got rid of the ball. It'd even gone through the goal. And you.." The umpire swung around to Miles, meaning to say that he was getting the kick but started when he saw the reporter, "..you'll have to go off."

"Meh!" Miles was suddenly aware his nose was blocked, and hurt.

"Blood rule, mate. Go off and get cleaned up."

Miles wiped his nose, aware that his opponent was suddenly cackling with glee. His hand came away with a bright streak of blood, mixed with mud. Oh great! If blood was showing he had to go off. He trotted away, past his opponent who could not resist another cackle and a shove. Miles staggered theatrically and the umpire rose to the bait. "Oy! Oy! Fifty meters up on the free kick for that!" A decent kick by the Lovett Bayers would get the ball into their goal square.

"Hey umppie, I just gave 'im a shove!"

"We weren't even playing!"

At the boundary line the coach jerked his thumb in the direction of dressing room and told him to lie down head back, which was fine by Miles. But then, with his nose still running with blood, who should he meet but Anne. She looked trim and neat as always, wearing an expensive coat and carrying a large umbrella as a concession to the rain. She had come to meet Tomasina and was just putting her umbrella down, when she looked up and saw him.

"Miles!" She yelped

For a moment Miles could not understand why she looked at him with such horror. The he looked down and realised that beside being covered in mud there was blood all down his football jumper and, for all he knew, all over his mouth and chin. He took out his mouth guard but, given the state of his nose, it did not make him more understandable.

"At beast I'b not drunk," he said.

"Miles, just go somewhere at get cleaned up," she said, waving him away and averting her eyes. "Please don't just stand there, dripping blood."

He trotted off, his feelings a little hurt, and lay down on the concrete floor in the changing rooms where he heard the final whistle. His team mates soon came in, boots grating on the concrete floor. Jake loomed over him.

"The girls think you're dying in here."

"Don't worry mate I'b am," said Miles opening his eyes. He got up, and blew out each nostril with force, ejecting two large wads of blood and mucus into a wash basin. "It's stopped, maybe." he flopped wearily beside Jake keeping his head well back for, despite his brave words, it felt as if blood was going to leak out. The philosopher started taking his boots off.

"How'd it go at the end."

"Henry," this was the full forward, "got another goal after you left. "So we ended only three goals or so down. Not so bad, considering it was mostly in their half."

"Rough game."

"Nah! I went to a workshop once on post modernist concepts in existentialism; now that was real intellectual violence. Never mind these amateurs. My opponent, however, did seem up on the Greek philosophers. I'll give'im that."

Miles was going to ask both what existentialism and post modernism were when the coach blew in. As his team had held one of last year's finalists to just a three goal win, despite a big turnover in players he was reasonably hopeful for the season. That meant, for once, that he was almost human.

"Good game Miles! Nose okay?"

"Just a knock"

The coach nodded. He was an electrician who had played with minor clubs in Melbourne in his younger days. "And not so bad Jake but, mate, we've gotta teach you about tackling in Aussie rules."

"In this game if you start manhandling guys, everyone starts screaming."

"It's that thing called the rules. Try 'n make it to practice on Tuesday and we go through some basics," said the coach.

"So I can tell the girls you'll live?" said Jake after the coach had gone.

"Guess."

"They don't understand why they we do this stuff," said the philosopher. "They don't see the fun."

"You mean the fun of having your nose flattened and being trampled on in the mud by half yer own forward line? Then getting sent off."

"'n don't forget the blood," said Jake, eying Miles' football jumper. "The chance to get covered in your own blood. Women just don't get sport do they?"

There were no showers in the changing blocks on that field. After sticking his head under a tap to get rid of the worst of the mud and blood, Miles walked out in time to see Anne in the passenger seat of a new Porsche, driving out of the car park. He could not see who was in the driver's seat but Anne was laughing.

He met her again during the week, by chance. He always walked around a little during lunchtime, if the weather was bearable. It was part of his business to inspect the retail establishments that made up the Koala Bay shopping precinct, or so he told himself, but he also got away from Angela for a time. On one of those excursions he saw Anne in the crowd.

"Oh hello," she said. Her greeting was neither warm nor cold. "Not drunk, hung over, bruised or covered in blood I see. It's an improvement."

Miles had the impression that Anne's glance had

taken in his clothes. He wore elastic-sided boots, an elderly pair of jeans and a gray jumper, a little the worse for wear, on top of a light blue shirt. Wearing a suit for interviews in Koala Bay seemed over the top, but the uncomfortable thought occurred to him that his clothes might not be considered fashionable.

"I've taken a vow," he said, pushing that thought aside.

"To give up drinking?"

"Not to drink port - not with beer, anyway."

That earned Miles a small smile. "Something to be thankful for," she said.

"You work for a family company up here?"

A slight shadow crossed Anne's face. "We have investments up here."

"So why don't we go somewhere to get coffee?"

"Too busy just now. Got some shopping to do. She began walking and Miles, naturally, walked with her. "How come you're walking this way?" she asked.

"To keep you company. You know, you find someone you know in a big city you walk around with them. It's a bush thing. So how about coffee this week?"

"Busy, I'm afraid Miles. I have to go in here." They had stopped outside a shop. "I'll probably see you at Emma's party this weekend."

"I could go in here too."

"Miles."

"Um, yep." He like the way she said his name.

"It's a lady's lingerie shop."

Miles looked at the shop window and realised that it displayed women's underwear. "So it is. Well, maybe I have business in a lady's lingerie shop."

She smiled. "You don't seem like the type, somehow, Miles. I'll see you around."

Miles had half formed a plan to ask her to Emma's party but she would not even have coffee with him. She was not interested, and that was that. He was disappointed of course but at least, so he told himself, he did not have to persuade her to ride in his Orange Ute.

In the end, Miles decided to leave his akubra at home. He had a red silk shirt – his only decent shirt – his best pair of cotton pants and a reddish-brown cord jacket. Country with city flair, or so he hoped. He thought the best way to set off his outfit was a genuine bushies' hat. Of course it was not a real bushman's hat, as it was both clean and unmarked. It was a bushman's hat fit for a city party. He examined himself in a long mirror inset into the front of a recently acquired, second hand wardrobe. The main attraction of the wardrobe had been the price, despite a smell that reminded him of visits to his grandmother, but its mirror was coming in handy. He tried a few different angles and tried emphasising his drawl. Nope! In the end he decided that it made him look too much country and too much obviously on the prowl, so he dropped it on his desk, which was also recently acquired. He thought of a tie, and then decided to button up the top button of his shirt instead. Was that fashionable? Miles had no idea. He undid the top button, as that seemed to suit him.

By the time he got to the party, a pack of imported stubbies in hand, the ice dumped in the bath tub for the drinks was starting to melt and the noise from the guests, scattering throughout the modest, rented brick house, was rising. Emma kissed him on the cheek and introduced her fiancé – a tall, taciturn man with a beard, who Miles would never have picked as a partner for Emma. But as he had come without a partner himself, he was not one to judge.

Jake was in the living room with Tomisina, who inspected Miles critically.

"Your eye is all healed. I told pain here," she whacked Jake on the shoulder to emphasise her point, "that if he gets into fights like that again he can look for someone else to get the ice for the bruises. I won't be there."

"Okay, okay," said Jake. "Next time I'll try Eastern philosophy... Lot of beer here to discuss, mate." Tomasina had started talking to Emma.

"Maybe. Thought maybe I'd give Darwin a work out."

"Yeah..," said Jake, nodding sagely. "Couple'a sorts here. Rejection's a bit of a pain, but philosophers can handle it. We get rejected a lot."

"How do philosophers handle it? I may need to know."

"Hmmm.. welllll... It all depends on how you define 'no' or 'get lost arsehole'. From the speaker's point of view then, okay, it's a rejection. But you're not looking at it from their point of view, but from your own. And from your own it's one scene in the absurd tragi-comic theatre of your existence."

"Theatre?"

"Well, maybe heroic journey is better." Jake was warming to his theme. "That's right, we're all heroes in our own personal heroic journey, so someone appears and has a bit part – a one liner. They are merely an obstacle; one of the barriers that must be circumvented in your quest to find the true female lead."

"I'm on an heroic journey?"

"That's right, you're voyaging through life."

"That's such bulldust!"

"Hey, man, I'm on a roll here.. please no simple negativity. We philosophers value only reason and dispassionate argument."

Before they could discuss the issue any further, Anne came into view obviously in the company of the man. Miles had been expecting something like this, and had to push aside a surge of jealousy. It did not help that Anne was looking particularly chic in black pants and a skivvy that clung to her figure. Her companion was blonde, tall, clean cut and was wearing a suit without a tie, as if he had just come from a meeting which he had.

As they were with Tomasina, Anne came to them first. "This is Allen," she said a little nervously.

"Gentlemen."

"Hey!" said Jake.

"Hi!" said Miles. He did not look at Anne and, out of the corner of his eye, he noted that she did not look at him.

"Miles and Jake are both journalists."

"Oh right!" said Allen, his face lighting up. "So who are you guys with – the Herald, Channel Nine; one of the magazines."

"Not exactly up that high yet," said Jake. "I'm on the *South Forest Bugle*."

"*Koala Bay Bugle*."

The light in Allen's face was abruptly switched

off. Anne had turned to talk to Tomasina and Emma, leaving Allen temporarily alone with the journalists. He glanced at her, plainly hoping to be rescued from such undistinguished company, but then thought he should try to make the best of it.

"What are you messing around with those things for? You want to get up onto the big papers, or the networks."

Miles had previously encountered, and would encounter again, people who may look at a newspaper once in a blue moon giving unsolicited career advice to journalists. He had quickly learned there was no point in trying to argue with them, so he just said "uh huh". Jake, however, gave the advice the treatment it deserved.

"See, Miles mate, that's what I've been saying all along. We're wasting our time on the locals. What we should do is march right up to the Channel Nine office, brush aside the heaps of people wanting jobs, and tell them 'we've decided to give you the benefit of our experience'."

"They'll go for it mate," said Miles, catching his cue.

"They'll see our vast experience - me four months on South Forest and you, what? A few weeks on Koala Bay.."

"And two years part-time on a weekly in the bush."

"..Mate, they'll wet themselves offering us contracts.."

"That personal journey you were talking about before, that'd really speed up."

"F'king oath It'd speed up – especially if security gets a hold of us. Whadda ya reckon Allen?"

Allen brows knitted over this. "Personal journey? It's not that far to channel nine – maybe an hour by car."

That response stopped both journalists cold but then Tomisina called Jake away to meet someone and, as Anne had not rejoined her friend, Miles was left alone with Allen and had to make the best of it.

"You go in for any part of the law?"

"Property law," said Allen, becoming animated now that the conversation had returned to his favourite subject – himself. "I was putting together a trust structure today for a client to buy land. The object is to minimise tax but retain flexibility in a family trust structure. We do that and the tax work and the trust management in another section. We're a one-stop shop on trust structures, if you like."

"Uh huh," said Miles, thinking that his new lawyer acquaintance would not be keen on a chorus of the philosopher's drinking song. "Been keeping you busy, have they?"

"Yes, it's a good time for property. Thinking of getting in myself. Been checking out the market. Don't think much of residential but commercial property is looking good. Are you invested in property at the moment?"

"Not really."

"Oh well then equity?"

"I've got investments in information technology and the automotive sector," said Miles, thinking of his beaten-up car and dodgy computer, "but I would like to invest in land." Miles tried not to smile. Allen missed the joke.

"Well if you think of property then Anne's family are the people to watch."

"Oh yes?"

"That's why I thought you might know something about property if you know Anne."

"We've only met a few times. I know her because I know Jake."

"I see." Allen was losing interest, which suited Miles fine. "I thought you must be in that crowd. But you must see property investment opportunities as a journalist. You have to move around and talk to people. Then you can invest and talk it up in the paper."

"Sadly not ethical, and there are some terrible killjoys in the Bugle Group who'd spot tricks like that a mile off. You don't become a journalist to get rich. The calling comes with a vow of poverty and everything."

Talk of poverty made Allen restless. "I just realised I don't have a drink," he said, "I must go and see what Anne has done with the drinks we brought. Nice to talk to you."

"Same to you," said Miles, and he escaped out onto the back porch.

The night was still and cold but a few of the partygoers, preferring the night air, leaning on posts and railings and talking in hushed tones. Miles walked around a little, and then talked with a sub-editor he knew from the Bugle Group, then a male photographer that the sub editor introduced. He was avoiding going back inside where Allen and Anne lurked.

"Miley!" It was Emma clutching the arm of another woman of about her own age she had just dragged from inside. "This is Fiona. She's not long moved up from

Melbourne." She turned to Fiona, "This is Miles. He's from the country in Victoria."

"Oh right!" said the friend, embarrassed at being strong armed into an introduction. "So how come you're in Sydney?" She was built along the same lines as Emma, which was good, but with longer hair. The chin was perhaps longer than it should have been, but bright eyes made up for it. Miles glimpsed briefly, in his mind's eye, her long hair, wet against her slim back.

"Fresh start. Time to move away. And you?"

"Me too, time to move on. Got a job with an advertising agency here, as a PA. Hoping to move up."

They chattered for a few minutes, before the inevitable question.

"So what do you do?"

"I'm a journalist."

"Ohh! I love journalists. I always think they are so interesting. So who do you work for? The Herald? The Telegraph?"

"Not exactly. Locals I'm afraid. The same one Emma takes pictures for."

"Oh right." The light went out of Fiona's eyes. "Oh yes, I'd forgotten, the Koala Bay thing, and, um, the Lovett Bay paper."

"I do the *Koala Bay Bugle*."

"Right."

Just then Jake burst through the back door to confront Emma, who was talking to another girl.

"Hey listen Emma, it's a real disgrace. There's a major emergency in that bath tub of yours."

"For heaven's sake, what is it?"

"There's no more Fosters. I ask you, how can a

photographer have a party, invite a bunch of lawyers and not have enough Fosters on hand, instead of the foreign stuff."

"You got away from Tomasina, I see," said Emma.

"I snuck away. Say Miles," he said, catching sight of his friend, "how come you're just standing there?" He was half drunk, and working on the other half.

"Well I was.." Miles looked around, meaning to say something to Fiona, but she was not there. He glimpsed a back with long hair going into the house. "..I was just thinking to myself what a right bastard that Darwin is."

"Wasn't a philosopher, mate. He was a scientist, and they're bad news. Ignore him mate."

When he got home in the small hours of the morning, Miles had to admit to himself that the evening had not been very successful. After striking out with Emma's friend he had fallen into conversation with two accountants – a husband and wife who knew Emma from her days as an accountant. They had been amused to find that he was a journalist on, as they put it, a "dinky little paper" like the Koala Bay Bugle. They asked what sort of stories he wrote and giggled over the fact that he wrote about parking restrictions, street upgrades and sporting ovals. Miles laughed along with them but found the conversation tiresome and moved on. He had spent the rest of the evening avoiding both them and Anne and Allen. He has nothing against Anne but hanging around when so clearly selected out was not cool. In any case he did not like Allen. Well stuff them all. He would read for a time – he was a reader – then go to bed.

Just as he reached that healthy conclusion the phone rang.

"Miles?"

The voice was girly and breathy. The memories rushed back.

"Elizabeth? Do you know what time it is? Is everything alright?"

She giggled and then, when she slightly slurred her next words, Miles knew she was drunk. It happened very rarely but it did happen. It did not sound as if she was using a mobile. Maybe it was from her bed room?

"I just rang to tell you I'm getting married."

Oh great! That was all he needed. Was there any alcohol in the house? He needed to get blind drunk.

"You rang me at this time on a Sunday morning to tell me? Couldn't you have gotten your mum to tell my mum, or something? Did I have to know? How did you get the number anyway?" He knew that was a silly question the moment he asked it. In the district he had come from there were few small secrets, but there had been one very big one and it was the reason Miles had left.

"I wanted to tell you myself."

"Well, okay, consider me told."

"Is that all you are going to say?"

"Oh – um – I hope you'll be very happy."

"Don't you want to know who I'm going to marry."

"No." He thought he could guess.

"It's Ben."

"Okay, well, it's Ben." Until very recently Ben had been Miles' best friend.

Her voice sank to a whisper. "You left before I could explain anything."

"I'm not good at those scenes. Anyway, wasn't it a bit late for explanations? I must've been the only one who didn't know what was going on. I just wondered why people kept on smiling at me. I was blind."

"Are you still blind, Miles?"

"Dunno. Probably not as stupid as I was, but that wouldn't be hard."

She giggled slightly. "I miss you Miles."

"I miss you too."

"Are you ever coming back?"

"I haven't been gone long enough to think about coming back."

"Jas said you wouldn't even see him, when he was there. He was upset."

"Fuck Jas! He picked his side he can stay on it."

"Miles don't be like that," she said, slurring her words and sounding close to tears. Miles remembered that she was the local beauty, with long brown hair and oval face. "I hoped we'd all still be friends."

".. Well, we're still friends - sure." What harm could there be in saying that?

"Are you seeing anybody?"

"Nope. No one wants me."

"Poor Miles," she giggled.

"Yes, poor me."

"So you could come back?"

"What to you and Ben? It'd get real complicated."

"They still talk about you at the newspaper."

Miles was sure they did. There was not much else to talk about.

"They'll get by without me."

"You could come back for the wedding – it'd be a nice gesture."

"You're drunk. You've got your fiancé to think about and it's not me."

"That's true," she admitted.

"Can't we leave it now? It's getting late and I have to get drunk by morning."

"So why do you have to get drunk Miles?"

"Seems like the thing to do. Lots of people get drunk in Sydney."

She lowered her voice. "You know, I still have your ring."

Miles swallowed This was hard. "Keep it to remember me by."

"Try to make it for the wedding," she said and hung up.

Well, that was just great. He had been trying to adjust to life in the big city and his past had come back to wallop him over the head. Why did she have to call? He gave up the thought of reading and, to distract himself, watched a violent action film that belonged to his landlord. Despite what he had said to Elizabeth he did not want to start drinking alone. Unexpectedly, he fell asleep in the chair.

CHAPTER ELEVEN

"So what do you think you owe your long marriage to?" asked Miles.

"Eh?" said the old lady.

He had forgotten to yell.

"SO HOW HAVE YOU MANAGED TO KEEP MARRIED FOR 50 YEARS?"

"OH! ITS ALL ABOUT MAKING AN EFFORT TO GET ON. YOU KNOW WORKING AT GETTING ON?"

"What's that dear?" said the husband, who had been sitting by her, smiling inanely.

"I SAID IT'S ALL ABOUT WORKING AT GETTING ON!" she snapped, irritably.

"Oh!" he said and went back to smiling.

The happy couple were sitting on a modest lounge suite in the front room of their double fronted brick house two blocks from Koala Bay's surf beach. Set on a coffee table beside the sofa for the occasion was a large black and white photograph of the pair at the ceremony 50 years before. He had been a strapping man; she a pretty bride. Their looks had long gone but they had children, including the middle-aged daughter who had arranged this interview and was sitting with them, grandchildren, and a good TV with cable. Most days they walked along the beach. They also had each other which, Miles supposed, was an advantage.

"YOU'VE LIVED IN THIS HOUSE 30 YEARS?"

"YES, YES, 30 YEARS.."

"HAVE THERE BEEN MANY CHANGES IN THAT TIME?" asked Miles, searching for something interesting to put in the story.

"OH. EVERYTHING HAS CHANGED."

"ANYTHING IN PARTICULAR?" he asked hopeful.

"OH EVERYTHING!"

"CAN YOU GIVE AN EXAMPLE."

"JUST EVERYTHING HAS CHANGED. YOU KNOW A LOT OF CHANGE. BUT WE'VE ALWAYS WORKED AT GETTING ON."

"What did you say dear?" said the husband, springing into life.

"THAT WE'VE ALWAYS WORKED AT GETTING ON," she yelled.

"Oh, okay," said the husband, unaffected. "Mary still looks the same as she did when I met her," he told Miles. He was a good deal older than his wife, and had made that observation three times previously.

"DARLING BE QUIET AND DON'T INTERRUPT THE MAN," snapped his wife.

Miles excused himself as Emma arrived to take the photographs, and Miles went outside to wait for her to finish. They were rarely at the same job at the same time but as they were going to put in a rare double appearance for the next job, which might be a story of substance, for once, he was going to wait for her.

The wait also meant he was in one place long enough to be cornered by the daughter - a large, commanding women, who wanted to know things.

"When will I see the story?"

"Might be in the paper next week. Depends on paper sizes and how much material we have."

"That's fine but when will I see it."

"If you mean before it goes in, sorry. We don't show stories beforehand."

"But why not?" she exclaimed.

"It's our story. We don't show it to sources to vet."

"I don't believe it. It's my parent's fiftieth wedding anniversary."

"That's why we're taking the trouble to talk to them. But the story's ours."

"What happens if there's an error in the story?"

"Then you can complain."

"What good would that do - the story's already in."

He shrugged. "That's the way we do things."

Miles was being hard line in this. Other journalists might figure that a 50th wedding anniversary story was not worth fighting over and send the daugher their version in an email. However, after a couple of bad experiences in the country where the sources thought they had some control over the stories - and that the story should express only their point of view - he had decided never to show stories to sources.

"That's not good enough."

"I'm not going to say she snapped at him," Miles said, guessing that was the error that the daughter wanted to correct in any story. By their nature such stories had to be played straight and cheerful, with only veiled hints at any deeper troubles. But that meant sentiments like "we've always worked at getting on" would not stretch very far. Maybe he would just write a caption. He should have done the interview by phone.

"I should think not, indeed! She did not snap, you arrogant puppy." Miles smiled and that made her angrier. "I'm going to complain. What's your name?"

She made a great show of taking paper out of her purse and asking Miles to spell his name. In response he took a copy of the latest Koala Bay Bugle out of his car and handed it to her. She made to hand it back after ostentatiously writing his name but he said "keep it madam" and left her holding it.

"You mark my words, I shall complain."

"Uh huh!" said Miles. The thought of what Justin would make of a complaint about a story that was not even in the paper made him smile again, and that made the daughter even angrier. Emma finally came out and he had an excuse to walk away from the still-spluttering daughter. They took her car a few blocks to the next story. For Emma had taken one look at Miles' orange utility on a previous job and refused to be seen in it.

"I've been cruised by guys in utilities heaps of times. One time they even had a can of weed killer in the back."

"Yeah? What brand of weed killer?"

"Eeyouh! Miley, who cares what brand? You still need a different car for Sydney girls."

This was true, as Miles had to admit, but his bank account did not agree. Maybe with a little more saving it might.

"They weren't as bad as some anniversary couples,"

said Emma, when they got into her car together, and Miles had mentioned the wife snapping. "There was one fiftieth anniversary I did where I couldn't get them to sit together on the same couch, 'cause they'd had a fight. Best I could do was to get them sitting at the opposite ends of the couch looking away from one another, arms folded. I rang the daughter and said 'you've got a problem'."

"What happened?"

"They couldn't work out how to write the story without saying the couple fought all the time, and the daughter begged us not to put it in so they didn't do anything. Still got it at home, but – it's a classic!"

"Must show it to me."

"Must, and while we're on the subject of people's love lives, how did it go with you and Marie?" Since the party the photographer had arranged for him to meet a girl called Marie who, as it happened, was experimenting with different ways of interacting with potential partners for a sociological thesis she was doing. As Miles understood the concept, and he had spent a little time on the phone with Marie working it out, this meant that she did not go out on "dates" as such. Instead, she insisted that Miles come along as part of a group of friends going to a night club. He knew no one else in the group and Marie's idea of interaction with him had been to ignore him the whole evening. He scored a dance with a complete stranger – she was interested but devoted to her boyfriend, who was out of town - but otherwise he thought he could chalk another one up to Darwin, or sociology. He wondered if he would be mentioned in her thesis.

"But what was wrong with her?" asked Emma.

"Nothing was wrong with her. She doesn't believe in dates so I went out on this group thing and she was surrounded by men. I never even spoke to her."

"Who was surrounding her?"

"A John and a Martin – I think."

"They're both gay."

"The gay guys got to talk to her? If I was gay, do ya think women would talk to me, at least. Strange ways in the city."

She smiled. "No chance of you turning out to be gay, Miles."

"So whadda reckon about internet dating sites? Should I put my picture up on that?"

"I think you're a traditional guy, Miles. Better stick to the traditional ways."

"Have to find a traditional girl. One who believes in dates, anyway."

The story for which Miles and Emma had taken the trouble to put in a rare joint appearance was a substantial development on the foreshore - just how big, Miles did not appreciate until he walked in and saw a scale model of the development. Koala Bay was shaped like a shallow horse shoe with rocks on either promontory, to make it a smaller version of the more famous Bondi and Coogee beaches. Along the southern curve of the horse shoe, at almost the edge of the usable beach and barely 10 meters back from the high tide line, the recently formed Koala Bay Development Corporation proposed placing an eleven-storey building, combining shops and offices in the bottom two storeys with five storeys of luxury apartments in the top. Not only that, by cutting a deal to move an impoverished bowls club, buying up a couple of houses and closing a piece of redundant road the developers had found room for a cluster of units and a small village green. As part of the trade-off for building this monstrosity and associated units almost on the foreshore, a set of tennis courts was to be built on the other side of the Koala Bay CBD, plus two multi-use playing fields.

The head of the KBDC was a red-faced, thick-set man in a dark suit called Graeme Clark – certainly not the hearty, black-slapping type wearing gold chains and white shoes which Miles, in his bush innocence, thought was the prototype for all developers. Clark had also brought his lawyer, a heavy jowlled man in an expensive suit. Miles was to discover that, as a general rule, lawyers at press conferences spelled trouble, but for the moment he could only see endless weeks of front page stories. The development was still a proposal as it had yet to be put to council for approval, so a lot of community consultation lay ahead.

Emma went first, taking her pictures and left. Then it was Miles' turn.

"This is a large development. The building is much higher than anything else on the foreshore, and closer to the beach. Will you be able to get council approval for this?"

"We've had preliminary discussions with council members and offices in the council, and believe that the project will meet with success," said Clark.

The answer was word for word identical to a sentence in the press release which Miles had been given.

"Okay.. so do you reckon you're gunna get much community reaction from this proposal."

"We will consult with community groups about the proposal, and point out the advantages to the community when the development goes ahead," said the developer.

Again, this echoed a statement already in the press release. Miles tried again.

"What stuff have you guys done before. What other developments have you done?"

Clark and his lawyer exchanged glances. "There's background information on a separate sheet in the folder," said the lawyer. So there was. This minimalist form of interviewing went on for a few more minutes until the reporter gave up and began to excuse himself.

"We will need to see the story, of course," said the lawyer.

It seemed to be Miles' day for sources thinking that he was some form of glorified copy writer, with the job of writing ads for their development proposals.

"But you haven't told me anything beyond the release!" he exclaimed. "Everything you've said is here on the release."

"My client must be able to see the story to check it for factual inaccuracies," said the lawyer. "He is about to raise a great deal of money from private investors. Public announcements must tally with the information we give to investors."

"We won't touch any matters of opinion," said Clark, in an exasperated voice. "We only care about the facts."

As if that changed anything.

"Sorry. It's our story not yours. Anyway, you can show the investors your press release. That's all you've told me. No doubt I'll be speaking to you soon." He stood up to go.

"I shall complain to your superior," said the lawyer, briefly peering at notes to remind him of the name, "Mr. Justin Brock. We will tell him that we find your attitude is unsatisfactory."

The lawyer said this with a stern look, lips tight, as if uttering some terrible threat. Miles gave them what he hoped was a disarming smile and shrugged. "If you want to complain about me to Justin join the queue." The lawyer's face turned a shade of red that matched that of his client. "Now if that's all you're going to give me, I've got a lot to do."

He walked to the office, which was only two blocks away, thinking he would collect his car with a stiff walk after work. On his way he encountered Anne and did his best to smile and wave politely as she passed, to show that he was not upset at being selected out, but did not stop. She half-smiled back, but he thought she seemed preoccupied. Well, he had his own preoccupations.

When he reached the office, he found someone was sitting at his desk using his phone. The stranger had the angular features of a film star, carefully brushed brown hair and small moustache, and wore an expensive black suit. The stranger cut such a sharp contrast to the mess on Miles' desk, that for a moment the reporter thought he must have come out of a space ship. Then he caught the flash of a gold chain on the stranger's wrist and it occurred to him, finally, that he must be connected with Angela. To compound his offence of being so well-groomed, this stranger was sitting back with both immaculately tailored legs up on a corner of the desk. Miles did this himself, sometimes, as it was just possible in that cramped space, but it was tiresome for a complete stranger to do it. Then, when the stranger realised Miles was standing at the newsroom door, he pointed forcibly at Angela and resumed his conversation, which seemed to be about a property deal. He had assumed Miles was a visitor like himself and was referring him to Angela who worked there.

Miles' reply was to reach over and drop his note book and biro onto the desk with a 'thwack', that made the stranger look up again, irritation showing on his face, and point more forcibly at Angela. That reporter was having one of her lengthy, irritating conversations and had not seen Miles come in, not that she would have bothered to ease the situation. Miles snatched the coffee cup from his desk – this time the stranger looked surprised – and went to make himself coffee, but by the time he came back the stranger was still on the phone, still with his feet on the desk. Miles put his cup, pointedly, on the desk and stood there, arms folded. The visitor looked up puzzled.

"Hang on, Geoff, hang on – what is it?" said the strange, the last question being directed at Miles.

"Get out of my chair and desk, please, 'n use someone else's phone."

The stranger looked puzzled then looked around him, as if only now realising that he was in Miles's desk.

"I'm with Angela."

"Fine! Use her phone."

"She's using it."

"Look, mate, do you want to hang up? It's been a long day. Go 'n use someone else's chair and phone - please."

The visitor's first response was to the person on the other end of the line. "Hang on, Geoff hang on, some guy here wants his phone back. It's his desk, seems like. Yeah all right. Yeah, hang on mate." Then the visitor spoke to Miles. "Look, can you use your mobile for a mo, this is really important."

"Work doesn't pay for the mobile, and I want to sit at the desk. I've got stuff to do. Wind it up."

The stranger stood up while Miles edged around him, but still kept talking. "Hang on Geoff, hang on. Listen mate it's not that desperate, the property will sell at the price we want. We just have to wait." Then, after listening for a few moments, "well, just talk to them. There's room in the deal for them… Oh come on, everybody's after something."

This went on for several minutes, while Miles tried to start his story. He actually only needed the phone to call Jake about football practice, but it was the principle of the thing. In any case he could not work with this person shouting almost in his ear. He finally caught the stranger's eye and made a hanging up motion, and after saying a few times "gotta go, Geoff, yeah I'm with Angela. I gotta go. I'll call you on the way to her place. I gotta go. Yeah mate. We'll talk about it. Gotta go. Bye!"

"Sorry about that," said the stranger, making an effort to smile. "Partner's a bit edgy."

"You sound like a busy man," said Miles, picking up his phone headset.

"Steve," said the stranger, holding on his hand.

"Miles." They shook, very briefly.

"So whadda you do around here?"

"I write stories for the paper. I'm the reporter here."

"You help Angela?"

"We work independently. Here's a paper." He handed Steve a copy of last week's paper, which he looked at as if he had never seen a newspaper before. Perhaps he had not.

"Oh right, this is what you guys do in here."

"Uh huh."

"So I see your name here and here.." He then flicked through a few pages, looking for Angela's name."

"You've passed it. Page four."

"Oh right, I see. Good story, Ange."

Angela had finished her conversation and put her bag up on the desk. It was the end of another day of doing nothing.

"Yeah, guess so," she said, glancing at the paper he held. She did not deign to look at Miles. "Always do police notes."

"Say, what sort of commission do you guys get on the ads?" said Steve, looking at a large ad for a real estate agent.

"None," said Miles, "this is editorial. Kate in the other office does advertising."

"Oh right!" Steve's eyebrows lifted.

"C'mon, Stevo let's get going."

"So you guys sell the words?"

Steve's knowledge of newspapers was not deep, it seemed.

"We don't sell anything. We write. We're editorial."

"You must get a bit under the counter then," said

Steve, grinning, making a motion with his hand as if receiving a small bundle from someone behind him.

"Nope! Good way to get fired."

Steve's grin faded slightly. "Nothing in it for you guys."

"Apart from our meagre salaries, nope."

"And no mobile phone."

"Nope."

"You should get 'em to give you one as part of your salary package. I know an accountant who can work out tax effective stuff on a car and mobile."

Miles had a sudden mental image of himself asking Justin for a car and mobile phone and chuckled.

"Listen mate, the only packages we know about at this end of the office, come in the post 'n have addresses on 'em."

Angela led a still puzzled Steve out at that moment but Miles could hear them talking as they were walking out through the reception area.

"Do you work with that guy?" Steve asked her.

"Not really, he's no one."

CHAPTER TWELVE

The next few weeks were busy for Miles. The announcement of the Koala Bay tower development, as the proposal soon became known, drew sharp reactions. First cab off the rank was a Graham Gleick, an energetic 30-something man representing an organisation called the Australian Natural Foreshore Association. He came in, unannounced, perched on the corner of Miles' desk as if it was something he had done every day to that point, and started to tell Miles about how the planned tower would be an appalling disaster for the environment.

"There's just too much pressure on the foreshore as it is," he told Miles. "And in the bay itself."

"But they're not building in the bay."

"Look mate, this tower will increase activity on the foreshow and put real pressure on the bay environment."

"Right!" said Miles, taking notes in his self-invented, doggerel shorthand. He had never been through a proper traineeship which involved being taught shorthand. Instead, he had found an old shorthand textbook in the town library back home and had adapted the outlines to his own uses. His notes were largely an aid to his memory of the conversation. "Is there any specific danger?"

"Yeah, yeah, the orange striped custard fish is in real danger."

"The – um – orange stripped custard fish."

"The bay is one of the last six known breeding grounds of the fish."

"Right – er – how do you know this?"

"The state government did a study 10 years ago which showed they were in danger from further development in the bay."

"Ten years ago – what was the name of the report?"

"Development balance in Koala Bay," said Graham, "it's on the department web site. I wrote down the link for you."

In all of this, Graham proved considerably more media savvy than his developer counterpart, Graeme Clark, or Clark's legal advisor. He also gave plenty of quotable quotes and, above all, he never made the basic blunder of demanding to see the story.

No sooner had Graham Gleick finished telling Miles what a disaster the development would be and had gone, than Councilor Coustas rang to say what a great thing the development was for Koala Bay.

"Mate, can't do better. This'll make those bastards in Hornsby sit up. When these guys build some'n that big there'll be others right behind them. Soon we'll be just like Chatswood."

"Yeah right – say, how come it's so close to the foreshore?"

"Cause there's no beach just where the tower's gonna be – anyway, town planning says it's okay, so it's okay. You should go to Surfers Paradise mate. Buildings lined up right behind the beach. Anyway, this will be great for house prices – remember to put that in the story..."

What did Miles think of all this? He thought that getting the first names of Graham the developer mixed up with Graeme the greenie was an accident waiting to happen. He also hoped for more controversy, as more controversy made for more stories. In that he was disappointed. Residents were initially surprised by the size of the development but when they read that their house would become more valuable because of it, the vast majority thought that the orange striped custard fish could take its chances.

In the middle of this frenzy of editorial activity the email system died. It expired quietly and mysteriously, while Miles was out to lunch one day. He came back to find a system message saying that it had lost connection with the server. The internet connection worked, but not the email.

"My email's got problems," said Kelly from the next room.

"So's mine," said Kate, the ad sales lady, yelling harder to be heard from her room. "I've called tech support."

"Mine too. Techs get back yet?" Miles also raised his voice to make himself heard.

"No, no response so far."

"Okay.."

Ros did not contribute to the conversation, although Miles knew she was in her room. It was her job to sort out this problem, but she never seemed to do anything but laugh on the phone, abuse Miles and get in Kate's way. Kate would dearly have liked her boss at South

Forest to tell Ros where to go, as Justin had done. But the sales side of the business could not display the same independence from management as editorial.

The next day, when Miles came back just before a little before going home time from a meeting with a group of residents who were concerned about the morning shadow from the proposed building, Kelly started complaining the moment he walked in.

"Miles, my email is still not up and the techs just aren't returning our calls."

"Can't we get our office manager on the job?" asked Miles, without really expecting that Ros could be made to do anything useful.

"She told me to get it fixed. She says she's too senior to deal with it."

"GET TO WORK MILES, AND STOP CHATTING WITH THE OTHER STAFF!" screamed Ros from her office.

"ROS DO YOU KNOW WHY THE TECHS DON'T RETURN OUR CALLS?"

"THAT'S NONE OF YOUR CONCERN. KELLY FIXING IT. GET ON WITH YOUR WORK."

Miles did not bother to reply. "So much for Ros," he said quietly to Kelly. "Have you any idea why the techs don't return our calls."

"The people at South Forest say that the techs always call them back. No one knows why they don't call us back."

"Doesn't someone in admin have a direct number for these guys?"

'MILES! YOU'RE STILL TALKING"

"I just keep being given the same number to ring," said Kelly.

"Hmmm!"

"And Miles, I've got all this work waiting to sent off." Kelly did not work solely as a receptionist but did some basic clerical work for ad sales, some of which was for Kate – work that was shunted around the company by email.

"Okay, well at this point we'll have to give up on the techs. Do you know how to set up an email address on a free email site?"

"I – I think so.."

"Okay, set one up. Then get one of your computer savvy mates down in South Forest to log onto the system as you, and set up your inbox so that all your email is bounced to your new address."

"Got it – I think."

"Just talk to someone who can do it down there. Also, set it up for Kate."

"What about Ros?"

"MILES GET ON WITH YOUR WORK!"

"Do I really have to answer that?"

Miles walked to his desk to again find Steve in his chair with his feet on the desk using his phone. This time, at least, he stood up immediately so that Miles could edge by, but kept talking for several minutes. Again, it was all about a property deal, in which the party at the other end was having unspecified second thoughts.

"Anyway, gotta go, using another guy's phone," he said eventually, "we're going back to Ange's place now, n' I'll drop in after that. Sure..." he laughed, "Whatever!

Catch you." He hung up. "Stories to write, ay!" he said
to Miles, grinning. His teeth had been capped.

"Something like that." Miles managed a weak smile,
then forgot about him. The next time he looked up both
Steve and Angela had gone. It turned into a regular
routine with Steve dropping in regularly at the end of
the day to pick up Angela. Each time he spoke briefly
to Miles who would nod and say a few words in return.

He naturally never bothered to tell Angela how to
jury-rig an email system and paid for it the next week,
when Eve nearly had hysterics over both the police
notes and the community notes being missing in action.
Rather than try to confront Angela he got Eve to tell her
to copy the material onto a memory key and put it on
Kelly' desk. Kelly then gave the key discretely to Miles
who sent the files. That was the way they did things at
the Bugle Group.

On the same day he arranged the file round robin
with Kelly and Eve, he accidentally overtook Anne in
the street, and gave her a pleasant "Hi!"

Since she had judged that Miles did not need any
further discouragement, her response was civil. "Miles,
hi! What have you been doing."

For a few minutes they were walking in the same
direction and he muttered something about helping his
co-worker with the email system.

"I think I've seen her," she said. "She's the drop-
dead gorgeous one. One of the juniors at my work hangs
around on the street sometimes hoping to see her."

"That'd be Angela."

"What's she like to work with? Is she nice?"

"She's a poisonous bat."

Anne gave a startled laugh. "Go on, tell us what you think Miles," she exclaimed. "Don't hang back."

"No chance of your junior running off with her, is there?"

Miles had to get to an interview but they were to meet again soon. That Friday, Miles and Jake cut their usual beer and video games night because Jake was on a promise to get back early. As he did not have a car that day and they started out from South Forest, Miles dropped him at his flat. He was invited up to find both Tomasina and Anne sitting at the table but, he was pleased to note, no Allen. On seeing Miles in a decent suit and tie, Anne raised an eyebrow and smiled. Miles liked the way she smiled.

"Miles! You're sober – again," said Tomasina.

"No lecture in philosophy today."

"I should hope not."

"Aw, Thommo, I've been easy on 'im so far," said Jake. "We haven't even started on deconstruction as a concept yet."

"Deconstruction sounds bad," said Miles. "It involves heavy liquor, right?"

"Mate, three bottles of cheap Yarra Valley Riesling involves heavy deconstruction the next day, trust me!"

"So how come the suit and tie, Miles?" asked Anne.

"Had an interview. Was trying for a job on the *Manly Daily*."

"Do you think you'll get it."

"They were interested but a lot of other applicants, I think."

"They're saying at work that the Herald is looking for juniors," said Jake.

"Manly sounds like a better shot – or Newcastle. Don't reckon the Herald 'd look at me, yet."

"They're all raving on about the *Herald* at work. Half the reporters in the group are lining up, I reckon. They won't even look at Newcastle."

"What's wrong with Newcastle? I reckon youse blokes are all stuck up." Tomasina and Anne grinned and exchanged glances – a byplay which Miles noted, and was relaxed enough with them as a group to ask the reason for it.

"Youse blokes.." teased Anne trying to imitate his drawl. "You're such a Bogan."

"Bogan!" exclaimed Miles. "Bogan, you North Shore Princess. Youse is a perfectly good plural form of the pronoun you. Youse blokes can all go and bite your bums."

They all laughed.

"Fair enough," said Tomasina, "but Miles, one thing we really want to know."

"Um, yes?"

"Your fashion model – weather girl, co-worker – why is she a poisonous bat?"

After talking about Angela's faults to Anne and the others – he had stayed for another half hour before they all vanished to a live theatre show, where Allen would also be - Miles felt better about being cooped up in the same office with his co-worker. But on the following Wednesday, when he turned up for work as usual, Angela was not there. Miles was puzzled - she had never taken a sick day in the months they had been sitting in the same office - but was too thankful to have the office to himself for once to question her absence. After lunch Kelly came to the newsroom door and asked him where Angela was.

"Dunno. Did she ring in?"

"Nope. Haven't heard from her."

"What about Ros or Kate? Maybe she's doing something for Ros."

Kelly was back in a few minutes. "No-one knows anything."

"Okay," said Miles, reaching for his phone headset. "If you find out anything let me know so I c'n avoid her."

"But aren't you going to do anything?"

"About what?"

"Angela."

"I've been told by Justin I'm to have nothing to do with her."

"..Nothing to do with her?" Kelly repeated his statement, puzzled.

"That's right. Anyway, she hated my guts from the moment I came here. I'm the last person she wants calling to find out what's happened. So if you want to tell someone tell Justin at South Forest."

"Ring him!" said Kelly, looking alarmed.

"Before you do that, maybe you'd better ring her at home, or ring Steve if you have the number. Maybe she's there."

He turned away, puzzled over why Kelly thought he would have the slightest interest in where Angela had gone. It was not until later that he realised Kelly thought that Angela was a full reporter, instead of editorial ballast. She might have known better if she looked at the Koala Bay Bugle or any other newspaper, but she never did. After a few minutes she drifted back into Miles' field of view.

"Nothing but answering machines at Angela's. South Forest doesn't know anything."

"Uh huh," said Miles absently without looking up.

"So whadda I do now."

"Oh, em, er, do you know any of her friends?" Miles had since thought that because Angela was extremely good looking her disappearance - he hoped she had disappeared - might cause more than the usual stir, so he should at least be seen to be making an effort.

"A couple, I guess. I can ask."

"Okay, do you mind? At least before we start ringing her family. With any luck she's just gone off with Steve, or decided to take a day off. Not that I care."

"Sure."

Miles heard no more about Angela that day, and was so thankful for an Angela free newsroom that he was reluctant to ask Kelly if she had found out anything. The next morning when he walked in past Kelly, with his usual "morning!" she was on the phone but started to tell him something. Too late! Miles found two men in suits, one with a small moustache, rummaging through the news room. His first thought on seeing them was that they were far too neatly turned out to be local hard men, and his suspicions were confirmed when the one with the moustache thrust his identification in Miles' face.

"Police," he said. He was the older of the two and perhaps the brains of the operation, if there was any brains to be found in it. "You the other reporter that works here?"

Miles nodded.

Moustache man picked up a clipboard folder he had left, opened up, on Miles' desk. "Miles Gregory Black?"

He nodded again, startled that his name was in a policeman's folder.

"We have a warrant to search these premises, including this room," he thrust a folded piece of paper at Miles who took it and glanced at it. The document seemed official enough. "Which was Angela Feldman's desk?"

"Your mate's almost standing on it."

"The other is yours?"

"Uh huh!"

"Sorry, but we'll have to search that as well?"

"Um, sure." Miles' mind was racing. Journalists do not welcome policemen who come with search warrants to rummage through their desks, but he had nothing whatever to hide and, if he played up to them a little, he might get a story. "If you find a story in it, give us a shout."

The policeman smiled slightly.

"Don't give you much room in here, do they?" said the younger one.

"Not wrong there," said Miles, and meant it. They smiled again.

"Do you know Steven Gerald Coombes?" said moustache.

"If you mean Angela's friend, Steve, just to nod to. Use to come to pick her up sometimes, in the last few weeks."

Both men nodded. Ros chose that moment to appear, semi-hysterical beside Miles. Anything to do with the police and lawyers terrified her.

"What have done, you bastard!" she yelled at Miles, "was it something in the paper?"

"I haven't done anything," snapped Miles, "'n they don't send the police round if we get stuck into the mayor or someone. The mayor issues a writ."

"They mayor is suing us?"

"It's nothing to do with me! These gentlemen have a search warrant," he held out the warrant to Ros, who snatched it from him and started studying it intently. "And they are looking for Angela and Steve."

"Who is Steve?" She asked, looking up. It was the first words she had uttered to Miles in months that had not been hostile.

Miles noted Kelly at her desk, listening to every word.

"You must have seen him. Guy in a good suit, brown hair, moustache. Comes in to pick up Angela."

She thought for a moment. "Oh him! I thought he was an advertiser, in to see Kate."

"Well he wasn't and these gentlemen.. youse guys going to arrest the man?"

"He's a person who can assist us with our enquiries," said moustache.

"What about Angela? She's a co-worker. My own boss will be asking."

"At the moment she is also a person who can assist us in our enquiries, but we have no reason to believe our dealings with her will go further."

"Thought she couldn't have done anything, she's not bright enough."

Again the two policemen smiled.

"We haven't met her," said the younger man, "we understand she's very good looking".

"The cops down at the local station would know about her, more than me." The two policemen exchanged looks. "She does the rounds – goes down there on Monday for the local police briefs."

"Maybe we shouldn't 've gone there first," said the younger policeman to moustache. The older man gestured him into silence.

"Did Coombes make any telephone calls from here, sir?" said moustache.

"As a matter of fact he did. A few, and on my phone. I couldn't help but overhear. Something about a property deal where the other side was proving real reluctant to do the deal." The information was of no use to Miles by itself. If it had amounted to a story he would never have told them, but now, almost unconsciously, he was playing the age-old game of trading information. He hoped that they would tell him a little of what they knew. The policemen exchanged looks again. Beside the door, Ros was reading the search warrant with fierce concentration, her lips moving.

"Don't do anything until I get back," she snapped to the policemen, then raced off to her office.

"It's a properly made out warrant, madam," moustache called after her.

"Ignore her," said Miles, "they sent her up here to keep her out of head office." The men grinned. Kelly suppressed a giggle. In the end, the two policemen just glanced through the filing cabinet which was, very obviously, full of dusty council reports, and the equally unexciting contents of both Miles' and Angela's desk, but they did disconnect Angela's PC to cart it away. "Say fellas," he asked as they were going, "what brought all this on, anyway. I mean has Steve committed a murder?"

"No, no, nothing like that," said moustache. "We're fraud squad. We can't tell you who he did for, but a local business is short a lot of money – a lot, and that's all I'm gunna say." He tipped Miles a wink. "It'll come out into the open, soon enough."

"Thanks. Well, if you find him give him a belt for me."

"If we don't find him soon," said moustache, whose name was Sergeant Owens, "a few people may give him a belting for us."

"See ya, Miles," said the younger one, who had introduced himself as Frank.

"See ya, Frank."

A local business, thought Miles, and if the police were involved it was a lot of money. He remembered reading that the fraud squad never became involved unless the amount was really worth the trouble of chasing. That meant it must be something like $1 million. Anything less and they relied on the business to collect the evidence before interrogating the suspect, if the suspect could be found. Perhaps this might be a nice page one story with a breakout on the police raid of the Koala Bay Bugle's office? But what business in Koala Bay had a million dollars to steal? The first stop in the investigation process was Kelly.

"Did you find out anything from Angela's friends?"

"Oh yeah! They dunno where she is, but they're pretty sure she's with Steve. 'Been talking about just going. Doesn't reckon she's cut out to be a journo."

"Well, she learnt something from being here."

"Wasn't she any good?"

"Couldn't say she was. Do you happen to know where Steve worked?"

"He was a solicitor down the road somewhere?"

Miles had in fact, suspected either a real estate agency – a couple of property sales in Sydney would add up to a lot of money – or a solicitor, as they had trust funds that could hold money from property sales. But he would have put money on Steve being in real estate.

"That salesman was a solicitor?"

"That's what Angela said. Reckoned he had a degree from a Uni in England."

"England? Steve? I picked him for real estate. He was always talking about real estate deals."

Kelly shrugged. "I reckon Angela did real well. He was a honey and he knew about clothes."

"If those cops catch him they'll put him where they all wear the same clothes."

"Reckon they'll catch him?"

"Dunno. Steve didn't seem like a bloke who planned a lot, but I hope I c'n find him first."

"What, you want to hand him over to the cops?" Kelly was surprised.

"Nooo! I want to interview the man."

Miles went back to his desk to think for a few seconds about what he should do, and in those few moments the telephone rang. It was Justin, who had chosen to act as if their last conversation had not been a screaming match.

"Ros has been on the phone to the company lawyers about cops in the newsroom there."

"Gone already, mate." Miles had also chosen to act as if he did not loathe his editor in chief. "They were after Angela and her friend Steve."

"Steve?" There was a distinct note of anxiety in Justin's voice. "Who's Steve for Chrissake?"

"I just told you, a friend of Angela's. Use to come 'n pick her up sometimes."

Justin was silent for a moment, as if this was an enormous blow. Miles could guess why the editor in chief was upset, and thought 'you have a wife and children you bastard'.

"So do you know where Angela has gone?"

"Word is she's run off with Steve somewhere," Miles said cheerfully. "Told she's been thinking about leaving journalism."

"That can't be right!" Miles did not bother to reply. "Have you tried to get her back?"

"Why on earth would I want her back," blazed Miles. "She hated my guts and, the one time I tried to do anything about her total lack of skill after the subs begged me to help out, she called in the editor-in-chief to scream at me."

"All right! all right!" growled Justin, "so you don't know where she is?"

"Haven't the foggiest. I wish I did as I'd like to interview Steve. Skipped with a lot of other people's money."

"How much?"

"Cops wouldn't say, but I'm working on it."

"Humph! We should make some effort to contact her."

"Fine, I'm going to be busy with the story."

"Someone's gotta go and find her."

"Sound's like a job for the editor in chief."

"You didn't know anything about this?" Justin sounded as if he couldn't believe what had happened.

"Mate, I was told not to interfere, remember. We never spoke and she hated my guts, totally. Why don't you talk to Kelly."

"Who's Kelly."

"The receptionist here. She knew the happy couple a little better than I did, which is not saying much. While you're at it, why not asking around the women at South Forrest, she may have been mates with a couple of them."

"Humph! If you find out anything drop us an email."

"Sure, it'll be coming from a free internet service – our email hasn't worked for weeks."

"Well for chrissake you just ring techs here!"

"We've just about melted their answering machine down leaving messages! They don't call back. They don't want to talk to us. Why don't you help us work out why they won't talk to us?"

The editor-in-chief did not trouble to hide his irritation at being bothered with such petty concerns. "Just talk to Bronwyn about that stuff," he snapped. "She's got the time to talk to IT."

"She won't do anything either."

"Just tell her I said. In the meantime find out about Angela."

"I'll look for Steve – so I better go 'n do it." Miles hung up before Justin could argue further. There was no point in ringing Bronwyn. She would have even less interest than Justin, if that were possible, in the IT system issues of Koala Bay. But getting to the bottom of Steve's nefarious doings in the mean streets of Koala Bay, now that promised some fun.

CHAPTER THIRTEEN

One of Miles' first acts in investigating the allegedly criminal activities of Steven Gerald Coombes was to walk down the main street of Koala Bay. Kelly had said he was a solicitor in a firm somewhere along the street. An internet search did not show anyone by the name of Coombes working as a solicitor in Koala Bay but perhaps Steve had been using false names, and there was a lot to be said for checking out the territory. The legal firms were easy enough to spot. Each firm had a small sign on the building in which it operated, usually in the floor above the shops. There were a surprising number in Koala Bay's main street – scraping a living on property conveyancing, plus minor injury, accident and police work. The reporter started from the beginning, poking his head in the front doors to smile vaguely at the receptionist, who smiled back, in a business-like fashion. He then asked for a business card, muttering that he wanted to check out a few law firms.

On his third visit, at a firm called Werribee and Wilson, one narrow flight of stairs above street level, the receptionist, a 30s-something women in a blazer, did not smile back. Someone, not far away, was shouting into a phone.

"WHAT DO YOU MEAN YOU DON'T KNOW WHERE HE IS? WE'VE BEEN WORKING…. HELLO! HELLO!" The shouter had been hung up on.

Miles suspected he had the right firm.

"I was just checking out legal firms for a friend who wants to buy a house around here," he said. He had worked out a decent cover story. "Do you have anything about the firm. A web site address, maybe?"

There was a sudden, splintering crash in one of the offices. "DAMN IT!" said the same person who had been shouting, "DAMN EVERYONE TO HELL!"

"Is it always like this?" asked Miles.

"Bad day," she said distractedly, looking towards the nearby office door. She thrust a brochure into his hand, saying "The web site address is on that."

Miles had no further excuse to linger but as he walked out he heard a dull, rhythmic thumping which sounded very much like someone was beating their head against a desk. The firm was missing Steven Gerald Coombes badly.

Back on the street the intrepid investigative reporter looked at the brochure, which stated that the firm had considerable expertise in all legal matters relating to property transactions and development. It also listed two principals plus an associate, one Steven Archer. Mr. Archer's qualifications included a law degree from Oxford and he was studying for a Master's in Finance.

Miles bought a can of soft drink and a newspaper from the delicatessen on the ground floor of the same building.

"G'day," he said, deliberately broadening his accent.

The little dark man behind the counter looked at

him, puzzled, then yelled something in what might have been Serbo-croat at his wife who was stacking goods on shelves well back in the store.

"Yith," he said, eventually.

"Just up at the lawyers upstairs. Bloke in an office sounds real upset about something." Miles spoke slowly, now not because he wanted to disarm the man by pretending to be a country bumpkin but so he would be better understood.

The proprietor shrugged his shoulders. "Bad news, I heard someting. One guy going – nice guy upstairs, he go, take money, so I heard."

"Oh right." Miles tried to sound casual. "They're carrying on a lot up there. Must've been a lot of money."

The little man shrugged again, and yelled at his wife again. She looked briefly at Miles and replied.

"My wife, she knows the women upstairs who buys coffee down here. Dey is good friends She says 'Dree mil.'"

"'Dree?... you mean three million dollars, mate? No wonder they're having a yell."

"Happy I stay down here, you know."

Back at the office, Miles rang a couple of his contacts who might know something about either Werribee and Wilson or Steven Coombes-Archer and could be relied on not to run to the Telegraph or the Herald. The fact that a Koala Beach solicitor was short a few million was not major news for the metros, but they would happily run it somewhere inside the paper. One contact was Councilor Coustas.

"Yeah, I know him," said the councilor, "he's turned up to a few meetings with the Libs, talking big." (Coustas had tried for State Liberal preselection himself, and was happy to see the end of a potential rival. He had not yet realised that hell would freeze over before the Liberal preselection committee would nominate him.) "They were talking about making him branch treasurer. Don't quote me," he added hastily. "Give the branch president here a call, I'll get the number, 'n don't say I gave it to you."

The president of the Koala Park branch of the Liberals Party was a Mr. Evans, a solicitor who worked at the other end of the street from Werribee and Wilson.

"Oh yes, I know Steven Archer," the official burbled, when Miles said who he was enquiring about. "A fine young man, active in party affairs."

Miles debated about whether to lead this man on with some guff about doing a profile because the paper had decided to make Steve Citizen of the Year, but realised it was unwise. In the small community of Koala Bay deceptions would be remembered.

"Well I hate to tell you this Mr. Evans," he said, "but your fine young man is wanted by the police. His girlfriend was my colleague here and when I came in this morning I found the cops taking away her computer to check the emails on it. I only just managed to convince them not to take mine away."

Miles later became used to what followed – silence. Like so many others when presented with bad news and suddenly realising that they did not want to talk to the media after all, Mr. Evans did not gasp, or sigh or mutter. Instead he just went silent.

"Mr. Evans," Miles said eventually, "I'm not going to drag your branch into it, although I probably will have to say he was known to attend branch functions – maybe there's no need to say active. He wasn't a branch official or anything as I understand it."

"Yes, yes, that's right." Evans let out a sigh. If one of the branch members was wanted by the police that was unfortunate, but not much to do with him or the branch. It happened.

"All I'm after is some idea of where he might have gone… Why don't we go off the record for a while and we just talk about our mutual friend."

Fortunately, Mr. Evans proved sensible enough to relax and tell Miles what he did know, which was little enough but it included the suburb Steve had lived in, and a phone number – information tacitly given in exchange for details on what the police wanted to speak to Steve about. In later years Miles would encounter others who, when faced with a situation that even hinted at criticism of themselves, however indirectly, would become semi-hysterical. Evans, however, was a man of experience who listened carefully to what the reporter had to say.

"Dear Lord," said the solicitor, when the suspected amount was mentioned, "it must have been money in the firm's trust fund account. We've had that much in ours at times – a couple of deceased estates at once will do it - but it's not often. But how did Steven get his hands on it?"

"Trying to work it out myself. The firm's advertising says he was a consultant, not a principal."

"If you have a law degree you can be on the letterhead, but you can't practice as a solicitor without passing a bar exam in one of the states. He shouldn't have had access to the trust funds, but the rules in each practice can be different."

"What happens if they don't find Steve or the money?"

"Its covered by insurance. I pay too much in premiums for the insurance fund to refuse to pay up. The principals will face disciplinary action but I just don't know enough about this. We are not even sure what we are talking about."

"True."

The suburb, the name Archer and the phone number lead Miles to an ordinary, red brick suburban house perhaps 20 minutes away from the office, where the reporter found his police friends of that morning busy carting computers and boxes of files out into an official looking station wagon.

"Hey Miles," said Frank.

Sergeant Owens condescended to smile. "Wondered if you'd find us."

"You fellas have collected a few things for your note books."

"We've collected a lot of work, that's what we've collected," said Owens sitting in the open back of the station wagon, organising the collected files in a brown box. "There's not much for you here. Can't have you in the house, mate."

"No worries…. But I was wondering if you'd spoken to the local Liberal Party here."

Owens eyed Miles appraisingly. "Why them?"

"He was active in the branch here. Branch president is a solicitor his office is not far from Steve's."

"Was he involved with them in any way?"

"Doesn't seem so, but they might've had a lucky escape. He wanted the treasurer's spot."

Both policemen laughed.

"I'm sure he did. They might know something. But why are you helping us?"

"Well… I heard Steve had taken off with $3 mill, from the trust fund. He told the other partners in Werribee and Wilson he could get good returns on money just sitting there. They knew he was doing some fancy financing course, and they thought they just let him have the money for a little while. They wanted to make some money on the side 'n get out of Koala Bay."

Most of that was straight guess work by Miles but he knew he could not be far wrong. Owens did not much care for reporters one way or another, but Miles amused him.

"How did you know all that?"

"Oh I'm just a shrewd bush lad."

Both policemen laughed again.

Owens flicked through files in one of the boxes then, without looking up, said: "You're not going to quote me are you?"

"Never heard of you."

"Then yeah, that's about right. Stick to the three mill figure. Its close enough. Another point that'll come out soon enough is that our friend forged his qualifications.. better to say, some doubts about his qualifications."

Miles nodded but deliberately did not reach for his notebook.

"You can check on qualifications, can't you?"

"You can check," said Owens. "You might also ask around about the problems that occur when two solicitors let money from a trust fund out of their control."

"Hmm! I was down at Werribee and Wilson today."

"You get around Miles."

"It's a nice day; good to get out of the office. Anyway, it sounded like one of the partners was banging his head against the desk."

Owens smiled. "Can't say as I blame him. Now Miles, nice talking to you, but that's enough."

The reporter raised both hands and stepped back, then walked away and got into his orange utility. He noted that Frank, the younger policemen, looked curiously at the vehicle's Victorian number plates. Back at the office he found that Ros had succeeded in creating more work for him. There was a message from a female solicitor at the company's firm who wanted to know what was going on.

"So what story was Angela working on?" the solicitor asked, when Miles rang back.

"Um, none that I know of. She was junior. She did police rounds stuff and community notes – that kind of thing."

"Then what were the police after her for?"

"They weren't after her, they were after her boyfriend. They wanted to search her desk for evidence about him and they wanted her PC to check the emails they sent to each other."

"Oh right! So this has nothing to do with the newspaper?"

"Not a thing. The only issue is that they have the PC from the office. I guess we'll want it back sooner or later."

"Okay – the story we got from Rosalind Charles over there was that people had been arrested and office fittings had been removed."

"They've taken a PC."

"And no one been arrested?"

"Not even Angela. If they find her they'll ask her questions but I doubt if she knows anything."

"But no one's seen her."

"Its voluntary as we understand it – she's run off with this guy."

The women solicitor snorted. "Miles, women don't run away with guys anymore."

"Tell that to Angela."

The last call was the most difficult. It was to Werribee and Wilson itself. This time Miles identified himself and asked to speak to Mr. Werribee or Mr. Wilson.

"Mr. Wilson is in a meeting at the moment," she said. There was a muffled crash, and her voice became tense. "Can I ask what it's regarding?"

"Well its over what he's in such a bad temper about.." Miles briefly explained what he knew; the response being an extended silence.

"One moment," she said, eventually. Miles waited a minute, listening to inane elevator-music "on hold" music then a male voice shouted, "hello?"

"Is that Mr. Wilson?"

"Is that the reporter?"

"Um, yes, its Miles Black from the *Koala Beach Bugle*.."

"You rat fuck shit, piece of garbage."

"Yeah?"

"Print a single word – a single word of this and I'll sue you and that shit publisher of yours for every cent you have."

"Three million dollars is a lot of money."

"How.." Mr Wilson choked himself off, "it's a load of garbage. Print a word and I sue. In fact, I'm getting an injunction to prevent your rag from publishing, you blood-sucking parasites."

"Isn't that what they say about lawyers?"

"I'M GETTING AN INJUNCTION" Wilson slammed the phone down in Miles ear.

When Miles wrote down a few additional notes about the conversation he saw, to his surprise, that his hands were shaking. A few harsh words should not bother him. People with thin skins and sensitive souls did not last long at the Bugle Group. But perhaps he was shaking not over being abused but the excitement of being abused for a good reason. Miles had a good story and, by heavens, Miles was going to write it. Nothing could now get between him and the story.

Koala Bay legal firm Werribee and Wilson is missing about $3 million from its trust fund. The firm has called in the police who are now looking for a consultant employed by the firm to assist them with their enquiries.

Police want to question Steven Gerald Coombes who also called himself Steven Archer, listed on Werribee and Wilson advertising leaflets and on the web site as a consultant specialising in advising on property sales.

David Wilson, a principal of Werribee and Wilson,

had no comment to make when approached by the Koala Bay Bugle. But it is understood..

Miles was careful to ring the police PR unit for an official comment and got a "neither confirm nor deny", but otherwise thought that the story told itself. This was better than writing about visits by the state governor general to bush schools. He decided he liked being a reporter.

Miles decided he hated being a reporter. The Werribee and Wilson story almost wrote itself and was destined for his front page until a dead hand belonging to a different set of lawyers – those retained by his own company – descended. Eve took one look at the story Miles sent in and promptly referred it for legal advice. The lawyers equally promptly convened a meeting in the office at South Forest where they all sat in Justin's office, along with Eve. It was only the second time Miles had been in Justin's office.

"You can't possibly print this," said the younger of the two lawyers, the same one Miles had spoken to over the search warrant. She was not at her best in a moment of crisis. It was the first time Miles had seen anyone literally wringing her hands. "This firm's already been on the phone to us threatening the company with everything."

"Don't much blame 'em," said Justin, "but isn't that what we pay you guys for? To make problems like that go away."

"The way to make the problem go away," said the second lawyer, with a slight, self-satisfied smile that Miles wanted to wipe off his face, "is not to print the story at all." Owning to the name of Mr. Bosworth – no first name was mentioned - he was a heavy set man with silver hair and a dark suit. He also had an old fashioned attitude, for lawyers retained by a newspaper group, that stories should not leave their clients open to legal actions. Bosworth and Ms. Moore, the female solicitor, were from a recently retained small firm in Chatswood which thought it knew as much about communications law as any expensive lawyer from Sydney's CBD, but neither journalist had encountered journalists in the rough before. It was proving to be a revelation.

"You mean we should prevent the public from knowing that there's a bunch of bent lawyers who've just had their trust fund emptied out because they had someone on staff benter than they are," said Justin, "just because our own bunch of lawyers won't get off their fat arses and fight legal actions?"

Bosworth was taken aback. "I wouldn't have put it like that," he said. "Part of our job is to advise clients on how to avoid legal actions. We've seen a potential legal action and we're telling you to avoid it."

"And this is very damaging," said Ms Moore.

"Damaging!" exclaimed Justin. "Great! Eve put a bigger head line on it."

"Sure!" said Eve. "So we go with it as is?"

This startled the two lawyers.

"But you can't print this, they'll sue us," shrieked Ms. Moore.

"So? Truth is a defence in defamation actions, isn't it?"

"In a way," said Bosworth. He could have lectured the others on the issues of truth and public interest in defamation law but he sensed that the editor in chief was not the sort of person who would sit still to be lectured for very long, so he got down to brass tacks. "But do we know it's true?"

"Of course its fucking true," said Justin, "look at the way they've been acting. No baffled denials. Instead we get abuse and injunctions – they're desperate to stop the story getting out."

"But they can sue if we run with the story."

"So? Mate, if they're missing three large from a trust account then they'll have a whole lot more problems than us once the story gets out. Trying to take an injunction itself is so fucking unusual for a small firm that if the dailies found out about it, they'd wanna know why they want it."

"But they'd get sued, too?" protested Moore.

"Their bigger; nastier. Their lawyers are braver."

"I don't mind a fight," said Bosworth, irritably. "But can we win it? What happens if they get the money back? You don't carry three million around in a suitcase you have to transfer it. You have to know how to hide that amount of money. This Coombes person can't know much about international transfers just from working in Koala Bay."

"Betcha that's why they told the cops," said Justin. "The cops tell Interpol, which can trace the transfers and freeze the money."

"Exactly," said Bosworth, "then the money comes back, eventually, and no-one is the wiser unless the police say something officially. The Law Society will only start an investigation if someone complains. If the money comes back, then no-one knows anything."

"Aren't their books audited?"

Bosworth shrugged. "I suppose.. but if the money comes back and the lawyers are desperate enough then a few book entries can be made to disappear. Even if an audit finds something the result may be just be a fine for not keeping proper records of the trust fund."

"Difficult to hang a fucking story on that."

"Exactly."

"So it comes down to a question of what we can prove in court," said Moore.

"What about it Miles, what have we got on the record?"

That was a problem. In his inexperience, Miles had not really thought about evidence that could be brought before a court. He had written what he knew. No-one involved so far could be dragged into court.

"Not a whole lot," he said reluctantly. "Cops said everything off the record."

"We can't work with that," said Moore.

"Even evidence wouldn't matter if three large takes a walk. They'll be too busy skipping town to sue us," said Justin.

"But if the money comes back.." said Bosworth.

"Yeah, that is the problem. 'Fraid Miles, you're going to have to sit on this one."

"But it's the best story I've had since I've been up there!" wailed Miles.

"Mate, the reason I'm in this hell hole is because I didn't listen to lawyers once. They're scum, but they know how the scum working for the other side thinks."

"Thanks for that," said Moore, looking grim. Justin ignored her.

"You can't be serious about having me sit on this?"

"You can eat it if you don't wanna sit on it," said Justin, "but it ain't running until we know the money is gone. What else you got for this week?"

Miles was too numb to answer.

"Council action on graffiti on local, buildings is okay," said Eve, "then there's council's worm farms losing heaps of money."

"Worm turns, eh. Go with that. Miles we haven't lost your story, we're just hanging fire. Now get out and find stories we can put in the paper." Miles did not quite believe what had happened. He had a good, local story and at the last moment it had been snatched from him.

"The story's been killed?" he heard Bosworth ask.

"No way," said Justin. "If the money doesn't come back, just watch us run it."

"But you still couldn't prove it."

"So? It's like I said, if they're missing three mill they're not going to start hiring barristers are they?"

"But it's very damaging."

"If it's not damaging it shouldn't be in the paper. Miles?"

"Uh, yeah?"

"I told you to bugger off – but if you're still here, did you find out about Angela?"

"No – gone."

Leaving Justin to argue with the lawyers Miles went back to his office. On his way up the back steps, he stopped on a whim at the back door frame. He backed up against the frame and touched the back of his head against the lintel. This had helped last time.

"WACK!" Okay, that helped. "WACK!" Still

not quite there. "WACK!" Ouch! He slumped on the back step. The back door opened out onto a strip of concrete edged by an ordinary suburban wooden fence, but wide enough for a few parking spaces. The Bugle office was entitled to one car space which, of course, was occupied by Ros's late model Ford. Miles thought briefly of slashing its tyres, but put the idea to one side as unworthy of him, not to mention pointless. For all her incompetence Ros was not responsible for his current frustrations.

In fact, as he realised much later, he should have felt complimented that the story had been the subject of a conference, rather than simply killed on the spot. Large dailies would have hesitated to run a story for which there was so little direct evidence. All Miles did know at the time, sitting on that back step, was that he still had no place else to go. He had not got the job at the *Manly Daily* or another at the *Newcastle Herald*. He just had not been in journalism long enough to be taken seriously. If he got some decent stories in the paper – stories like the one which lawyers had just managed to squash - then maybe he would be taken seriously. Maybe! With an effort he stood up and dragged himself back upstairs. The paper still had to be filled. He could make a few more calls before he went home.

CHAPTER FOURTEEN

After all Miles' efforts the only item that appeared in the paper was a tiny story on page three to the effect that the police had raided the *Koala Bay Bugle*'s offices in search of, an "associate" of a member of staff. The police were hoping that associate could "assist them in their enquiries concerning a sum of money missing from a Koala Bay business". It sounded like one of Angela's police reports, but it was all the lawyers would allow him to say. He argued that it was ridiculous not to even mention the member of staff, but the lawyers were adamant. His one consolation in this sorry business was that Angela seemed to have gone for good with her departure – as he later realised - occurring shortly after the office email stopped working.

The Monday following Angela's departure, still feeling sorry for himself because his story had been blocked, Miles did his former colleague's job of walking two blocks to the police station to get that week's news. The station was a large, cream brick building within sound of the surf, separated from the street by a tiny hedge and a short stretch of lawn. The reception area was covered in bright, white and green linoleum and the sort of light brown veneer endemic to police stations.

Behind the reception desk were no less than four young constables.

"Miles Black from the Bugle, doing the police rounds," he said by way of introduction, when he stepped up to the front desk.

"Angela's not coming?" asked one on the far left, the shortest and youngest of the four. Miles recognised him as the constable who had told Angela about the service station in his first week.

"'Fraid not. It's just me this time – but haven't you guys heard? Two of your fraud squad guys came and took her computer away. They wanted this friend of her's Steve. Haven't seen her since.

"Steve?" said the youngest constable, blankly.

"As far as we know she's run off with this Steve.." Miles stopped when he caught the expression on the young constable's face - he looked as if he was going to cry – and hastily changed tack, "but we don't know anything for sure. We just haven't seen her for several days."

The young constable abruptly left. One of his colleagues hesitated and then went after him. The third shrugged and wandered away, leaving Miles with a young constable who seemed amused by the turn of events.

"Used to invite Angela back to the lunch room for coffee," he said. "Highlight of our Monday. Boys are a bit disappointed."

"Don't doubt it. 'Fraid you'll just have to settle for me. At least I'm taller. Anything much happening this week?"

"I'll get the senior sergeant."

That senior police officer proved to be a balding, affable man in his late 30s. It seemed to be a happy station.

"So you're the new guy," he said. "Bit of a change from Angela."

"Your guys are disappointed."

"Eh! They'll survive. Anyway the head of detectives is a women - you go up the stairs to her once you've finished with me. She didn't like Angela much; didn't think she was much of a reporter." Miles shrugged and half smiled but did not commit himself. While there was any chance Angela might come back, he was not going to say anything to an outsider that might get repeated. "So what sort of reporter are you?" the sergeant asked.

"Me? I'm just like any other reporter."

The sergeant, who had dealt with journalists before, thought about that for a moment.

"Crawl over cut glass for a story but otherwise alright?"

"You've got it."

One minor penalty for the loss of Angela was that Miles had to do the community notices. These were mostly the notices of various clubs and organisations in the area about meetings, events, changes in office holders and so on sent in by email. Miles cut and pasted these into a larger file without doing anything more than glance at them. The subs could read them if they wanted. As with the other email addresses many of these were forwarded on automatically from the company issued email to the free email box, but increasingly he and the others were giving the non-official email to others as a contact, and that seemed to cause problems with the people in administration.

By that time Miles had done all he reasonably could to restore the proper email address. At his request Eve had asked a passing technician whether his section had heard anything about calls from the Koala Bay Bugle office, with the only response being a puzzled look and a shake of the man's head. He had even tried to explain the problem to Justin, when he went down for the disastrous meeting with the lawyers, in a few quiet moments before the lawyers turned up, but the editor in chief was not going to trouble himself with such trivia.

"Are you still farting around with that stuff? Just ring IT for chrissake," he had snapped.

"I've melted down IT's answering machine with calls and they just don't return them," Miles snapped back. "So whaddam I supposed to do? Tell me that? Where is the guy who takes the messages anyway?"

"Ohh this is just such bullshit. He's off site somewhere. It's outsourced."

"Okay, where?"

"I – I don't know. Some service. They handle a lot of people besides us."

"Well can someone find out? Tell me where I can find this guy so I can work out what the problem is?"

"Miles I'll get someone to look at it, okay. Just don't hassle me over this total fucking trivia. This is an IT thing."

Then the lawyers arrived. Later, Justin told Bronwyn that Koala Bay was having some sort of problem with their IT system and they needed help, but gave her no other explanation. Her sole action was to ring the same

number Miles and everyone else at Koala Bay had been
ringing and leave a message telling the service to ring
the Koala Bay Office. There you are, problem solved!
Why did she have to do everyone else's work as well as
her own? The message was, of course, ignored. No one
else had any luck, including trying to prompt Ros into
any sort of action.

Miles wanted to forget about the problem after that.
They had tried, and the jury rigged service worked after
a fashion. He should have known better. The next week
he came in to find the normally cheerful Kelly sobbing
quietly at her desk.

"Kelly, what's wrong?"

Kate was out on calls and Ros's door was closed
which probably meant their office manager was on the
phone to her mother, as that seemed to be all she ever
did in there.

"One of the people in administration rang," said
Kelly, between sobs, "and really yelled at me for
allowing unofficial email addresses."

"What! What's it gotta do with you?"

"That's what I told her," said Kelly recovering a
little. "But she didn't listen. She was just yelling about
having unofficial email addresses and how it was
causing problems, and how Ros had told me to work
it out and how I hadn't done anything. She even called
me lazy, and said she would tell people in South Forest.

"Oh for heaven sake. I asked you to set up those
email accounts because we had no choice."

"Yes, that's right. But Ros told me to get IT to fix it
and now this women says it's my fault."

"Aren't they just a useless pack of bastards. Next

time, just tell her to ring me. Yell back. Say I've grabbed all the responsibility." This chivalrous gesture on Miles' part was prompted just as much by total disgust at South Forest, as by a desire to help Kelly. Unlike the vast bulk of journalists in Australia Miles lent to the political right rather than to the left, but after spending a comparatively short time with the Bugle Group he thought he could understand the revolutionary urge.

"She really yelled at me."

"She should try the editorial side, we're always yelling at each other."

Back at his desk, Miles rang the IT help service again, but this time pretended to be a sub at South Forest with a problem, even putting on a slightly different voice for the occasion. Half an hour later a tech called Carl rang back.

"Listen Carl, I'm not at South Forest I'm at the Bugle in Koala Bay. We've just about melted down that answering machine of yours with calls, but no-one there ever returns the calls. Why is this?"

"Oh right!" said Carl. He sounded reasonable enough. "Someone at South Forest was asking me about this. I've never heard of you guys, are you part of the group?"

"We're a branch office up in Koala Bay itself, and our email doesn't work. We were told if there's trouble to ring your service, but the calls are never returned. I'm trying to work out why you don't want to talk to us."

"'Erm well its Liam that takes the messages from the answering machine, and the Bugle calls he gives to me or Rachael. I never hear any of the messages on the machine, I just do the jobs."

"Okay then, is this Liam person in?"

"Um no, I can't see him at his desk. I can take a message, if you want."

"No thanks. Does he have a mobile number, or any other number I can get him on?"

"Sorry, it's more than our job is worth to give out any other number here to clients but the answering machine."

Miles had feared as much. "Okay, then, can you do me a very small favour. All I want is just some idea of why we're being ignored, so then I can tell our own administration. Just ask Liam what the problem about the *Koala Bay Bugle* is – no, come to think of it, just mention that someone at South Forest was hassling you about the Bugle and you'd never heard of it, so what's the deal? I just need to know why we're being ignored. Can you then send me an email?"

"Well, I guess I can do that."

Miles gave the man his free service email address and then went back to his reporting work. A little later the tech kept his promise and sent him an email.

"Sorry Miles," it read, "told not to deal with you guys. Not in service deal with the Bugle Group. Your machines don't have a maintenance contract. Liam is really angry about some woman there. Had a real fight with her a few months back."

There was no need to ask what 'woman' Liam had his fight with – Ros had messed things up again. Armed with this information, Miles rang the woman who had yelled at Kelly. She was called Mrs. Turner and turned out to be an aristocrat of the old regime, horrified that a mere journalist should dare to speak back to administration.

"I will consult with Ms. Rosalind Charles, the office manager there, and see if there is a problem," she said stiffly, after Miles had pointed out, as tactlessly as possible, the true cause of their IT problems. "We have heard nothing of this. South Forest Networks handle the PC and network calls. They have always proved most reliable."

"Glad to hear it. So you'll get right on to them, shall you?"

"I shall consult with Ms. Charles." There was an edge to her voice.

"She's already given you the wrong story once. My guess is that she bought the PCs from somewhere 'n tried to cut maintenance costs, 'n probably still doesn't realise what she's done." Until very recently, Miles did not realise that PC networks needed help desks or maintenance contracts, but the Bugle Group was a learning experience in many ways.

The response to this piece of impertinence was a few seconds of spluttering and then, "well.. I will go straight down to Mr. Brock.."

"Complain to whoever you like," said Miles, raising his voice. "The fact is you were told the wrong story by Ros and rang up and abused Kelly here for no good reason. You want this problem fixed then get busy and fix it. Do you want us to take the problem direct to Mr. Charles and say why we're having problems with email?"

"I think this conversation has gone on long enough," said Mrs. Turner.

"Too right. And we're agreed that it's an administration issue."

She hung up.

CHAPTER FIFTEEN

It was the final quarter in the first finals game, months after Miles had confronted Mrs. Turner over the email system. Now Miles had forgotten everything except the fact that his team was three goals plus a couple of points behind a bunch of Southern Sydney low-lifes who called themselves Botany, and who had the temerity to challenge the Lovett Bayers on their home turf. And look like winning. After a mixed season with the side still raw, Lovett Bay had pushed and shoved its way into the draw for the finals. Now it seemed they might be pushed straight back out again by losing the first game.

Playing in bright September sunshine Lovett Bay fought hard after the final quarter bounce, but with initially little result. Then the ball dribbled over the boundary on the Lovett Bay half forward flank, near Miles' stamping ground at center half forward, where he had played most of the season. His opponent, a taciturn man with a red beard and arms covered with tattoos, trailed along suspiciously as Miles edged nearer the action. He and his opponent had been having quite a duel. The Botany half back was not as fast as Miles but he was a hard man to beat in contests for the ball. Tackling him, so Miles thought, was akin to tacking on a front-end loader. He had tackled him anyway, but in the preceding three quarters had not managed to get an edge.

The boundary umpire – as it was a final the game had a full complement of umpires – threw the ball in. Jake, as ruck man, contested the hit out and won, knocking it squarely to Ben, the rover. Ben had to take two steps to catch the ball and that momentum sustained him for several more seconds amid a pack of opponents, while he looked around for a constructive way to get rid of it. Seeing his chance, Miles jerked away from his opponent and ran towards the boundary line. Ben spotted him and handballed cleanly, aiming it so that the reporter could take it on the run. Miles turned, saw a lead from a forward pocket player, and booted the ball so that it landed squarely on his team mate's chest, just before his own opponent caught up to him. As he was turning Miles glimpsed a flash of white by the ground's fence but forgot about it as the forward pocket player scored a goal. The crowd, mainly wives and girlfriends of the players but a fair number of curious, or idle, cheered.

Something clicked with the Bayers. A psychological switch – something any coach wishes he knew how to turn on – clicked. Previously they had played as a team of individuals, not quite connecting. Now they starting to connect. At the center bounce following the goal, both ruck man got their hands to the ball but by chance it fell at the feet of the Lovett center who soccered it off the ground to Ben. The rover had little time to do anything but kick it low, to one side of Miles. The reporter and his opponent dived for the ball but Miles wrestled it clear and rolled to his feet a few heartbeats ahead of the Botany player. That was enough of a break for him to turn and kick it long to the goal square, and hope for the best. Their full forward, Josh, took a screaming mark in the goal square then kicked it in and, this time, the crowd really did roar. Just one goal the difference. The game had come alive. The coach looked down at his clipboard, shook his head tossed it away and screamed "'c'mon Bayers".

Miles did not know why he played so hard. The prize for winning was just to do it all again in the semi-finals the next week. Perhaps he was blowing off frustrations over Ros. Or perhaps he just liked the game. Botany fought back but the next time it came Miles' way he grabbed it, handballed past two Botanites who wished him harm, then ran on and took the ball back from the same player he had passed it to while the Botanites were still turning – a move worthy of the League itself – then he had a clear run at an open goal and scored. They were just points behind.

The rest of the game was a blur. He took marks, sharked balls from packs, smothered one kick, which was painful, flew high twice and scored a second goal from a snap shot out of a pack. At the final whistle with the score one goal and one point in Lovett Bay's favour Miles sank to grass. He did not feel as if he could make it to the boundary. His opponent trotted by but stopped for a moment.

"Game, mate!" he said, holding out his hand.

"Oh yeah! G'd game," said Miles, shaking hands, not to be outdone in courtesy. "You're a hard man, mate. Next season, eh!"

His opponent nodded, smiled briefly, gave the thumbs up and trotted off to his wife and child waiting by the fence. Jake came by and pulled Miles off the ground, although he could barely walk himself.

"What do philosophers have to say about football?" asked Miles as they lurched off the field. His vision was swimming.

"Not much, mate. While they're arguing about whether the ball exists or try to place the game within the currents of western philosophical thought, the other team's guys will bugger off with it and everyone start screaming that the philosopher has to get it back. It's too anchored in reality. It ruins you for philosophy – just like journalism."

"Yeah, what's wrong with journalism and philosophy?"

"Tom's always after me to write stories that people can read. I mean, I ask you. No philosopher writes stuff that the public can understand. The less understandable it is, the more they think the writer must know his stuff." Jake shook his head. "Mate, I'm just ruined for philosophy."

"Miles! Great game! You played really well." It was Anne at the boundary rail, with Tomasina.

"Thanks – wow!" Both were in tennis costume with short skirts. He was tired but not that tired. The two tennis dresses together were the flash of white Miles had occasionally seen during the game. "Like the dresses, ladies," he said looking both Anne and then Tomasina in the eye. "I'm gunna have to start watching tennis." Anne picked up her covered racket and flicked it at Miles's head, making him step back. "But I hate to tell you, this is a football oval."

"We're playing district doubles at the courts here in 20 minutes if you think you have time to watch, Mr. Black," said Anne. There were a set of tennis courts next to the field.

"For those dresses I'll make time."

"Another guy who really appreciates the skill of women's tennis," said Tomasina dryly, although she was by no means displeased. "Just what the game needs Annie."

"I'm a guy, I'm shameless. Summer's coming - you girls into beach volleyball?"

The girls were rolling their eyes over that one when Allen walked up in spotless cream trousers, a blue shirt with the name of his law firm monogrammed in gold on the breast pocket, and a brown, zip up jacket.

"So is Grace here, Miles?" asked Anne, hastily changing the subject. Miles was dating Grace.

"Never tried to get her to a football match," said Miles before he was pulled away by Jake. Anne watched him go for a few moments before turning to Allen.

"I tell you that Allen guy drives me loopy," said Jake.

"Yeah? What's wrong?" Miles had kept well away from the lawyer but Anne and Tomasina occasionally did things together which meant that their respective boyfriends saw a lot of each other.

"Always carrying on about some bulldust or other. If it's not getting a better car" (Tomasina had a modest hatchback) "it's about how there are really expensive flats available, or about the state of the property market, or about him arranging trusts for millions of dollar's worth of assets."

"All useful stuff," observed Miles, keeping a straight face.

"Its all total shite that's what it is. Anyway, what's happening with Grace."

"Not much. Seeing her tonight but I don't reckon it's a go. Reckon she's put off by the ute."

"Yeah? Bloody useful vehicle that. Color's a bit off and a few dents," Jake said, judiciously. "But it gets you around, what more do the chicks want?"

Miles had helped Jake and Tomasina move flats recently with his utility doing the heavy shifting. As that had saved Jake the cost of hiring a truck for the day he was now an admirer of the Milesmobile. It was during that move Miles made the mistake of calling Tomasina, "Thommo".

"Excuse me," she said, folding her arms, "my name is not Thommo – I hate that - it is Tomasina."

Miles was about to protest that he had even heard Tomasina's sister call her Thommo, not to mention Jake, but swerved at the last moment. "Then what's your second name?"

"Jane."

"If you want the full name I should call you Tomasina Jane."

"That will do," she said and smiled.

That exchange later prompted Tomasina to do a little quiet lobbying on Miles behalf to Anne. She had her own motives. Initially she thought her friend had done well for herself in taking up with Allen but would now be happy if she never saw the lawyer again.

"I think Miles is a gentleman," she said to Anne after the move.

"I think he is."

"Maybe, interesting?"

Anne shrugged. ".. Guess. I hope he meets someone nice, but he's not for me."

"Why not? What's wrong with Miles.

"A reporter on the *Koala Bay Bugle*! Think what my dad would say if I had started dating him."

"Who has to go out with him – your dad or you?"

"No one has to go out with him – although I hope someone does – I'm going out with Allen."

"Yes," said Tomasina and left it at that for the moment, although she noted that Anne had not said Allen's name with any conviction. She thought that later she would casually mention how useful Miles' utility had been, despite its appearance. Girls should not bother themselves over what sort of car guys drive, she told herself, but it might be best to soften up Anne.

Miles's love life in the months preceding the football game could best be described as checkered. The first item of note was his association with Ursula. He met her when Karen, the second reporter at Lovett Bay, had left to take up the ABC radio job in Karratha, joyously shaking the dust of the Bugle Group from her feet forever, or so she hoped. The departure of a reporter was a frequent excuse for the others to socialise, and the usual after work drinks turned into a marathon which ended up at Karen's flat. Ursula was a flatmate of Karen. By the time he left – Karen gave him a farewell kiss on the cheek, although Miles was not sure what he had done to deserve such an honour – he had Ursula's phone number.

The problem was that he was forever crashing into her ideological barriers. Going out on Saturday to play football, for example, was a "reaffirmation of gender stereotypes".

(Jake's reaction: "Mate, I thought we wuz just playing footy.")

She insisted on going to vegetarian restaurants and was horrified when Miles – tiring of tofu – suggested that they go somewhere she could order salad and he could eat meat. It seemed that she simply did not know anyone who ate meat and did not care to be associated with any person who did such an unnatural thing. That crisis was smoothed over, only to be replaced with another far more serious one. Of all things it was over the general principle of rich countries forgiving poor countries their debts, which came up in a general conversation at a party they attended. A youth in the second year of an arts degree, one of Ursula's circle of friends, was holding forth about third world countries being forgiven their mountain of debts.

"Why doesn't the country concerned just refuse to pay?" asked Miles. This was not Miles opinion but one he had read recently in a newspaper, and thought he understood.

"Huh?" said the youth. "They can't do that." He never read newspapers on the grounds that they were "biased and inaccurate". Instead he occasionally hopped on the Internet to glance at blogs which reinforced his own opinions. That meant he had never previously heard the argument Miles put forward. Having survived a whole first year course in politics, however, the youth believed his level of political understanding to be several steps above a mere suburban journalist. "They can't refuse the debts."

"Yes they can," said Miles. "They can walk away any time. Just refuse to pay – 'n there's nothing anyone can do about it, except invade or not lend'em any more money."

"Yeah, that's it," said the youth triumphantly, "no one will lend them more money. How will they develop if no one lends them money?"

"They didn't develop before when they were lent the money. The idea behind the loan is to build stuff that helps repay the money. The elites pocketed a lot of it and the rest went on stupid projects pushed by multinational corporations that turned into disasters. No more money no more disasters." Miles then remembered some more of the newspaper article. "Or what the lender countries could do is tie forgiving the loan to the borrowers adopting rule of law and cleaning up corruption."

"That imperialistic," said the youth, "you can't dictate to them how they should run their country. They have their own cultures."

"Mate, if they've borrowed several billion bucks then they've borrowed a heap of Western culture – subtle stuff about bankers wanting their money back."

This was at least a defensible argument, but it was not one that the youth wanted to hear. He called Miles a fascist. The reporter laughed and told the youth he should pay more attention in lectures. But later he was confronted by Ursula, white-lipped with fury, also saying that he was a "fascist", that he had "embarrassed her in front of her friends" and for those crimes he was "dropped". Miles did not bother to defend himself. Instead he went home, heated up a frozen meat pie and ate it with relish. He would stay dropped.

Then there was Grace, who said she had been named after the actress Grace Kelly, and looked a little like her namesake. Jake reckoned she was "a sort". They both met Grace, as did Tomasina, when she and a girlfriend turned up at a party connected with the football team, trailing along behind a girlfriend. Miles decided to try his luck by ringing where she worked as a librarian.

He discovered that Grace's idea of a night out was a performance of Moldavian folk dancing, alternate theatre, recitals of obscure classical music pieces, or showings of French art films of the 1950s. This was initially interesting to Miles who thought it might be cultured and urbane to acquire an interest in such subjects but he quickly discovered that most of the material was obscure because it had little interest for the general public, which included Miles.

After one experience of an experimental art film he suggested a popular romance film, but that suggestion horrified Grace. In fact, anything that could be considered mainstream, commercial or even mildly entertaining she seemed to find repulsive. How could anyone want to watch the nonsense that Hollywood turned out? What was wrong with Iranian films about camel herders suffering in the desert? People simply had no taste.

Miles found the folk dancing, in particular, an ordeal. He paid for extremely expensive tickets – at least Ursula had insisted on splitting everything – then drove for what seemed like hours through the suburbs to an old, unheated town hall. There he sat through a series of dull, indistinguishable routines, executed by dancers in faultlessly correct peasant costumes. Miles wished he could sneak off to a pub. Grace was absorbed. At the end of the performance she enthused over it with some people she knew in the audience, mainly older ladies. A couple of the ladies insisted on being introduced but otherwise Miles was left out of the conversation. At the end of all of this he returned Grace to her flat, only to have her leap out of the ute, smile sweetly, wave goodbye and walk away. He had to get out to close the wonky passenger side door properly, and by the time he did that she was out of sight. After driving for so long, Miles thought that it would have been courteous to invite him in. Coffee, at least, would have been a nice gesture.

Despite coming to almost dread their evenings out Miles persisted with Grace until he sprained his ankle. He did it in the third quarter of the semi-final against the Pennant Hills side, jumping for a contested mark. He took it but on his way down the shifting pack pushed his leg to one side. His foot hit the ground at the wrong angle and his ankle exploded with pain. For the next minute or so all Miles could do was writhe on the ground, fighting an urge to vomit, as his team mates clustered around asking if he was "alright". He wasn't. Eventually he was helped off where the girlfriend of the center half back who was a nurse, told him it was most likely badly sprained, but he had better get it X-rayed on Monday. That was the end of the season for him, but his team mates were also out of the season shortly afterwards when Lovett Bay lost by two goals. Well, they had made it to the semis.

Miles was driven home in his ute by Jake, who took him to a chemist to buy a constriction bandage and an ice pack, and to rent a single crutch – he did not need doctors to tell him how to treat a sprain. When they reached home, Miles hobbled around painfully having his shower and changing. Jake helped by drinking some beer he had found in the fridge.

"You wanna play that up for Grace," he said, as Miles hobbled past.

"Mate we were booked to see Persian folk dancing down near the harbour somewhere. The sprain's almost worth it to get out of it."

"What's wrong with Persian folk dancing?"

"You've gotta sit through it to really not appreciate it." Miles had to think for a moment for the right comparison. "It's like seeing home videos of weddings."

"Oh right!"

"Except that with the home movies at least you c'n get up and get a beer."

Tomasina came to pick up Jake, but came bearing a Pizza and insisted on making a fuss over Miles – settling him the couch with his foot up on cushions and the remote control to hand. That was what he needed, Miles decided, a bit of sympathy. A bonus was that Tomasina was in her tennis dress again.

"Is this yours?" she asked holding up a book that had been on the coffee table.

"P. G. Woodehouse, sure!"

"Minor classic," said Jake, almost dismissively. Having read several of the works of the French philosopher Derrida, he had decided that reading for pleasure was for wimps.

"Annie reads him."

"She does?" said Miles. "It sorta amuses me – for the Bertie Wooster character not dressing for dinner is the same as going bush for three days. He does absolutely bugger all except get himself into stupid scrapes in grand old English houses and change fiancés like he changes socks."

"You should talk to Annie."

"Sure.."

After Tomasina and Jake had gone he faced up to the job of phoning Grace to tell her the evening was off, at least as far as he was concerned.

She was not in the slightest sympathetic.

"What do you mean you can't drive?" she asked.

"I mean my right angle is sprained. Moving my foot is painful. If I pile on lots of ice and constrict it maybe I c'n drive to work on Monday or maybe it's a bus for the first two days, if I can hobble to the bus stop."

"So you can't come?"

"Nope! Its out of the question."

"But I'm expected!"

"There's still time to call people, or get a lift. And I can give you the ticket numbers. You can talk your way past the ticket guys. You seemed to know them last time."

"Umph! This is very late notice to say you can't come out. There are lots of other men I could've gone out with tonight."

"Then ring 'em back and say there's an opening. They'll even have better cars."

"Umph! And you got this sprain at this football game thing."

"'Fraid so."

"Then I'll just have to make other arrangements."

"Whatever. Do you want the ticket numbers?"

"Ohh – sod the tickets!" She hung up.

Miles put the phone down with a sense of relief. After that reaction he was under no obligation to call again. He looked at the films he had stored on the pay TV service. One was billed as a "hi-octane action thriller" set in Los Angeles and promising lots of gratuitous martial arts scenes. In other words, the sort of entertainment which would have sent Grace into convulsions. He watched it with relish.

In the following weeks the weather started warming up. Daylight saving came and Miles abruptly found himself going home with plenty of sunshine left over. The grim task of finding stories in Koala Bay continued, Ros and Bronwyn had given up trying to bully the high countryman, Justin never called or came near Koala Bay and Angela was a bad memory. About the only direct contact he had with head office was the occasional call from the sub editors. This complete lack of supervision also meant that he never had to attend staff or internal meetings of any kind, which was a blessing he did not appreciate at the time. Sometimes when he rang contacts he would be told they were "in a meeting" and, after leaving a message, he found himself wondering what people did in meetings. A football team mate once mentioned that he had undergone a performance review, and Miles asked what it was. The team mate just laughed and said it was "a form of corporate torture". As one women who left newspapers for a time put it, when she returned gasping: "there are some people in companies whose job is just to hassle you."

When he was contacted by anyone from South Forest, apart from the sub editors, it was for the most bizarre reasons, such as the call he took some weeks after he had sprained his ankle.

"It's the pay office here," said a man's voice, "I was trying to contact Angela Feldman."

"Good luck to you – I haven't seen her in months."

"But she hasn't been working there?"

"Nope. She upped and left with her boyfriend, one step ahead of the cops yonks ago."

"But she's still on the payroll."

Miles laughed. He thought that if he left then his pay would be cut off the moment he walked out the door. Angela seemed to be in a different category. He discovered later that the pay office relied on Justin to tell them if someone in the outer offices went, but the editor in chief never told them about Angela initially. He had his own reasons for hoping that she would reappear. Then he simply forgot to tell them. The pay officer only found out that a staff member had been missing for months through casual office gossip, but that was life at the bugle Group.

"You can always pay me her money. I'm doing what she did here."

"Humph!" The pay officer was not amused. "We need a resignation letter."

"Uh huh!"

"We need it straight away, dated from the time she left."

"Uh huh."

"So when can we get it?"

"You'd have to ask her – if you can find her."

"You will have to ask her immediately!"

"Me! I'm not asking her anything! As far as I know she's in Hong Kong but I dunno where, and its nothing to do with me. So good luck sorting it out. Anything else you wanted."

"But just a minute! You were her boss there?"

"Nope. Justin specifically said that I was to have nothing to do with her. I had no authority over her at all." The editor-in-chief's outburst earlier in the year was now proving very useful. "You have to go to either Justin or Ros Charles, the office manager here. I'd go for Justin as he might make some sense."

The pay officer was not happy with this advice. "This is most irregular."

"Uh huh."

"I mean sorting it out after all this time."

"Uh huh."

"We have to pay out her holidays. Even take legal action."

"Uh huh."

"You have no idea where she's gone?"

"As I said, overseas somewhere. Why don't you try her family? You must have the number for next of kin in your records."

"Can't you ring her family?"

"I told you, I was told specifically to have nothing to do with her. Anyway, you have the number on record,

I don't." (Actually Miles did have the number, although he was not about to tell the pay officer that, and had tried the family a week after Angela had gone. They had known that she was alright and that she was with Steve but little more beyond that. Miles' uncharitable thought at the time was that incompetence ran in families.)

"Who said you were to have nothing to do with her?"

"Justin."

"Oh!"

Finally, the pay officer hung up.

The phone rang again and, thinking that the idiot pay officer had come back, Miles picked it up as if he was at home, without putting his headphones on, and snapped "Miles Black!"

"Oh! Have I called at a bad time?" It was Anne.

"Um, no, no! Caught me at a bad moment. That's all. How are you?"

"Fine.. good! How are you?"

"When I'm not arguing with people in admin here, pretty good."

"I'm in admin."

"If you were in admin here I'd never argue with you."

"Why wouldn't you argue with me?"

"Um – because I'd just know you'd be in the right. I'm from the bush, so I know this – it's an instinct we have."

"Miles, that's a good instinct. I'm glad you realised I'm always right, it saves a lot of time. But I should be angry with you?"

"What have I done?"

"You never came to see me play tennis. I saw you

play football that time, but you didn't come to the tennis."

"I did too."

"You did not."

"Did too.. I watched almost a whole set of you and Tomasina playing against the blonde and big red haired girl."

"Humph! She wasn't that big, and the other one was barely blonde."

Miles had actually meant that the red haired girl had been big breasted but thought it best to change the subject.

"You played well. You two were two games up when I left."

"Why didn't you stay?"

Allen had shown signs of being sufficiently bored to want to speak to Miles, so he had decamped.

"Had to go," was all he said.

They spoke for a few more minutes, with Anne saying she understood he liked the author Woodehouse. Flattered that she remembered that detail, passed on by Tomasina, Miles told himself he would read all he could of the man. Then she wanted to know why he had argued with administration.

"So the drop dead gorgeous witch was still being paid."

"Seems so."

"You even have an office manager, and still took all this time for them to work it out, and then they still wanted you to get a resignation letter out of her - which they don't need by the way."

"Loopy isn't it. We didn't talk at all even when she

was in the next desk. Mind you, they could've sent me to Hong Kong to talk to her if they wanted."

"Is that where she is?"

"Think so, but I dunno where in Hong Kong. Could've stayed there for weeks, on expenses, looking for her."

Anne giggled and came around to the point. "Miles, the reason I'm calling is that I have a bigggg favour to ask."

"You do?" Miles was now curious to know where this conversation was going.

"Jake said you were trained as a fire fighter in Victoria."

"I was a volunteer in the CFA down there. 'Lot of people do that down my way. Got called out to fires a couple of times. Um, why?"

"Well, see, you know it's coming to bushfire season."

"Yes." In fact, Miles had recently done a front page story on fire authorities warning about how the area was at risk of bushfires.

"I'm house sitting for my aunt, a bit further North from here, along the coast and, well, it backs right onto bush."

"Oh!"

"I was hoping you could come out to have a look at the place."

"Me as a bush fire expert? You've got the wrong bloke."

"It's just that I don't know anyone else who knows much about fires. I could stand outside with a hose if a fire comes."

"You're better off inside the house. Fires are dangerous. Can't your aunt fight the fires? It's her house."

"She's in a Buddhist retreat in Tibet."

"She's meditating and her house is in the bushfire front line?"

"Well, yes…"

"Um, well I'm happy to take a look at the place if you want if you want, but I'm not sure how much I can help." If Anne asked him, he would be there.

"Oh good. I was going to invite Tomasina and Jake .. and Allen."

Would that man never go away?

"Are they bushfire experts too? I thought I was the only one."

"No. I just thought I'd make a social event of it. Why don't you bring Grace."

"I haven't seen her in weeks."

"So that's all over is it?"

"I can't say it ever got started."

"There was an Ursula wasn't there?"

"Yep, also gone."

"And a fiance."

"Yep! Lost one of those too."

"You don't seem to have much luck holding onto women."

"True. So what's your opinion as a woman - what am I doing wrong? Am I being too masculine and bush?"

She chortled. "I don't think of you as too masculine, Miles. I'm not sure what being 'bush' means."

"Then tell me what I'm doing wrong?"

"I haven't seen enough of you to say? Anyway, there are some things a girl has trouble saying."

"Yeah? Ursula never had trouble saying things - mostly stuff I didn't want to hear."

"Poor Miles, always in trouble."

"True. Poor me."

"Miles, I've thoroughly enjoyed talking to you but I must go. Can you come?"

"Sure, I'll come. When and where is this social event?"

On his way home Miles always past a bushfire indicator outside a NSW Rural Fire Service station. Since he had been at the Bugle the indicator had been pointing at low. It had been pushed up to moderate. Bushfire season was coming.

CHAPTER SIXTEEN

The house owned by Anne's aunt was a timber affair with a tiled roof, painted a smart white. Outside was a Porsche which belonged to Allan. Miles fought down an urge to scratch the paintwork. A little further along was Tomasina's small hatchback. He parked his own beat-up utility on the far side of Tomasina's car where he hoped it was less likely to be noticed. It was a warm, cloudless day and there was no shade in street. Miles left the windows down a fraction and throw a towel over the steering wheel, thinking that he should try to find out why the car air conditioner did not work - although he was not sure it had ever worked - before the hot weather started in earnest. He was let in by Anne, in a white T shirt which did wonders for her figure, but behind her was Allen looking smug. In the living room was Tomasina and Jake, who waved the can of beer that was in his hand by way of greeting.

"Oh right, um, Miles," said Allen, although he must have known the reporter was coming. "I've been trying to remember, what paper you're on again?"

"Koala Bay Bugle. Your aunt's house is nice, Anne."

"Thank you. Do you want to see out back?"

Everyone followed Anne and Miles, who felt

ridiculous at being thought of as a bushfire expert, to a standard, suburban backyard sloping gently towards the back fence. On one side of the lawn was a ramshackle, wooden garage and on the other a large above ground pool on a level concrete platform, shaded by an awning and skirted by the required child proof fence. Apart from those items all the backyard could boast of was two stunted trees that looked as if they bore apricots, when they bore anything at all, and a large pile of chopped up bushes at the back fence.

"You've been busy," said Miles, pointing at the pile.

"My aunt cleared away some bushes along the back fence before she left."

"That's nice, but I wouldn't leave them there. Better get rid of 'em somehow."

"Oh, okay."

There was a gate in the back fence which Miles opened and walked through into the narrow, grassy strip beyond, kept clear by council regulations. Beyond that strip was bush – a mixture of gum trees and scraggly undergrowth on a gentle slope. Anne's house was one of a long, straight row that backed onto the bush, most of them with man-high, timber fences as if the owners wanted to shut out the bush hinterland.

The moment Miles walked through the gate a massive Samoid, apparently allowed the run of the bush from the neighbour's house, started barking furiously at him.

"What about the houses on the other side of the street?" asked Miles, ignoring the dog. He meant to ask whether they also backed onto bush, as he had not thought to look closely at the street directory before he came in. But then he realised he was talking to himself. Anne and the rest were still inside the back yard. Miles had no idea why they had stopped at the gate, but to ask them to come out meant yelling over the dog's barking.

"Shut it, you!" he growled, pointing his finger at the animal. The dog promptly ran a few meters to just inside what must have been its own back gate in the neighbouring house which stood open. There it turned and started barking again, albeit with less conviction.

"You big wus!" said Miles indignantly.

"I've been terrified of that dog," said Anne peeping out from her back gate. Allen was behind her.

"Do you know its name?"

"Sam, for Samoid."

"Hey Sam!" The dog stopped barking in surprise. On an impulse, Miles pulled a stick out of the nearby bush, waved it enticingly at the dog then threw it. Sam hesitated then ran and grabbed it. He hesitated again, then ran back to drop it a short distance from the newcomer before retreating back to his own gate.

"He's alright he just wants to play."

Miles retrieved the stick and threw it again, and Sam instantly sprinted after it. The others came out onto the cleared strip.

"You back right onto the national park?" the bushfire expert told Anne, while Sam trotted back, holding the stick in his mouth.

"That's right."

"And you're on top of a slope, in a wooden house. That's interesting."

"What's the problem about being on top of a slope."

"Fires travel real well up hill. It gets up speed."

He went forward and ran his hand through one of the bushes, because he felt he should. He had seen that the undergrowth was dry from the back fence. The Samoid trotted up and dropped the stick at Miles feet. He obligingly picked it up and threw it again. "It was a wet winter so there's plenty of undergrowth, but now it's all bone dry. They should have burnt this stuff off in winter."

They walked back through the gate, Miles pausing to throw the stick for the Sam a final time.

"I just don't believe it," said Anne.

"Believe what?"

"That dog playing with you like that. I've never even gone out there because of that dog."

"He's not much of a watchdog. Just take a stick along next time and he'll be your friend for life."

They sat in garden chairs in the shade of the back porch. Out of the sun the day was pleasant. Jake handed him a can of beer.

"Just one and I'll go," said Miles, looking meaningfully at his friend.

"We were all going out to dinner," said Anne, "you should come with us."

Miles saw Jake roll his eyes at the thought of having to put up with Allen for an evening.

"Prior plans, but thanks." Actually Miles had little to do but go home and read, play computer games, or watch a film; or maybe he could sulk. There were lots of things he could do. One thing he would not do is be the odd man out in a fivesome.

"Got a date?" asked Tomasina.

"An arrangement," said Miles.

The Samoid bumped against the gate and made a noise that was somewhere between a howl and a growl.

"No more game now," the high countryman called, "go home to your owners!"

"Ruff!"

"We should let him in," said Jake, "he sounds like a lonely guy."

He walked to the gate and let the Sam in. The dog bounded up to Miles. In his mouth was a short piece of thick rope with knots on both ends, which he dropped in front of the reporter.

"His rope toy," said Miles, "he's a smart pup. C'mon boy." He got up, picked up the toy and held it out to Sam who grabbed the other end in his teeth and tugged. Miles was almost pulled off balance but tugged back, whipping the rope from side to side. The Samoid growled, delightedly.

"Is he – is he, getting angry?" asked Anne.

"Sounds dangerous," said Allen.

"Nah, he's just enjoying himself. Sam thinks its a great game." They all watched Miles play with Sam for a time, then Miles became self conscious. "Here, Jake, you let him in you play with him."

Jake stood up and took the rope in one hand, still holding his beer in the other. "Strong pup, isn't he," he said after a few seconds of tugging.

"Is he what!"

"So what do I do now, about the fire situation I mean?" asked Anne, as they watched Jake and Sam play tug of war, Sam growling enthusiastically.

"You have to prepare the house. Get rid of the garden rubbish against the fence, and clean the gutters of leaves. Your garage being wooden is also unfortunate. Is there much in it? Extra wood, paint, cans of petrol…" Warming to his role as bushfire expert, Miles got up and opened the peeling, wooden side door. Anne followed and, inevitably, Allen. There was little stored in the building, apart from an ancient side board at the far end, on which stood a couple of old tins of paint that might have once contained the paint now flaking away on the side walls. There was also a neat, red BMW sports.

"Wow! Is this yours Allen?" Miles was envious.

"No its mine," said Anne.

"I'm the Porsche out the front," said Allen hurriedly, in case anyone would think he belonged to Tomasina's plebian hatchback.

"You can afford this on your salary?"

"Not really," said Anne. "It's sort of a family deal."

"Oh I see." He remembered what Allen had said about her family. He glimpsed a neat as a pin interior and resisted the urge to open the door and sit behind the wheel. Anne would probably not have minded but he did not want to appear to be a country bumpkin who had never seen a luxury sports car before. She did not invite him to get in. "Impressive," he said, and to cover his momentary confusion – realising why Anne might not be interested in a poor and decidedly undistinguished reporter from country Victoria – he glanced in the sideboard and found a pump.

"You have a pump and hoses to take water from your swimming pool."

"A pump?" said Anne, without enthusiasm, as Miles lifted the piece of machinery onto the bench.

"It's a good one too; petrol powered. Let's see.

221

Tank's still full. it's a pull start like the lawn mower." He showed Anne the handle for the starter cord. Your Aunt has this for a reason. Didn't she tell you about this?"

"I think she expected to be back by now."

"A lot of places have these. You connect it to the hoses, drop one end in the pool and start the pump. Its real good for fighting fires, while the water in the pool lasts. Let's have a try."

He took the equipment out to the pool, the others trailing behind. Jake and Sam were obliged to break off their tug of war game, but Sam came along thoughtfully bringing his rope toy. At that point, Allen's mobile phone rang and, excusing himself, he walked around the side of the house to talk. It took Miles a few minutes to assemble all the components and then pull-start the pump, which shot out an impressive spray of water at the back fence. It was efficient and comparatively quiet, but still noisy enough for a suburban back yard. Miles let it spray water over the back fence for a couple of minutes to see what affect the pumping had on the level of the pool and then, to let it run for a little while longer, pointed the hose back to the pool, accidentally splashing Tomasina.

"Sorry!"

"It's okay."

"We should have brought bathers," said Jake, raising his voice to be heard over the pump.

"Didn't even think of it," yelled Anne.

"Sam! Dinner!" The call was from next door. Sam picked up his rope toy from where he had momentarily dropped it then dashed off.

"See ya, Sam," yelled Jake.

A moment later, when Miles switched off the pump, they could hear: "there's Sammie. There's my Sammie wam, looking for his dinner wasn't he."

"Dog knows where its dinner is," muttered Miles.

"When the fire comes why don't I get in here," said Anne.

"In where?"

"In the pool. Plenty of water. Jump in and shoot water out."

"Worse thing you could do."

"Why is that?"

"If a bush fire gets as close as that line of trees, the heat'll be intense. It'll boil the water in that pool like it was a billy on a fire. Everything w'd be so hot, you wouldn't even know it was boiling until you jumped in."

"I see."

"If you must, get someone not so important – maybe Allen - to jump in first."

Anne giggled. "Then what should I do?"

"Get in the house and wait for the fire to pass over or finish. Bushfires are broad but thin. In theory, if you're caught out in bush by it you can put a woolen blanket over your head and run through it, but I don't know if I really want to try it."

"People die.." said Tomasina.

"The people who die are mostly the ones who panic. When they see a fire they get into their cars and race away so fast they crash and the fire catches up to them. This is the suburban edge so the fire's likely to stop here, mostly - unless it's a real fire storm - but it'll set your house alight. When it comes you go in the house, wait until the fire passes over, leave the house and put the fire out. House saved. Or you can stop it at the fire break line with this. He pointed to the pump. Some people do that."

"I'd – I'd prefer that," Anne said, although without much conviction. "I don't want the house scorched."

Miles shrugged. "Better get Allen familiar with the pump".

She looked doubtful but, as Allen came back at that point, said nothing.

Having completed his brief spell as a bushfire expert, Miles tried to slip away quickly but they kept on saying 'are you sure you won't stay' and offering him beer. Pleading a fictious arrangement, he finally managed to get out of the back yard into the house. Anne felt that as hostess she should see him out, Allen following. He tried to shake them off at the door.

"It's alright I can find my own way from here."

"No, no, we'll come out with you."

"Look, us bushies have a good sense of direction. I'm sure I can find my own car in the street." The real reason he did not want her to come out was so that she would not see his car. For someone who drove a red BMW, a rusty, battered Ford might prove a shock. He was embarrassed.

"It's okay," she said, "this is the city. Its big, its bad, its ugly, and you get drunk and get into fights, remember."

"Only when I'm with Jake."

"He gets into fights?" asked Allen dubiously.

"Long story Al."

"Allen."

By that time, Miles had lost the argument as they

were at the front gate, with his car only just up the road. He let them come with him up the street.

"This is yours?" asked Allen.

"All mine, and like a brother to me." Miles now had no choice but to put up a jaunty front.

Anne said nothing. In fact she had been told about the ute by Tomasina and had seen it in passing before. Allen, unfortunately, could not let the opportunity pass.

"Are you.. are you, going to be able to get this through inspection."

"In New South Wales, no way. Could cut away some of the rust I guess. But its registered in Victoria."

"Oh I see, yes. But you should get it registered here, if you're living here."

"Yep, I should do that."

"Or get something better."

"Yeah, well, you know the price of Ferraris these days."

Anne giggled. Allen, nettled, was not about to let the subject drop.

"What happened here," he said, pointing at a noticeable dent in the right front panel.

"Well, it was me mum. She borrowed the ute and parked too close to a tree at the bowls club one day. Or at least that's what she told me. There are two trees at the club which don't have a lot to do with the car park, and they had been celebrating a big win, but difficult to argue with your mum."

Anne smiled at this story.

"You didn't claim on insurance?" asked Allen

Jake had said that Allen seemed to be on a different planet to everyone else. Miles could see why.

"Allen, mate, a pro panel beating job would be more than the car is worth. Even the annual insurance premium on a comprehensive policy w'd be worth more than this thing."

"Right.. yeah."

"Some mates helped me knock some shape back into it, but maybe the finish is not so smooth."

"What about this dent," asked Anne, pointing to the back tail-gate, which was distinctly misshapen.

"My sister. She said she was backing and a tree jumped out behind her."

Anne laughed. "Quite a family history in this car. Had she been celebrating a win too? How old is your sister?"

"In her case I think it was men. Some guy a couple of farms away she's been seeing without telling Mum by taking my ute down back lanes. Anyway, I reckon that's what was going on. I never got to the bottom of it, before I left."

"When your own engagement ended?" said Anne quickly.

"Yep! See ya!"

As Miles drove off he could see Anne in his rear view mirror standing in the street, looking cool in her white Tee shirt and jeans. He did not see Allen at all.

CHAPTER SEVENTEEN

One result of Miles' stint as a bushfire expert was that Anne started to call him for more advice. What does one wear to a fire? Answer: cotton or wool, no synthetics, and it has to be long sleeved shirts and pants with boots. No thongs, shirts and Tee shirts, unless you like being burnt. How do you put water in the gutter? Block the down pipe, perhaps with a tennis ball wrapped in a Tee shirt. Then put water in it with the garden hose. Should she put out the pump now, to make sure it was ready. Leave it be; if its left out someone might take it.

The conversation usually wandered onto other matters. Anne recommended that he read 'Right Ho Jeeves!" as the classic Jeeves and Bertie book by P.G. Woodehouse, and he did, thinking himself a besotted fool. They talked about other matters, with Anne trying to trap him into talking about his broken engagement - a subject which seemed to interest her. Eventually she caught him off guard.

"So what happened to your fiancé?" said quickly during one of his bushfire advisory conversations on the phone at home.

"By now she must be married to my former best mate," Miles replied, before he could stop himself.

"Oh!"

"Yes, oh! Time to come to Sydney and become a bushfire expert."

"Lucky for me, but these things happen. There's no need to run away."

Miles sighed. "That's what my mum says, but running away is an under-rated survival mechanism. Anyway, it sorta helps if the person who has changed their mind, tells you they've changed their mind."

"You mean it was going on before hand?"

"Yep."

"You found out?"

"Uh huh."

"Don't just 'uh-huh'. How did you find out?"

"I've been trying to forget."

"And.."

"I've forgotten."

"Ohhh! Well, tell me how did you feel about it?"

"I felt awful, how do ya think I felt!"

"I guess you would, but did you talk to your fiancé afterwards – what was her name?"

"Elizabeth. I didn't think there was much to say."

"You're the silent type. You walk away from an engagement without a word."

"Guess."

"Miles, you're meant to give details with these answers not just single words."

"I am?"

"Two short words will not do either. Now, how do you feel about all this now? Are you still angry at Elizabeth and your best friend?"

"Um, hmmm!" Miles thought he should say

something, if only to keep Anne quiet. "I don't blame Elizabeth and Ben, so much. Maybe I didn't really want to stay. Maybe I couldn't see myself helping Mum and Dad with the stud for the next fourty years while it went down hill. Dad has been doing things his way and he just wasn't going to listen to me, but at the same time I was expected me to save the place."

"I see. So you think you may have not been whole hearted with this Elizabeth."

"Something like that."

"Was she pretty?"

"District beauty."

"Oh! So this was quite a district scandal?"

"Yep."

"Miles!"

"Whaaat?"

"This question-single-word-answer thing is becoming wearisome. Details please."

"Why don't we talk about your romantic disasters? Didn't you say when we first met you'd just had a bad break up."

"That was all too boring for words. I had decided that we had grown apart. I was noble about it; he was tiresome."

"You dumped him for his own good?"

"He was better off. He certainly didn't pine for long. Anyway, we weren't engaged. Breaking up with a fiancé is more interesting. So, you don't have bad feelings towards this Elizabeth now?"

"No not her. The people I've got it in for are me mates – or me former mates. They didn't tell me what was going on, 'cause they thought it was 'fun' to watch it all happen, like it was some big practical joke. That's the point when you decide you don't want to know any of them, and bugger off."

"Perhaps now they're sorry for the way they acted?"

"Maybe they're fuckwits."

"Hmm! I wouldn't want to get on the wrong side of you."

"You're different. I told you," said Miles. "I know you're always right so there's no problem."

"That's boring. I don't want people to just agree with me."

"You're right."

"Miles, stop that!" she said laughing. "You are coming to my pool party?"

"No."

"I don't want you to start disagreeing with me now, for the sake of disagreeing."

"I'm not disagreeing with you for the sake of it, I'm not coming."

Miles had been told about this lazy afternoon by the pool, which would include the usual three other suspects besides Anne and himself, but he had a good excuse.

"What? And why not, Mr. Black?" This was said very sharply.

"I've got a summer Saturday job as a stable hand cum riding instructor, if one of the regular instructors doesn't turn up, at a riding stable over at Dural."

"Why are you doing that?"

"Money. You remember, the folding stuff you put in wallets and purses that pays for things."

"Humph! Well, what time does this job finish?"

"Four, about."

"Then come after that."

"Nope. You two happy couples will be just drying out and doing heavens knows what."

"..we won't be doing heavens knows what.."

"..And single me will turn up. No good. Pass."

"Oh, what does coming alone matter?"

"Like I said, you blokes will be preoccupied with one another."

"We won't be preoccupied with one another."

"..and there'll be me," he said, ignoring the interruption, "sitting in a corner by myself, drinking beer and smelling of horses."

"We'll talk to you."

"You'll be able to spare a few words for me, while gazing into each other's eyes over a candle lit dinner table. Nice of you."

"Oh! You're being obtuse."

"I dunno about being obtuse, but I will be working."

"Humph. I'm put out." She did, indeed, sound put out.

Miles thought of the red BMW sports in the garage and the rich lawyer Allen – the man she had chosen - sneering at his car, and hardened his heart.

"Okay, you're put out."

"I'm annoyed."

"Fair 'nough, you're annoyed."

"Men are such boys!" she said and hung up.

Jake also rang to try to get him to go to the pool party, pointing out that he'd be stuck with Allen. Miles did not want to desert his friend but thought again of the red BMW and declined.

"Anne in a bikini is worth the trouble, trust me," said Jake.

Miles thought that argument was a strong one but remained unmoved.

"Seeing Thommo w'd be worth the trouble too, but they are both off limits."

"Don't think Allen's living there yet. He's moving in for the kill but he's not there yet."

"Did I have to be told that? Why can't people leave me in ignorance? Allen's established there so I'm not going to be the fifth wheel."

"Then bring someone."

"I haven't got anyone to bring. Is this a crime in Sydney now is it?"

"Not a crime mate; a misdemeanor," said Jake, who had recently been doing the police rounds. "You have to fill in forms then go in for counseling."

"Yeah? What are the councilors like? Sorts?"

"Nah, the cops reckon they're all gays who want to convert you."

"Just my luck."

He never went to the pool party. Instead he went to the football club's Christmas bash. Anne found out that he had gone to another party instead of her's and, he was told, was very angry with him. For his part, Miles did not know why declining an invitation to a pool party was such a serious crime in Sydney. It must be a piece of city culture that he had yet to understand.

Anne complained to Tomasina on the phone one day in the following week.

"Why couldn't he come?"

"Allen was there. You're with Allen. I don't see how you could've expected him to come?"

"Humph!" Anne decided to change tack. "Well, why does he have to be suburban reporter?"

"What's wrong with being a suburban reporter? I'm living with a suburban reporter. He'll do other things."

"Humph! He's a pain."

"He's a honey, I think," said Tomasina trying to keep a note of amusement out of her voice.

"Oh shutup!"

While all this was going on, with both Christmas and the bushfire season approaching fast, the Koala Bay Tower Development reached approval stage with various, tiny protests making little headway against the general community approval for the project. There were a few stories about the giant development in the metro newspapers. The story was also considered for a current affairs program – Miles knew this because one of their researchers rang him and they discussed the unusual height of the proposed building – but no story went to air. The researcher soon found out that there was no significant local opposition to it, and no opposition meant no controversy which meant no story.

The beach also started to come alive, with Miles and Emma making another double appearance to do a story on a local champion surf lifesaver team, ready for another season. He was finishing up his interview – standard stuff – just as she arrived.

"How is it going, Miley," Emma asked.

The interview had been conducted in the shade of a big oak on the edge of Koala Beach, looking over golden sand and waves rolling into the foreshore. The full heat of summer had yet to arrive, but the beach looked inviting. Miles thought that he must bring bathers into work and have a dip sometimes after work. Living well inland most of his life a visit to the beach was always a treat but not today, not with one more story to write - about the controversy over council's new waste management site (where he came from such a facility was called a tip or a rubbish dump) heaven help him.

"Don't ask how things are going, I might tell you."

"Not so good, huh!"

"Thinking of turning gay."

"Miley, you and gay I don't see."

"It's a big city, I can experiment – behave yourself with these guys now."

The surf life saving crew, as one man, had run an appraising eye over Emma's summer attire of skimpy top and jeans, as she strolled up, and had switched their attention from him to her. Just as well the interview was over.

"They're only men," she said, waving her hand as if to dismiss them but not minding the attention. "It's you and women I worry about."

"No chance of problems there."

Then there was the welcome distraction of a major case at the Koala Bay court house. Most of the cases were speeding fines that had somehow made it to court, or those involving interaction between an otherwise honest citizen and a breathalyzer. Now and then, however, there was a juicier case.

Miles had been told about it by Sergeant Wooldridge, police prosecutor for the district, who Miles knew slightly through people at the football club. As this police official was also not averse to getting his name in the paper, he was quite willing to tip the reporter off about the occasional "good" case. Police co-operation was important in another respect, as court clerks at Koala Bay did not consider it part of their job to give out information, any information, about court cases past, current or pending, to the media. In America, routine information about court cases might be online but in Koala Bay the clerks glared suspiciously out of the window where they took applications and notification, and waved reporters away.

That week Sergeant Wooldridge was prosecuting an assault in a super market by an 18 year-old making his first judicial appearance outside the Children's Court system. He was a tall lad with a long face, prominent cheek bones, lank brown hair and long arms with large fists on the end. Miles would have been wary of him at school and, as the trial showed, his caution would have been justified. Amazingly the youth had decided to represent himself.

After charges had been read Wooldridge led his first witness, a bespectacled youth about the same age as the defendant who was the victim, through his testimony. The facts were simple. The defendant had asked for a packet of cigarettes at the supermarket front counter, and the older women serving had asked for proof of age. Although the defendant had just turned 18 he did not have proof on him and he became resentful, yelling at the women and pushing over a stand of cigarettes. The police were called. The youth, who worked at the supermarket, asked the defendant to leave, and received a whack on the jaw for his trouble – an act which detained the defendant just long enough for the police to arrive. Only the victim's ego had suffered any significant damage, and it was the sort of thing the defendant had been doing to school mates in a hidden corner of the school yard a few months before, without the police being called. But he wasn't at school any more.

"So what happened then," Wooldridge asked.

"I was hit on the jaw, here." The youth pointed at a spot on his jaw.

"What happened after that?"

"I fell back into a tray of bread and knocked it over."

The defendant looked grim and scribbled furiously on a folder in front of him. At that point, he received reinforcements in the form of a mate of the same age who walked into the courtroom and sat down beside him, at the defending legal team's small table. The newcomer was obviously overawed by the proceedings, gazing around the room open-mouthed and open-eyed at the assembled prosecutor, magistrate and witness in the witness box.

"Fuck me dead," Miles heard the newcomer whisper to his friend. If the magistrate heard the whisper he chose to ignore it. "This is awesome. This all about you?"

"It's nothing," said his mate. "Be out of this soon."

"Your witness, Mr. Adams," said the magistrate. He was a red-faced, white-haired man who did not like the thought of lunatic eighteen year-olds asking questions of witnesses, but had to follow procedure. "You can ask questions of the witness."

"Yeah thank you, your honour," said Adams getting to his feet.

('There were a few dropped charges on his sheet,' said Wooldridge later, 'maybe he'd been able to talk his way out of charges in the Family court and thought he could do the same here. We had a victim, a witness and police who grabbed him at the scene and stupid comments he made later, and he was trying to play TV lawyer. No wonder the pro bono guys walked away.')

"So you reckon I hit ya?"

"You hit me and I fell over," said the witness, defiantly.

"A likely story, you tripped."

"I did not. You hit me."

"You tripped on the bread stand, when I asked you to leave me alone."

"I was asking you to leave. You hit me."

"You know, I can have you sent to jail if you lie in the witness box."

"You can do no such thing!" interrupted the magistrate, appalled. "You have to ask me and.. oh, just ask questions and don't make stupid threats."

"I'm just trying to get at the truth, your honour."

"Just ask the questions!"

Adams managed to get himself deeper in trouble with cross examination of the witness, the older lady – his mate scuttled away after that - then with a statement made under oath from the witness box which Wooldridge demolished in a few questions.

"I find the charges proven," said the magistrate, relieved that the TV lawyer had finally shut up. "Anything known?"

"Several offences, your honour." Wooldridge handed up a sheet, which the magistrate glanced through, grunted and put down.

"Well what am I going to do with you?" he asked Adams.

"Your honour?"

"You experienced a minor frustration in a super market and went and assaulted someone working there, and damaged property because of it. Not only are you not contrite about the matter, you made up a pack of transparent lies in order to get out of it. I have a good mind to send you off to prison straight away, and would have had the victim suffered anything more than minor bruising. But prison might just make you worse. Do you have a job?"

"Looking, your honour."

The magistrate sighed. "A fine is not going to do much either, so it's community service. Twenty hours. You will be told when and where to go for it. And Mr. Adams, I urge you to pull yourself together and not come before the courts again. Go and find a job and stop hitting people, now get out of my court before I change my mind and send you off to jail."

When Adams left the court he looked puzzled, Miles thought.

On his way home that day, he noticed that the fire danger indicator board had been changed from moderate to high, and he thought of Anne.

CHAPTER EIGHTEEN

Christmas came on with a rush. One moment Miles was writing about a new set of warning signs placed at the beach in preparation for a busy summer season and the next moment, or so it seemed to him, he was writing the usual police warnings that holiday makers should cancel newspapers and arrange to have their mail collected, before going on holiday. One of the last lead stories for the year was that the Koala Bay Tower Development had cleared all of council's regulatory hurdles, that the handful of objections received had been dealt with and that residents generally supported the proposals. All the efforts of Graham Gleick to stir up interest in the environmental aspects of the decision had met with little response.

"Still might not mean anything," Councilor Coustas told Miles when he dropped in to give him a few quotes 'face to face', as he put it. "Other councilors still talk 'o the time Lovett Bay Council wanted to sort out a few traffic problems in an area next to the main shopping area in Lovett itself. So they worked out something that sounded reasonable with one-way streets and two roundabouts and stuck heaps of pamphlets in people's mail boxes; had stories in the local rag, and called community meetings. A few people turned up at the meetings and make comments about the proposals, but there wasn't much reaction so council thought it'd be alright. So they did it, they changed the streets around and all hell broke loose. Residents came from everywhere saying 'we didn't know you were going to do that!'. Councilors couldn't use their own phones for people ringing in to abuse 'em. Even had guys with placards coming to the council meetings."

"But they put stuff in their letter boxes."

"People must be too used to getting junk mail; they tossed it all out without looking. Same with the local rag; lotta people must stick it in the recycle bin without even looking at it (From personal observation, Miles knew that many people left the paper on their driveways or front lawns where they had been dropped for weeks.) But that's the worst I've ever heard of. Mostly if it means something to the area, someone who does look at the stuff will pass it on. And they look at the local rag – most times."

"So is the tower going to cause problems when they start it?"

"Doubt it. It'll stand out a bit, but it doesn't affect very much and sparks up that end of the foreshore. Houses will go up in value; everyone's happy."

The building certainly was going to tower above everything else on the foreshore, and Miles did point this out in a number of the stories, but he could not think of any way to make the fact of its tallness a separate story. He needed some sort of hook to hang the story on – someway to lead into it, such as a resident's group speaking out about how tall it was, but nothing eventuated.

Then the start of the bushfire drove his suspicions about the tower development to the back of his mind.

The Bugle Group traditionally celebrated Christmas by requiring its reporting staff to take two weeks leave, but only after they had produced the bumper Christmas issue and made arrangements for the first issue of the new year. As some papers had to be in the printer's hands the moment the reporters returned from their enforced break, news gathering would be more of a challenge than usual. That year, perversely, the seasonal shutdown was timed to coincide with the likely best news stories of the year.

Strong rains in winter followed by sunshine meant that the bush around the city had grown nicely. All that extra fuel had then been thoroughly dried by a succession of hot days in early summer. As Miles was writing his last stories for the year, the wind started blowing in hot gusts from the west. Bush fire brigades went onto alert. Pleas by reporters for special issues were flatly rejected by senior managers, pointing out that there were no advertisers during the Christmas break.

By then a battle-scarred veteran of the Bugle Group, Miles did not bother to complain. In any case his particular patch of suburb was not to be threatened that year. The Brigade commanders he spoke to were looking further west and north, towards Anne's house. There were still some danger, however, and in the heartless way of reporters Miles hoped that something would burn down before his final story of the year.

It would be unfortunate for those whose houses were destroyed, but Miles could help relieve their anguish by reporting on the event. Emma lightly suggested that the solution lay in kerosene and matches, which would certainly be more convenient than an accidental fire as she could be "on hand" to take pictures. The reporter put the idea to one side, with a sigh. He was not that desperate to get out of the Bugle Group, at least not yet.

In the end, despite fires to the west and north, Koala Bay buildings perversely refused to catch fire. When Miles drove to work on Monday, a few days before Christmas, the penultimate day of the working year for him, he listened to news bulletins on his car radio about fires all around Sydney but not at Koala Bay. He had already written about the area's preparations and about how the surrounding suburbs were at risk, and the subs would fling together general stories to be slotted into all the Lovett Bay Council papers at the last minute. As he had already sent almost all his other stories over, at the request of the subs, there was little more to do but listen to the reports, and for that there was nothing quite like radio. He had bought a cheap radio to continue to listen to the bulletins in his room. This was sensible enough for Ros to object to it.

"Turn off that radio and get to work!" she shouted, from Kelly's desk.

For once Miles rose to the bait. "Half of Sydney is burning up and you want me not to listen?"

"We just care about Koala Bay, that's what this newspaper is about, young man."

"Hey I know how you can make yourself useful around here," said Miles, rising and walking to her.

The light of battle came into Ros' eyes at last, instead of simply ignoring her, that hateful reporter was biting back. "You can tell us what you've been doing about the email?"

"And what does that have to do with me?"

"Everything. You bought the computers here, remember?"

That revelation caused Kelly to switch her gaze from Miles to Ros. Kate came out of her cubby hole to also stare at the office manager. The light of battle went out of Ros's eyes, and she started sliding back to her office.

"I – I don't know what you're talking about."

After finding out exactly what the problem was with the email, Miles had put off telling anyone until the right time. After much delay the right time had arrived.

"You bought the computers, didn't arrange a service contract and argued with the guy who runs the help desk for the group. No wonder we couldn't get anyone; you stuffed it up and tried to shove it on to Kelly."

"I did no such thing," she said, continuing to shuffle backwards.

"Admin in South Forest knew nothing about it, until I told 'em. They had no idea you'd done that stupid deal."

"Nonsense!" said Ros, before she slipped back into her own office and slammed the door.

"I hate the free email," said Kelly, "I get all this junk email, but looks like I'm stuck with it."

"If Ros is in charge; it's permanent," said Miles. "No point in even mentioning it, but it was sort of worth it to shut her up."

"Stupid bitch!" said Kelly.

After that little piece of office drama Miles was flicking half-heartedly through some of the bushfire websites when the phone rang. It was Anne. His heart did a small flip, as it always did when she called. The last thing he had heard from her was that she had been angry over him going to the football party, rather than her pool party.

"Miles!!"

"What?"

"I'm at home - there's a bush fire coming this way."

"I heard about one on the car radio coming in. Said something about Mount Colah."

"That's the one, only it's not going there, it's coming here and, well, my aunt is still overseas, and the police have been telling people to leave and, well…"

"There's no chance of you leaving? Your aunt wouldn't want to come back to find a corpse in her house."

"You said houses could be saved if you stayed."

"Me and my big mouth."

"Can you come? I would really appreciate it."

Of course he would. Although he did think it hard that he should take the lead in fighting this fire and not Allen. The lawyer would just hang around like he always did. As Miles had even done the police notes on Friday, at the special request of the subs, he could cut work for a few hours and check with them from Anne's place.

"How long before the fire gets there?"

"Don't know, but there's a lot of smoke. I'd really appreciated it if you can hurry."

"Okay, I've just got to dash home for some stuff. I'll be as quick as I can."

"That'd be good. Jake and Tomasina .. and Allen.. are coming so there'll be a few of us."

"The usual suspects. I'll be there."

One block from Anne's place, Miles was stopped by the police. A single policeman sweltering in a yellow reflective jacket wanted to divert Miles down a side street. He did not have a car, just two traffic witches hats behind him. The police were spread thin trying to divert people away from the houses threatened by the bushfires.

"Gotta divert, mate," yelled the policeman, an older constable, through the open passenger side window. "Fire's coming."

"But I've gotta help people in one of the houses."

The cop shock his head. "All evacuated. Move on!"

"Okay!" Miles acknowledged the direction with a wave, then gunned his engine, spun the wheel and veered around the witche's hat.

"OI! OI! COME BACK!" The policeman was not happy.

Miles' ute swerved over the curb - with two distinct thuds as he hit it then two thuds as it rolled off - then he took off down the street. The cop glared after the car fists on his hips but then, as the reporter watched a little apprehensively in his rear view mirror, turned back to his job waving a hand as if to dismiss the incident. Crucially, he did not write down the ute's number. Miles was not sure about the etiquette for defying a road block to a bushfire, but the policeman had probably decided that if a ute-driving manic was that anxious to go near a fire then he deserved whatever he got - or, at least, that's what Miles hoped he thought.

Tomasina's car was outside Anne's place, Allen's car was in the driveway in addition to a sprinkling of cars along the street, indicating that the police had not been successful in clearing everyone out. Apart from the additional cars, there were no fire trucks, fire fighters or hoses or anything else in the street that suggested a fire was on the way. Miles draped a towel over his steering wheel, wound up the windows – leaving them open near a fire was not a good idea - and got out, wondering if he would see the utility again. He stepped out into hell.

The day had been dimmed to a red twilight by an enormous plume of smoke that towered above him to the west, on the other side of Anne's house, and rolled down over the street even as he looked. A hot wind blowing in his face made him gasp for breath – he could never get use to hot winds - then cough as smoke caught in his lungs. Red hot embers fell through this grey shroud to drop on the asphalt or the yellowed grass of the nature strip. They would get larger, and hotter, as the fire drew nearer. Already it was close; just above the houses Miles could see the tips of red flame.

A helicopter flew by noisily its rotors swirling the smoke around, trailing a gigantic bucket dripping water. It disappeared in the smoke to the north, then another appeared shortly afterwards trailing an empty bucket. He knew that even helicopters with their big water loads could not put the fires out by themselves; they were used to prevent fires reaching certain strategic points, but what was so important to the north, that the helicopter were being used there rather than in front of Anne's house? At a cross road further along the street a fire truck appeared, then disappeared going in the right direction – towards the fire. If the professionals were still going towards the fire rather than away from it, then the situation could not be too bad. Another helicopter roared over from the East towards the fire, its water bag dripping. It was time to go in.

He found them all sitting by the house's sole air conditioner, dressed as he had recommended in long, cotton pants and long-sleeved shirts, as well as boots rather than runners or sandals, and cotton gardening gloves. They also had cotton baseball-style caps with thick peaks. This was Miles idea, as he thought they could pull down the peaks if they ever had to front a fire, to avoid the worst of the radiant heat. He had no idea whether it would work, but at least they had some chance if they went near the flames. He had heard tales of people trying to protect their homes dressed in shorts, tee shirts and sandals, as if they were going to a barbecue rather than fight a bushfire. (A better idea, of course, would be not to go near the fire in the first place.) Anne and Tomasina made their outfits look good, but were obviously nervous. Allen got up every now and then to look at the red glare visible through the kitchen window. Jake, however, was sitting in the house's best arm chair drinking beer. Miles promptly took the can away from him.

"Mate, after the fire hits is the time to drink this stuff. First the fire then the beer – fire, beer, got it!"

"Not beer-fire?" said Jake.

"That's right, the proper causal sequence is fire, beer – first fire, then beer – sure you didn't study engineering?"

"Watch it!"

"What wrong with people from engineering?" asked Allen.

"Just a joke, Allen."

"That fire is getting close," added the lawyer, looking nervously out the back.

"Did you set up the pump?" Miles asked of Anne.

She nodded. "It's out by the pool."

"And the blankets?"

"Just here," she indicated a chair on which was a pile of wool blankets. Polyester or synthetic fibers could melt.

"Cleaned out the gutters?"

She nodded again.

"Put water in them?"

"No, I haven't done that."

"Okay, I'll look at the pump. Jake you and the others put water in the rain water gutters around the roof. You got the tennis balls."

There was a sharp intake of breath from Anne.

"I don't have a tennis ball."

Miles promptly tossed her a tennis ball from the stuff he had brought and was rewarded with a smile. "Wrap an old tee shirt around that, and it'll stop the water."

"You came prepared." Out of the corner of his eye, Miles saw Allen look sour. "What's that other stuff?"

"The garden hose from my place," Miles said,

taking the item in question from his bag, "and my bush hat. Used it to muster horses." He stuck it on his head, to illustrate his point.

"You are from the country," said Tomasina.

"Even engineers w'd know that we're fighting fires, not wrestling horses," said Jake.

"True, but that same engineer w'd know about protecting his face from the radiant heat of a dirty great big bush fire coming his way, and how he didn't have a proper firefighter's helmet. Best I can think of is to use a cotton handkerchief…," he produced a handkerchief of red and white squares which he tied around the lower half of his face – making him look like a bandit from an early American western, "…and to pull the brim of my hat down…" He pulled on his hat until all his friends could see was the reporter's dark eyes. Anne's eyes gleamed. "It's not good but it'll have to do," Miles said, his voice now muffled by the handkerchief. He pulled on heavy work gloves which he had got his mum to send up to him. He knew they would not melt. "Now I'm the guy with the big hose. Jake starts the pump. Tomasina gets the garden hose. Wrap it in a towel so it doesn't melt into your hand."

"Goodness!" said Tomasina.

Besides the pump and the garden house, Anne had found a small fire fighting cylinder in a cupboard, and had carefully read the instructions on the side. She had also filled up the house's few available buckets and put them in the kitchen. It would have to do.

"Anne and Allen take towels and put out any spot fires. Also, put something over the plastic fittings on the tap." Miles felt as if he was a coach giving his team a pep talk before game time which, in sense, he was. "Remember to keep below the fence. It's sure to burn but it'll keep the radiant heat off you for a time."

Anne looked alarmed at the thought of her Aunt's back fence catching on fire.

"We're not going to go out when the fire's coming are we?" asked Allen, the disbelief evident in his voice. "Shouldn't we wait for the fire brigade people."

Allen was right. They should wait until the fire had passed or at least hit the back tree line where it would naturally peter out, before going outside to put out all the spot fires. Those spot fires would see the whole house burn down, if not attended to. But if Anne wanted him to go out to meet the fire, he would go.

"What's the matter Al," he said, voice muffled by the handkerchief, "don't you like barbecues?"

He walked out and the others followed, leaving Allen with no choice but to reluctantly step outside.

In the few minutes Miles had been inside the red twilight had given way to an inky, smoke-filled blackness that made them all cough. In front of him, above the fence line, he could see giant tongues of red flames. He remembered being told that the flames looked taller close up as the image was reflected off the smoke above, but that did not help. He still felt tiny. Then there was the noise. Already it was a deafening roar, like being in the slipstream of a big jet, and it was getting louder.

He coughed again. So far the fire's pace had been sedate but it had plenty of fuel and when it hit the slope, Miles knew, it would come on with a rush. He was suddenly aware of a ball of ice in the pit of his stomach and had to fight the urge to turn and run. What would they think of him of he did that? What would Anne think of him? What had he got himself into? Somewhere in the gloom he could hear the helicopters. He tried to think. What to do?

"Hey!" he said, screaming above the noise, "get busy and fill those gutters."

For something to do Miles moved the pump off the pool decking where Anne had put it, and checked to see whether its petrol tank was filled. He started the pump, pointing the nozzle back into the pool so that he didn't lose any water, adjusted the nozzle to get a satisfactory plume, then switched it off again. Out of curiosity he took off one of his gloves and tested the water in the pool. It was scalding hot. Well, even hot water would be effective against a fire. He dropped the hose ready for use and looked to see how the others were doing. Jake was already up a ladder at the side of the house, and had stuck a tennis ball wrapped in one of Anne's old tee shirts in the down pipe. As Miles watched Jake took the garden hose, handed up by Tomasina, and started spraying water into the gutter.

Allen crawled up to Miles, who had taken to crouching to in the hope that the closer he was to the ground, the better the air. "There are water restrictions!" the lawyer screamed.

If Miles had not been scared he might have laughed. What was Anne doing with this guy? "Tell that to the fire," he screamed back.

Miles crept up to the gate and to his surprise, in the gloom, he saw it move. He looked through the bolt hole to see two pleading eyes that belonged to Sam, looking back. He flipped the bolt – without gloves it would have been too hot to touch – reached through and dragged the terrified dog in by the collar.

"You've been left behind?"

"Sniffle." Sam wanted to jump all over him. Miles let go of the collar and pushed him away.

"Get in the house and stay low."

The dog shot straight to the house and Anne, seeing that he was terrified, let him in. He went to ground in the kitchen where any sensible dog should be in a bush fire.

"This is madness," coughed Allen, still lying flat Cough! Cough! "Just think of it as smoke from the camp fire."

"Aren't you suppose to be fighting it."

"No point." Cough! Cough! "Gotta wait until it gets to the break just outside here. The cleared area." Cough! Cough! "Then we'll hit it. We're trying to protect the house, not save scrub."

He crawled up to Tomasina. "You're with me with the hose down by the fence," he screamed. "We'll play with the big fire."

"Okay," she squeaked, then coughed.

"But let me face it."

She crawled off, looking distinctly apprehensive.

The roar intensified. The fire had reached the slope. It would be on them in a minute. Time to get the hose. Miles walked over, bent almost doubled, just I time to see Allen turn and fling himself at the safety rail around the pool. What was the man doing? After tangling with the fence for a moment and burning his face on the red hot metal, the lawyer fumbled at the safety latch on the gate – his gloves saving him from nasty burns - then pulled it up with a panicky jerk.

'Jesus wept!' thought Miles. The lawyer had lost his head and was going to jump in the pool. He hadn't heard Miles told the others what happened to water in a pool with bush fire a hose pipe length away. The reporter charged, got to the gate before it swung shut then flung himself at Allen, grabbing the lawyer around the waist and pulling hard. Allen held onto the pool decking for grim life with one hand, flailing at his opponent with the other. Miles could not budge him.

"JAKE!" He might as well have been shouting into a tornado. He jerked his head against Allen's shirt, dragging the handkerchief from his mouth. So much for that idea. "JAKE! COUGH! COUGH!" In the gloom he could just see Anne's head turn and her mouth fall open in surprise, then nudge Jake and point. "COUGH JAKE!" The philosopher, bent double, came at a run. "HE WANTS TO GET INTO THE POOL!"

"WHAT?"

"JUST STOP HIM! STOP HIM!"

Grasping that there was danger of some sort, Jake wrenched Allen's hand away from the decking and then the two of them literally threw him over the safety fence. Still panicking Allen got up and tried to get through the gate.

"STOP HIM GETTING IN THE POOL!" Screamed Miles into Jake's ear. "IT'S BOILING WATER."

At least realising the problem, the philosopher landed a good, clean, right to Allen's jaw. The lawyer fell as if he had been polaxed. Miles thought for a split second that the sight of Allen being belted had made the whole thing worthwhile then remembered he had a bushfire coming. He yelled "START THE PUMP COUGH! COUGH! THEN DUMP HIM INSIDE", then grabbed the hose and scuttled down to poor Tomasina, near panic herself, by the gate. .

The back fence was sagging from the heat. Then, with a whoosh, the fire arrived right at the tree line and the fence burst into flame. Miles put the hose above the fence, just as Jake jerked the pump into life and started spraying the area just outside. Tomasina poked the garden hose through the gate bolt hole and added to the stream of water. Miles put out most of fire in the cleared strip in a few sweeps of the hose, then doused the back fence, and the still burning trees behind the fence. He dragged Tomasina back and sprayed water all over the back yard putting out several spot fires. He moved back again, and dealt with some scrub that was still smouldering. A few more sweeps and the noise had almost stopped; they could hear themselves speak again. Tomasina dealt with a few sparks and a small fire that had started in the grass near the house while Miles, sprayed water on fires in the back garden of Sam's owners, dousing the back of their house while he was at it. There were houses on fires on either side of them and another plume of smoke from across the street but otherwise the air was clearing. He switched off the pump and left Tomasina to hunt for fires around the house with the garden hose. She pounced on another flame and then there was little left to do but clean up. Everyone except Allen, who was out cold on the kitchen floor, his face being licked by Sam, checked the house and garage inside and out, but it was all over.

"You're troopers," he said to Anne and Tomasina who grinned in appreciation.

"I'm hot," said Tomasina. "Wish we could get in the pool."

Miles turned on the garden hose again, checked to see the water was cool, turned the nozzle to spray and showered her. She took it in good part, swinging her hair in way which Miles considered to be very cool, despite the heat. Then it was Anne's turn. She did not have Tomasina's long hair but she smiled at Miles, with water running down her face and into the open V neck of her shirt. He found himself short of breath. Must be the after effects of the smoke. Jake was also doused but Miles thought he just looked soaked.

"Now beer," said the philosopher hopefully.

"You bet, beer."

Sam bounded into the midst of all this also to be sprayed, and shook himself vigorously.

"Oh migosh!" said Anne. "We forgot Allen."

They trooped into the kitchen to find the lawyer blinking and sitting up, holding his jaw.

"Are you alright?" asked Anne.

Allen thought about that for a second, fingering his jaw, glaring at the others.

"I'll sue," he spat.

"He'll live," said Miles.

CHAPTER NINETEEN

At Miles' insistence Allen reluctantly dipped a finger into some of the remaining water in the pool to see for himself how hot it was. It did no good. Miles and Jake soon retreated to a pub in another suburb in the hope that the girls would cool him off.

"What do the philosophers say about bushfires?" asked Miles.

"Mate, even Socrates would have wet himself getting away. I wasn't gonna argue about the meaning of existence with that fire. I took action against it."

After that Miles did not see anyone for almost two weeks. Jake and Tomasina went to Tomasina's parents who had retired to a spot further up the coast, and stayed for Christmas. Emma along with the others he knew from the Bugle Group and the Football Club also mostly vanished on holiday somewhere. His landlord was, as usual, overseas implementing an enormous computer system. Miles thought he was in europe. That meant he was by himself for Christmas. He had always known he would have a lonely Christmas but he had not bargained on not even speaking to anyone over the holidays. His mother had given up trying to get him home too late to send his presents in time, so all

Miles got on the day itself was just two cards - from Emma and her fiancé, and Jake and Tomasina. He had planned to spend time and some of his meager savings in touring the northern beaches, but just after he fought the bushfire the weather turned and it rained. Well, he would do the beaches after Christmas, he told himself.

He bought some more Woodehouse books and a book on a particularly gory bit of English history - reading about other people's long gone troubles diverted him. He also bought, second hand, a slim volume entitled 'Teach Yourself Philosophy' intending to ambush Jake. He watched films, exercised some and toyed with the idea of taking up skin diving, but put the idea to one side after checking equipment prices. Miles did not have the heart to check out night clubs and, in any case, did not fancy looking for girls by himself. Hunting in pairs was much easier. Anyway, everyone was away for the holidays.

He almost rang Anne. He had some excuse as he could ask what had happened after the fire, and whether Allen was still going to sue everyone as he had been threatening when they left. In the end he did not but he still thought – brooded – about her a great deal. She was with Allen, he decided, because he had money and prospects, and he had nothing. He was just a reporter on the Koala Bay Bugle – an honorable spot in the profession of journalism but, as he was constantly reminded, not a high one. The less he talked to others the darker Miles' thoughts became, and the less he went out. By New Year Miles was unable to rouse himself to con an invitation to a party, and spent the night alone, watching the countdown on television.

After that miserable Christmas, Miles was even glad to get back to the dysfunctional Bugle group. In fact, as Justin had originally promised, almost a year previously, there were certain advantages to being based in that remote outpost of the Bugle group. When he returned to his desk, brushing aside questions about how he had spent his holidays, the summer weather had come back in a succession of balmy days. With plenty of people still on holidays, that meant Koala Bay Beach was crowded. Miles often brought in his bathers and towel and went for a swim after work, as this seemed more acceptable than swimming by himself would have been in his brief summer holiday. Very brief bikinis were in that season, Miles noted with satisfaction, and occasionally someone went topless. This was all heady stuff for a lad from the bush. He tentatively suggested to Emma that a few beach shots might go well in the paper.

"I know what you want in the paper, Miley," she snorted. "You want the ex-schoolies topless."

"Can I help it if they're there? A nice family beach like that and girls flaunt themselves. I'm shocked, that's what I am."

"So that's why you brought in your bathers?"

"Guy has to keep healthy somehow. Have to keep exercising."

"The exercise you get is perving."

"But this is summer, and this is a beachside suburb. What is more natural than to have a beach scene with healthy bodies in there – girls and guys."

"Lots of guys."

"Okay, lots of guys, but some girls right? We live

in a society with two genders remember? We have to observe equality of the sexes!"

"You've been hanging out with Jake too much."

Emma later produced some very good beach scenes showing groups of friends on the beach and a classy mix of the sexes, which Miles praised hoping for some more. He had known perfectly well that anything of girls alone, let alone anything saucy, was most unlikely to get past the subs desk at South Forest. The Bugle Group papers were for families, but the subs desk was also a hotbed of feminism. Very occasionally when the English language forced Miles to pick a pronoun denoting gender he chose 'he'. This was always changed to 'she' by one of the subs. Miles compromised in this silent conflict by switching to the plural form, but he good reason to believe that shots of single girls in bikinis would be right out.

Along with the turn in the weather came a turn in the news with the Labor MP representing the northern half of Koala Bay, as well as a large area north and west of it, abruptly resigning from Parliament, citing family reasons. That meant a by-election and a minor faction fight over the preselection for the seat Labor expected to hold, which Miles was able to report. This was at least more interesting than writing about community groups and in this he competed directly with the metro dailies, which printed the occasional, small article about the preselection battle. He acquitted himself well. The eventual result was that the center and right aligned to choose a right-wing candidate, as more acceptable to that electorate, against some opposition from the left.

With all of this, and as his friends came back, Miles

regained his good humor. Then a letter arrived from a lawyer representing Allen, referring to the events in Anne's backyard.

In part it read:

"My client suffered considerable emotional and psychological distress, as a result of these incidents and in the altercation with both yourself and Jake Richard Dunleigh, and has since been certified as suffering from Post Traumatic Stress Disorder. This condition may severely damage his substantial career prospects. After computing his likely loss of income, and recompense for the pain and suffering to which your actions contributed, my client demands the sum of $487,000 as due compensation for his losses.'

Miles was dumbfounded for several moments when he read the amount, then he laughed out loud, startling Kelly out in reception. If Allen had asked for $5,000 he might have been mildly concerned. Thanks to cheap living, a fortunate rent and his solitary Christmas he had a few hundred dollars set aside, but Allen was demanding nearly half a million dollars. Was the man mad? Come to think of it, the letter said that he was mad, in a way.

He rang Mr. Evans, the lawyer who was head of the local branch of the Liberal Party. Evans never wanted to say anything on the record, but he was sufficiently amused by Miles to at least keep him up to date with the few rumours that came through the grape vine about Werribee and Wilson. As it happened Evans did have some news, in that he had heard that the firm in question had got most of the money back but not all and, most interesting of all to Miles, the Law Society had produced a report about the incident. After kicking that piece of gossip around a little, Miles told the lawyer about his own legal adventure.

"He's hopeful," said Evans, when Miles told him the amount. "Everyone suffers from psychological trauma these days."

"So is there any hint you can give me about how to deal with this. I've got a few dollars but it's an air fare. It won't amount to much in legal fees."

"Well, have you got any assets?"

"Beat up car and a second-hand computer."

Evans was amused. "Ah to be young and not tied to assets or mortgages. This is not legal advice, right, but you don't need to do anything. Just put it in an envelope and send it back to the lawyers."

"Just send it back?"

"Sure. Once they work out you don't have any money worth a legal action, they'll lose interest very quickly. Trust me. The lawyers should have known you weren't worth pursuing. I don't know if there's a public liability action in it, but they should be going after whoever owns the house, and the liability insurance."

"Oh!" said Miles thinking of Anne.

But he still did not ring her. He later spoke to Jake, who had also received a writ. He had consulted a lawyer who wanted several hundred dollars just to negotiate a settlement which would involve a payout of several thousand more. As he was in the same 'poor but honest' wealth category as Miles, he liked Evans's legal advice much better.

"Mind you," he said, "it's almost worth the money to belt that fuckwit."

As it happened shortly afterwards Miles managed to get a little of his own back at lawyers in a story concerning his old friends at Werribee and Wilson. From the moment Evans mentioned that the Law Society had produced a report about the firm, he had wondered how to get his hands on a copy. The Law Society was of little help. It counted the report as confidential and was not about to let an inconsequential reporter from an obscure newspaper group see it before it went to the society's disciplinary group. In fact, it did not intend to release the report at all. Any action taken against the lawyers would be mentioned in the annual report. Now would Miles go away? Important people might want to use the phones.

Undeterred, the reporter wondered who else would have a copy. Ah yes, the police! He rang Frank, the younger of the two policemen who had raided his office, with whom he had become friendly. They had discussed the merits of AFL versus Rugby League, with Frank proving to be a die-hard South Sydney supporter. It took all kinds. As it happened Frank's superior did have a copy of the Law Society report. The partners may have broken laws at some point but as all but about $50,000 had been recovered which the partners had agreed to pay out of their own pockets, any disciplinary action was a matter for the Law Society. However, a little publicity would not hurt in efforts to find Steven Gerald Coombes. Besides his misdeeds in Koala Bay, the man had been involved in other matters of interest to police.

With the tacit consent of his superior, Frank emailed him the report.

Obtaining the report marked Miles for a shining career in journalism. In America police investigators have been known to hand over investigation files to reporters, on the record. In Australia, getting police to talk out of turn requires effort.

Miles then managed to wring a formal admission from the Law Council that the report existed but with the warning that, "the report is confidential and cannot be quoted in any story. Any copy you have must be destroyed at once".

"Okay, thanks," said Miles who hung up and started writing a story quoting from the report – although this time he was careful to quote only from the report and keep the language to that of a police report. The result made for dry reading beyond the first three paragraphs but there would be less reason for lawyers to wring their hands over it.

He rang Mr. Wilson, whose comments were unhelpful.

"SCUMBAG! PARASITE! SHITHEAD! WE TOLD YOU BEFORE, YOU'LL GET YOURSELF FIRED! PRINT A WORD! PRINT A SINGLE WORD AND YOU'LL WISH WAS NEVER BORN. FUCKING LOCAL RAG!"

"Okay," said Miles, thinking of Allen and smiling, "your threats have been noted. So what about the report?"

Mr. Wilson hung up.

The story landed him back in Justin's office with Justin, Eve and yet more lawyers, namely Mr. Bosworth and Ms. Moore - who were not happy at having to reprise the dubious activities of Werribee and Wilson. But having a report, illgotten or not, changed many things. It meant that a supposedly responsible body – that is, the State Law Council - was saying that the partners of Werribee and Wilson had been messing with their trust fund, and not a down-at-heel, knuckles-dragging-on-the-ground reporter from somewhere out in the wilds of suburban Sydney. Mr. Bosworth, however, was still sufficiently untrained in the ways of journalists to suggest that The Bugle Group write to the Law Society and ask them to officially release the report. Justin laughed at him.

"Jim, you've spent too much time behind a desk, mate. We don't write to people suggesting courses of action, we fucking ring 'em up and tell them we're running this shit tomorrow and if they want to get their side of story in, they they'd better make some comment."

"It's a confidential report," protested Moore, weakly.

"Yeah, great isn't it," said Justin happily. "Eve, it's got the fact that it's a 'confidential report' high up in the story, hasn't it?"

"Yep, second par," said Eve.

"There ya go; it's in there. No need to worry."

Stunned, Moore looked at Bosworth.

"I think that my colleague is concerned about the ramifications of printing a confidential report," explained Bosworth, smiling diplomatically. "She is concerned over the possibility of resulting legal action from the Society."

"Of course I know what she's fucking concerned about," snapped Justin. "I've been raped by lawyers before and I've got the scars on the arse to prove it. The bottom line is this; if we sit on a report only because its confidential then we'd be the first newspaper group in Australia to do it. Didn't they teach you anything in communications law, Jim?"

"They taught me to respect the law," Bosworth said weakly.

"Then what the fuck are you advising me for? So if you wanna take that report and hand it back to the Law Society, go right ahead. Miles, is it okay if our law-abiding mate here hands the report back to the Law Society?"

"That copy? No worries." Miles had, in fact, made four copies, in addition to digital copies of the text. He had done his best to lose the original email. "But they've already got copies – it's their report."

Justin laughed and, for a moment, Miles did not think of him as the enemy.

"See, Miles already knows the rules. You go away like good lawyers and tell the courts they can't have an injunction, or suppression order, or whatever else Wilson 'n fucking Werribee want.

Bosworth and colleague left, muttering to each other, without the report, then Eve left with Miles right behind her. Having got what he wanted he had no wish to linger in Justin's office.

"Miles!" said Justin.

Curse! He had almost got away.

"Yes boss."

"Did you ever find Angela?"

Was that all the man was interested in.

"Police think they've gone overseas, but that's only a guess."

"With this Steve guy?"

"Uh huh."

The editor in chief grunted.

Getting the story in the paper was one thing, but as Miles discovered to his surprise, the aftermath was quite another. For when the story hit the streets, the excrement hit the fan as it is bound to do for those sort of stories. Werribee and Wilson's first action was to send a letter to the Bugle Group claiming damages of $4 million – an amount so large, and so far in front of any defamation settlement yet handed out in Australia, not to mention the Federal cap on such awards, that even Jim Bosworth laughed and put his books on communication law aside. In a rare show of humanity, Ms. Moore rang Miles (on billable time) to tell him that they would handle to matter so there was no need for him to worry about it. In practical terms, as the article had been seen by the lawyers and discussed in a meeting before publication he was tolerably safe from management backlash - or, at least, he would be at most newspaper groups. In any case, as Miles had recently survived a personal legal claim for half a million dollars (he never heard about Allen's letter again), a demand for a mere four million dollars that someone else might have to pay could be laughed off.

However, for everyone else in the offices of the Koala Bay Bugle – the entire group soon heard about the gigantic claim - the legal letter was no laughing matter. It was assumed that because a firm of lawyers had sent in a letter claiming that they were owed such an enormous amount in damages, that Miles must have done something wrong. To make matters worse, a letter demanding compensation was easily confused with a writ starting a formal legal action. The last person to consider the issue in a mature, balanced way was Ros.

"YOU!" She screamed at Miles the moment he showed his face at the office door on Wednesday, after lunch. "YOU IDIOT BOY! WE HAVE A HUGE WRIT THANKS TO YOU. YOU'RE SACKED! DO YOU HEAR ME? SACKED!"

Miles ignored her, smiled at Kelly – who looked up at him with round-eyed, seriousness, but was distracted by the sight of Kate, who also came out of her den expressly to stare, open-mouthed and wordlessly at him. He found this unnerving. He cared nothing for Ros' good opinion, but he did care what Kelly and Kate thought and, as far as they were concerned, Miles was likely to be dragged off to court any moment.

"Are they going to sack you?" asked Kelly, so softly that Miles could barely hear her above Ros shouting.

"JUST WAIT UNTIL MY BROTHER HEARS ABOUT THIS? YOU'RE GUNNA BE MATCHED STRAIGHT OUT. YOU'LL NEVER GET A JOB IN NEWSPAPERS AGAIN."

"Will they have to close the paper?" asked Kate. Both ladies ignored Ros.

"Close the pap.. no, of course not," Miles said. "Lawyers make lots of claims that never get paid."

"HAVEN'T YOU HEARD ME? YOU'RE SACKED! GET YOUR STUFF AND GO! DON'T

EVEN GO NEAR YOUR KEYBOARD. THE DISGRACE. WE'LL HAVE TO NEGOTIATE."

"I'm even in the clear…"

"YOU ARE NOT IN THE CLEAR, YOU STUPID BOY!"

"Because we had a meeting about it – the story was cleared by the lawyers. They even laughed about the letter."

"So this is.. okay?" said Kate, puzzled by this careless approach to a legal action (both she and Kate were among those who thought the paper was already being sued, rather than just threatened).

"THIS IS NOT OKAY! YOU'RE SACKED!"

"Its fine. I'll explain more when its quieter.

He walked off to leave Ros shouting for what seemed to be an age until Kate, raising her own voice for once, asked whether she had got someone in to look at the email. Ros muttered something about budget and stomped back to her own office.

Miles settled down for another week, although without any exciting story to put on his front page. He was tempted to follow up the Werribee and Wilson saga but he suspected that this might stretch the nerves of the lawyers a little too far. However, when he went out for an interview Kelly looked at him again with a peculiar intensity, as if she expected him to be sacked at any moment. Kate also stared open-mouthed at him. The insurance broker in the adjacent suite of offices, who happened to be standing in his own reception area as Miles was passing, also stared very hard. He must have heard Ros shouting – it would have been difficult not to – and guessed that Miles had caused some trouble.

Miles hesitated, considering whether he should ask the broker why he as staring, but then moved on. This was proving more difficult than he thought. Perhaps it would get better once the other newspapers ran the story. Or would they? Miles had the report, they did not. Hmm!

The next day Miles found the card that had been given to him by a Herald journalist he had met at a press conference, when the Premier had made an announcement in the area. She had handed him her card unasked. He quickly found out she lived with her boyfriend in Bondi, but he had kept the card as a souvenir.

"Hey, Nicole, its Miles Black from the Koala Bay Bugle, we met at a press conference a few weeks back."

"Miles, how could I forget. My man from Snowy River! What can I do for you?"

"Well, I was wondering if you wanted a copy of a report about lawyers mislaying a few million dollars…"

Nicole had to scratch around for a fresh way into the story, as the Bugle had already run the story about Werribee and Wilson. She found some recent stories about the dubious antics of other lawyers, and interviewed the Law Society President over the issue of trust funds in which he commented that the society may consider tightening the rules governing their use. Ha! Story! That legal worthy also made the mistake of telling Nicole the report was still confidential and so it could not be used in a newspaper article. When that demand was relayed back through the editorial chain of command, the story was given greater prominence along with the phrase "confidential report".

When the story came out Miles made copies,

highlighted the sections concerning his friends at Werribee and Wilson, and shoved the bits of paper under the noses of Kelly and Kate, to make sure they saw it. He also left a copy of the article on the reception desk of the insurance broker when it was unattended. Everyone stopped staring. Then one of the current affairs programs ran an item on lawyer trust funds being at risk, which showed part of the front page of the Koala Bay Bugle and Miles became a minor hero. A few days after the current affairs program, Miles went past the Werribee and Wilson building and saw that the sign advertising the firm had been removed. He never heard about the firm again.

CHAPTER TWENTY

While Miles was gaining his small victory over the legal profession, life at the Bugle Group went on with Justin topping his previous efforts at demoralising the group's reporters by hiring a political writer. The concept of a senior journalist being hired to write political pieces and comment focusing on state politics that could run through all the papers was not a bad one. Justin occasionally wrote such material, but it could be done more often and certainly it could be done better. The problem was in the execution.

As all the other reporters quickly realised the new writer - one Jeremy Blackrush – was an old mate of Justin from the metros who needed a job but would not stoop to working on a suburban for which, in any case, he was unsuited. This old mate was then paid double anyone else, or so the rumour went, to work from home producing a dull weekly column that said pretty much what the political writers on the metros were saying with some local adaptations, plus a few rewrites of state government press releases which were intended to be news stories. Blackrush apparently thought that he did not have to try very hard for local papers. To make matters worse on the few occasions he appeared at South Forest, he completely ignored all the journalists except for Justin.

The group political writer's continued existence became such a sore point that Ellen from the Lovett Bay Bugle, as head of the union house committee, made the grand gesture of going down to South Forest and confronting Justin.

"Is it true you hired that political writer off the scale?"

Justin shrugged. "I thought the group papers needed some more general political coverage to broaden each paper's appeal. To get the good writers you've got to pay."

"But he writes crap! Haven't you read his stuff?"

"It's good stuff," he said, unmoved. "This week's column really gets stuck into the Premier."

"He's just saying what the rest are saying but coming out with it later. If the readers want that stuff why don't they go to the Tele or the Herald? Why bother to read us?"

"They have to buy those papers, they get our stuff free."

"But wouldn't it be better if you had original stuff that was free? If you want politics why not approach it in a different way. You've paid heaps for a column that puts people to sleep, and a few rewritten press releases."

"We get reaction all the time to that column."

"What reaction, where? We don't even get letters about his stuff from the known loonies. They can't be bothered with him. The problem is, he's just recycling stuff and you've been paying him good money. Why not promote internally if you want that sort of material? You'd get the same result for less money."

Justin did not bother to hide his disgust at that suggestion. "I want some decent writing and to get that I have to pay money for someone good."

"So you're saying he's better than us, even when he just rewrites press releases."

"I'm saying he's a good writer 'cause he's been on metros and we need to lift the paper."

"So just because he's been on metros, he's automatically better than anyone here."

"Of course, he's better. That's why I'm paying him more."

When Justin's comments were relayed to the supposedly second class journalists who did the reporting work, morale sank a few more notches.

Miles never got involved in the affair of the political writer. He was just happy that Justin had supported him on the Werribee and Wilson story and then stayed away. And he had other issues to think about. He happened to ring Jake at home to ask about a company cricket match they were organising and got Tomasina. They swapped notes about being sued by Allen – neither of them had heard anything since returning the letters of demand – and he asked about Anne.

"If you want to know about Anne why don't you call her?"

"Um – should I?"

"It's up to you, but I know she was very grateful over the help you gave with the bushfire. So call her."

This was a strong signal. Miles did not know much

about how women interacted, but he was fairly sure that Tomasina would never have said a word unless she knew that Anne would not object. But there were still reasons for hesitating.

"Um, well, it's just that she seems a little beyond me."

"How so?"

"She has this wealthy family and a red BMW, brand new, and I'm this dirt poor suburban journo from the bush. And Allen is this lawyer who arranged trusts."

Tomasina hesitated slightly. "I don't think she cares about that sort of thing at all, Miles. You should call her."

"Hmm! Is she still at her aunt's place?"

"I haven't spoken to her for a few days, but I'm sure she still is."

A few days later Miles plucked up enough courage to call Anne's mobile only to get a 'this number is disconnected' warning. Humph! Tomasina could have told him the number had changed!

Then the declaration of the poll story swept other thoughts from his mind. Normally the declaration of the poll for the local state seat was a dull ceremony held in the State Electoral Commission office in Koala Bay CBD – a smart, stand-alone office just off the main drag. The local returning officer read out all the voting figures and declared the candidate officially elected. This minor ceremony was now required to declare the new MP, who had narrowly won a post-Christmas by-election for Labor. Although such an event was normally a picture story at best, but there were hints this event would be different.

Coustas was the first to ask him whether he was going.

"Wasn't going to. Why?"

"Dunno. Hoping you could tell me. There's word around that people should go along."

Then Evans the lawyer rang to ask whether he was going to the declaration of the poll and to see if he knew what might happen.

Mystified but hopeful of a decent story Miles and Emma down to the electoral commission office on Friday, his busiest day. Both journalists were surprised by the size of the crowd. The attendees were mostly dressed for business but at the front, near the electoral office itself, a contingent of three men stood out. The leader – he wore a tie – had frizzy hair, a thin face framing intense eyes and a hooked nose. In the 1970s he might have been an academic telling anyone who would listen he was building a worker-student alliance. His hefty mates were definitely on the workers side of that alliance – they wore overalls. No ties for them. The MP-elect, Geoffrey Bashaw, a round-faced school teacher and a decent enough man was standing in front of the crowd close to the commission office's window, eyeing the odd-looking trio with concern.

Miles saw Bashaw step forward and speak to the academic-with-tie, who shook his head dismissively, and waved Bashaw away. He two mates grinned thuggishly. The reporter spotted Coustas in the crowd and circled around to him.

"G'day Miles. Guy in the middle is Barry McKinnon. Seen him around. Always agitating for this 'n' that. Wanted council to declare that marina area a park, but couldn't get any support. He's on the left faction in Labor and tried for the pre-selection on this seat."

In fact, Miles had heard of McKinnon and had even tried to contact him for comment during the preselection struggle.

"Might be some fireworks then," he said.

"Maybe, and it'll happen outside. No way they'll get us all in the office."

That point obviously occurred to the returning officer, a gray functionary in an open-necked, short-sleeved shirt, who came out of the electoral office shop front to gaze open-mouthed at the crowd. Then he shrugged, went back into the office and dragged out an ordinary kitchen chair, which he stood on. Bashaw came out of the crowd to stand beside the office window. The official took a sheet of paper from his pocket and started reading in a monotone.

"I hereby declare the results for the by election for the seat of Eastern Hawkesbury. Geoffrey Bashaw, gained 17,280 first preference votes..."

"That seat's mine!" yelled McKinnon. The crowd murmured

"..And Bruce Akehurst gained 16,196 votes...." Akehurst had been the Liberal party candidate.

"You bastard Geoff, you stole it from me!" More murmurs.

"Barry, mate," pleaded Bashaw, "the deal's done, the seat's gone. This just looks bad."

"..Brian Tweed gained 3,854..."

"Bad, I'll show you what looks bad," snarled McKinnon. Lunging forward he pushed Bashaw against the electoral office window. The crowd gasped, and took out their phones. The electoral official looked around in alarm. McKinnon's two mates turned and folded their arms as if to warn off anyone who wanted to interfere. Emma immediately went forward and to her left, to get just the angle she wanted, taking pictures. The two workers eyed her apprehensively. Miles also surged forward, first thinking 'what a great story', and then hoping Emma would not try to get too close to the action. Meanwhile, Bashaw had the sense to grab his opponent's arms and keep reasoning with him. He did not want to start his shining new career as an MP by brawling with fellow Labor party members. "Barry, mate, quit this; it looks really bad."

"Do you want me to call the police?" asked the official, who had turned, on top of his chair to face the struggling pair.

"No, no! Not the police!" exclaimed Bashaw, still pinned firmly against the shop front. "It's okay! He's just excited. Please keep going."

"You bet I'm exited," growled McKinnon. The crowd murmured.

"..Um, after distribution of preferences," continued the official, hurriedly, "the votes were as follows..." He rattled through a list of figures which Miles did not hear. He had eased to the front of crowd and was trying, unsuccessfully, to hear what the two men were saying. They had both lowered their voices.

"..and I declare the winner of the poll for the seat of Eastern Hawkesbury to be Geoffrey Bashaw."

The crowd would normally have clapped a little at that point, but they were too intent on the piece of street theatre before them. By that time, one of the workers had noticed Miles, scribbling notes just behind Emma taking pictures, and eh crowd itself working their phones and finally realised that the whole incident was being recorded. They nudged McKinnon and whispered something to him. The disappointed candidate released Bashaw stepped back and looked around.

"Bastard!" he snapped at Bashaw and walked away, the workers following.

Miles then had to tackle one of the more difficult parts of being a journalist, of fronting up to potentially violent people at a time when feelings were running high and asking questions. He dove right in.

"Mr. McKinnon, Mr. McKinnon!"

"Fuck off!" said McKinnon, not slowing down. The two workers glared at him.

Miles trailed along behind, trying to match McKinnon's manic walking pace, speaking to the man's back. "Miles Black, *Koala Bay Bugle*."

"Never read the local shit!"

"You'll wanna read next week's paper. You're gunna be in it."

That made McKinnon stop, turn and glare at him. Out of the corner of his eye, Miles could see Emma take another picture, but she sensibly kept a few paces away. The two workers also stared at him.

"What are you going to say?"

"Just what happened. You're saying the seat should have been yours. Why should the seat be yours?"

"The left shouldn't have given it away," he said, staring Miles directly in the eyes and pointing a finger at his chest. "But if you know what's good for you then you won't print this."

Miles stared right back.

"That's a good quote, Mr. McKinnon, thanks. You

wanna say anything else? I've got a whole notebook here."

McKinnon, beginning to realise just what a mistake the whole incident had been, sneered and stalked off. His two mates stared warningly at Miles, who ignored them, then followed McKinnon.

"What did he say?" asked Emma.

"Told me, if I know what's good for me, I won't print this."

"So are you going to print it?"

"Of course!" Miles was surprised by the question. "Your pictures'll look a bit strange without any story."

She giggled. "'Suppose they would. Beats taking pictures of fourtieth wedding anniversary couples. Anytime you want to show a girl some action Miley, just call on me... I meant photographic action, Mr. Black."

"I didn't say anything."

"You don't have to. I know that you were thinking."

In that playful spirit they walked back to Bashaw, who sighed when he saw Miles and gave a wry grin.

"Going to be all over next week's paper, is it?" he said.

"'fraid so. I just had a yarn with our friend McKinnon."

"What did he tell you."

"The left should've had the seat." Bashaw snorted. "And not to write this up, or else."

Bashaw's eyebrows shot up. "Did he threaten you?"

"Um, yep!" Later Miles realised he had given Bashaw something to report to his central committee. Once they heard McKinnon had been making threats to reporters he would have a lot of trouble getting preselection anywhere. "So do you wanna tell me what all that was about? Why was he upset enough to manhandle you?"

Bashaw thought about this for a moment. "Okay, look, its officially no comment from me – the party secretariat will ring you with an official comment - but off the record, right?" Miles nodded. "It was just as you reported during the campaign, and I know you spoke to others about it. The factional deal was done and the left, bless them, had to accept me in the seat and they told Barry he couldn't have it. He didn't like it, and nobody saw him for a while. Then I heard that he's angry and he's going to make his point at the declaration of the poll. I thought he was just going to yell a bit, but he turns up and does this, with mates too."

"Hmm! Who were the other guys?"

Bashaw shrugged. "Seen 'em around. They're just mates of his. Barry's living in the past. That strong arm stuff puts voters right off. Um, Miles, are any of the dailies up here today?"

"If there were any, they'd be right here asking questions. Dunno if tghey'll pick it up from the social media though."

"That's true," he said relieved. The longer the dailies did not find out about the incident the less newsworthy it would become, and Miles was not about to tell them before his own paper came out.

CHAPTER TWENTY-ONE

The only notice Miles took of McKinnon's threat was to include it in the story. The real problem he had with the story – the best he had written so far - came from inside the newspaper group. He should have known.

He was sitting at his desk on Monday, writing up the police round material and a late story – the president of the local community radio station had died, again, with the position now being seen as a ticket to an early grave – when someone walked into the newsroom and tapped him on the shoulder. The reporter turned to see a dumpy, red-faced man perhaps in his 40s, in a fading tee shirt that said Brisbane Sun set out in the manner of the masthead of that distant paper. He had a hearty manner.

"Hey mate, I was after the newsroom for the Koala Bay Bugle."

"You're in it."

The stranger looked around the tiny room, puzzled. "I meant where the reporters are."

"You're in the news room and you're looking at the reporters, all of 'em. I'm sorta busy now. Is this about a story?" Eyeing the tee shirt, it crossed Miles' mind that the stranger might be a journalist.

The stranger looked around the tiny room in astonishment. "This is it?"

"All the news that's fit to print. What's on your mind? I'm on deadline."

"Justin said something about the cops being here."

Miles finally began to pay attention. "Did Justin send you?"

"Oh right, yeah, sorry mate. My name's Martin Towers." They shook hands. "Justin's an old mate from police rounds. He's hired me for a bit of consulting work on these things."

"Does that mean you're going to help out with a few stories?"

"Nah, nah mate." Towers seemed amused by the idea. "I've been hired to do the rounds of the newspapers and give you guys a few pointers. Show you what you've been doing wrong."

Miles was occasionally nettled by the way it was always assumed his work was inferior to the journalists who worked on larger publications, and Towers' casual remark about 'going wrong' was not tactful. In any case he was on deadline.

"Haven't been told anything about you."

"Oh yeah, well, you know Justin. Not exactly the best organised guy around."

"And I'm on deadline. Got a couple of things to get out of the way, so you'll have to come back. I can spare some time this arvo or tomorrow."

The visitor shook his head. "Can't do that, mate. Justin wants me to get on. I gotta get to the South Forest paper tomorrow."

"They'll be just as pleased as I am; their deadline

day is tomorrow. Maybe you wanna talk to Justin and rethink your schedule."

"I also want to talk to the subs..." Towers said, as if Miles had not spoken. He looked around, as if he expected to see another room with sub-editors in it.

"They're at South Forest, where they produce all the papers for the group. Why don't you go to South Forest to talk to them."

"What are they doing there?"

"Subbing the papers, mate. I'm writing now what they have to sub soon." Miles was beginning to find the newcomer annoying. That fact that he knew nothing about the work flow or internal structure of the group was about par for the course for a Bugle Group consultant. Perhaps he might even be useful, if he could be persuaded to come back at a reasonable time. For his part, Towers had never previously strayed far from newsrooms with more than 100 journalists scrambling around to get the next day's paper out. He was dimly aware that the *Koala Bay Bugle* was a small paper, but he thought that meant it had perhaps half a dozen journalists plus a few subs.

"Okay, I'll catch up with the subs later," said Towers, still puzzled. "Now I thought first I'd have a look at some of your stories and we could go over them, ya know..."

"Mate, I'm ON DEADLINE!"

"Oh right – but it's a weekly and you've got urgent stories now?"

"'Fraid so."

"Why didn't you write them last week?"

"Because I didn't know about 'em last week," Miles snapped. "Do you mind?"

Miles turned back to his PC hoping that the annoying consultant would go away. No such luck."

"Okay," said Towers, after watching Miles type a sentence, "why don't you print out some stories and I can look at them while I'm waiting."

"Fine." Miles printed copies of half a dozen stories on his list for the week, without looking to see which ones, and went back to work. The printer chattered and Towers went quiet for all of a minute.

"This is a great story, mate."

"Um, oh yeah its good." Miles look across the tiny office to see that Towers was holding a copy of his declaration of the poll story, then went back to work.

"You just need to sex up the bit about the factions."

"Um what?" Miles looked up from his PC in alarm. "All the stuff about the factions is in there."

Towers smiled pityingly. "You didn't believe the stuff about the deal being done, and this guy being a loose cannon."

"The metros wrote at the time a deal had been stitched up," he protested, "and I even checked with the rank and file. I know a couple now. They all say the same thing."

His reward was another pitying smile. "If they've got their stories consistent, it just means they've all been to the same briefings."

"So how do you know any different?"

"Got my own sources, mate," said Towers, tapping the side of his nose.

"About this story? You've only just found out about it."

Towers did not break stride. "What you need is some really good pics of the two guys."

"We've got pics of the event."

"No, that's no good. I mean of the two guys."

"We've got pics of the two guys at the actual incident; the event; the dustup." Miles was past the irritation stage. Now he disliked this consultant, who did not listen.

"Of these two guys going at each other?"

"The confrontation. I was there, like it says in the story. So was the photographer. It's there in the story." In his irritation, Miles prodded the paper with his forefinger.

"I'll have a look," said Towers grudgingly, although without really listening, and see if they're any good. "We can always reshoot with professionals."

"With prof.," Miles spluttered over the word professional, thinking of Emma's reaction. "What ignore our own photographers when they get pics of the actual event?"

"So where are the pics now?"

"South Forest I guess. Sometimes I see proofs but I haven't seen any this week. Not much time. You've gotta rely on the subs to set it out."

"Right, right! Listen Miles, I'm willing to help you a bit 'o help on this one, just to sex it up you understand."

"I don't need any help," said Miles, indignantly, "and I don't want you sexing it up. You go and find your own stories, with pictures."

Besides being accurate as it stood, the story did not

need any "sexing up" or "beating up" to get on the front page of the Koala Bay Bugle. The consultant, on the other hand, and through long habit, was thinking about getting the story up near the front of a daily. To a certain school of journalists that meant dragging factions and further controversy into the mix, whether they were meant to be there or not.

"I just need to check on some stuff," said Towers, without seeming to hear a word Miles said, "then I'll get down to this South Forest place. Thanks for that Miles."

He dashed out, clutching the printout of the declaration of the poll story, leaving the other stories for that week untouched on Angela's old desk. Alarmed, Miles rang Eve, who said the story had already gone through subs onto the front page and they weren't changing it for anybody. He sent a message to Emma warning her that there was a total lunatic on the loose and then called Justin, only to get Bronwyn who confirmed that the group had hired a consultant called Martin Towers to help. She did not see any point in passing on a message from Miles. After the distraction caused by the consultant, Miles went back to grinding out the last two stories, without the help of any highly paid consultant, or anyone else.

Towers had come and gone so quickly that Miles had almost forgotten about the consultant by the time he came in the next morning.

Kelly looked at him curiously. "You haven't been causing trouble, have you, Miles."

"Me? No! Good as gold; clean as a whistle, at least

until the paper hits the mailboxes this afternoon. Why what's up?"

In the absence of a readily accessible email system, Kelly had taken to writing his messages on note paper which she left at the front of her desk. Miles then thought to check his mobile which he had accidentally turned to silent. Several of the people he had spoken to about the declaration of the poll story, including Bashaw, had left messages concerning the "story in the Telegraph". His heart sank. The Bugle group's one effort at any sort of perk for its journalists was a copy of the Telegraph which Kate looked at in the morning, and Miles looked through for local stories in the afternoon. He grabbed that day's copy which was still on Kelly's desk and flicked through to the page five lead.

Bylined 'Martin Towers' and headlined, 'Factions battle in Koala Bay' it read,

'Labor party factions in NSW are shaping up for savage infighting following a fist fight between members of rival factions at a declaration of the poll in Koala Bay.'

Newly elected MP Geoffrey Bashaw of the right and left-winger and former pre-selection rival for the seat of Eastern Hawkesbury Barry McKinnon, tussled in front of the electoral office before a startled crowd on Friday.

The two men fought as Australia Electoral Commission officer, Bernard Crossman, called vainly for police assistance.

There were several paragraphs about how the left and right factions were at each other's throats with the center faction ready to stab the victors in the back. After that nonsense the tussle at the electoral office was as he had written it, except that Bashaw and McKinnon were described as "trading blows". Miles stood there stunned. He simply could not believe it. He had been scooped on the best story he had had, ever, having it stolen off his own desk by the a consultant hired by the company. He sat down in the empty news room simply staring at the paper and still only starting to comprehend that he had been "hornswoggled" as the Americans might say, when Towers himself came bounding up the stairs. In an evident good mood, he swept into the news room and perched himself on the edge of Angela's old desk. For a few moments, Miles could do nothing but stare at the idiot, opened mouthed.

"I see you've seen the story in the Tele. Good, good! See that's what Justin and I want to do with these good local stories is get the metros interested in them and then cross promote. I got a freelance gig at the Terror to bring in more stories like those. Now this week, I'm gunna really do the blitz on this story.."

"WHAT!" Miles had found his voice at last. "You mean, steal stories from me, add a couple of pars of bullshit at the top and scoop my own paper with it? Then call it cross-promotion?" Martin, you're a fucking lunatic! You don't cross promote the paper by scooping it! And you stole it, outright!"

"But you came out today," he protested, "so the stories came out together. They wouldn't let me change it at South Forest, so I wrote it up right for the Tele guys...."

"We didn't come out this morning, you LUNATIC!"

"Huh! But you were on deadline yesterday?"

"For the paper to be printed last night to get into mailboxes by today arvo."

"Oh!" Towers puzzled for a moment then shrugged. "Didn't get the timing right on that one but, anyway, you can see how the system should work, when it does." He smiled ingratiatingly, just to show that he could be human and make mistakes like the next man.

"And you didn't even give me a joint byline, bastard!" This was the really sore point for Miles. "No mention of the paper, nothing!"

"Oh yeah, well," Towers shrugged again. It had not occurred to him that suburban journalists might have feelings about stories. "I had to do a lot of work to that story Miles.."

"Bullshit! You added crap about factions in a new top, changed a couple of references to the fight and the rest is the same. You stole it, slapped your byline on it and gave it to another paper."

These allegations were so serious that even Towers paid attention, at least to the extent of explaining his position patiently, as if speaking to a rank beginner.

"Miles, I had to do a lot to the story…"

"Bullshit! Even so, so what. The story is still mostly mine and you weren't there, I was. I didn't get a joint byline, its plain STEALING."

Miles was on his feet by this time standing right beside Towers. He weighed less than the consultant, but he was a lot fitter and a whole lot madder. Finally, realising, dimly, that he might have gone too far Towers abandoned his perch on Angela's old desk and edged towards the door, still trying to explain the unexplainable. It would all be alright if Miles would sit down and listen to the explanation from his journalist superior. Miles did not feel like listening. Kelly was watching, fascinated. Kate had also emerged from her office to stare. It was another piece of exciting office theatre at the Bugle Group.

"Look Miles, this is just a shitty suburban rag. Who's going to care about the story in this thing. I gave it some space, some air."

"You shit! If the paper's small then it's okay to steal from it? Is that it?" By then they were out of the office proper and almost at the stairwell. "I'm a suburban hack, so it's okay to steal from me? Is that it."

"It's not like that, Miles. I was giving it real coverage. I didn't know it takes 'em so long to produce one of these things."

"Why didn't you ask?"

"It all happened in a rush Miles. I had to write the story. Look, I'm right against the stair well here. I need to move forwa…"

A mistake.

In order to move away from the stairs, Towers pushed Miles. He did not mean it as an aggressive move, but Miles was not in the mood to be pushed. He pushed back – hard. Caught by surprise the consultant stumbled and fell backwards, arms flailing. Kelly and Kate, who could both see what was happening, gasped. Fortunately for both the reporter and the consultant, one of Towers' arms caught the stair rail and only slipped down several steps before he stopped, feet higher than his head.

Miles gained some slight satisfaction from seeing the consultant sprawled against the stair wall, hanging onto the rail, mouth opening and shutting like a gold fish.

"Miles, WHAT ARE YOU DOING?" Towers said finally.

"Getting you to BUGGER OFF! THAT'S WHAT I'M DOING."

"Miles, phone."

"Huh!"

He turned to see Kelly waving the receiver of the phone on her desk.

"Its Justin."

Miles turned away from the consultant and took the phone.

"You've seen the Telegraph?" said Justin cheerfully.

Miles did not trust himself to do anything more than grunt.

"Have to speak to Martin about this cross-promotion thing. If he's going to work for us he can't just go out there and get his own stories and run 'em in the Tele."

"I've just thrown that lunatic of a consultant you hired out of here for stealing stories," snapped Miles. Justin was silent. "I made the mistake of showing him some of my stories yesterday, including the one about the declaration of the poll. I was at it, not him. He stole it, slapped some made up bullshit about factions on the top and sold it under his own name to the Tele, scooping me by about 12 hours. Then he had the hide to come back here and say it was cross promotion. No byline for me, no mention of the paper – nothing. Just a straight steal."

"Look.. he's a good journo.."

"That justifies him stealing?"

"But he said he got stuff about factions. new material." The charges were so serious that, for once, Justin had to pay attention to one of his own reporters.

"Look at the version that's in the paper being printed, then look at the Tele. He's got no other sources, the stuff about factions is just crap he made up. I checked out the factions angle and didn't put it in because none of it is true. There was a deal, not a dispute. If I see this guy here again; I'll throw him out again."

Miles slammed the phone down, before Justin could answer and walked out, watched by Kelly and Kate. Ros had gone out. He glanced briefly at the front stairs to see that Towers had wisely decamped and went down the back stairs. At the peeling doorframe he paused for a minute, thinking that this time he really should not bang his head against it in frustration, but he had to do something. So he stood with his back to the frame, as he always did when the Bugle group particularly annoyed him and banged the back of his head against it.

THUMP!

That felt good.

THUMP!

Better still. Perhaps if he tried harder...

THUMP!

OUCH!

Miles staggered, holding the back of his head, clutching at the frame for support, then sat down heavily on the back step.

"Are you alright?" It was Anne, standing a little way up the stairs. She must have just come in the front stairs, just missing Towers and asked Kelly where he was. "What were you doing that for?"

"You know - normal day at the office," gasped Miles holding the back of his head in agony.

"Huh! Well, I hope it hurts bad." She pushed passed him to stand at the bottom of the steps, outside the building, folding her arms. "I have a bone to pick with you."

Someone else who wanted to cause him grief, thought Miles. Well it was the day for it. He had not spoken to her since the bushfire.

"But what have I done?" he protested weakly, still holding his head. He felt sick.

"You think I'm a rich bitch!" she snapped.

Not for the first time in his troubled dealings with women, Miles was mystified. He tried to focus through the pain

"When did I ever say that?" he moaned.

"Thinking I'd be worried about a guy having money or not. Or about his car. You're a bastard Miles Black!"

"..A guy having money?.." Miles searched his pain racked mind for several seconds before realising where this accusation must have come from. "This is something I said to Tomasina."

"Yes, this is something you said to Tomasina," she said, glaring at him in a way that, Miles guessed, was meant to wilt him. He thought she looked very pretty. "You said I was only interested in rich guys."

"I didn't say that."

"You did too!"

"I did not. I said I was intimidated by rich girls with red cars."

"You did not! You didn't say intimidated."

"It's a lot closer than your version," he retorted. He

293

tried to remember what he had said. "I said you seemed beyond me."

"Ha! So you think I'm a rich bitch."

"I didn't say that."

"It's what you meant."

"I did not!" Warming to the argument, Miles was beginning to forget about his head.

"Anyway I'm not rich."

"Excuse me! Poor people do not drive a Red BMW sports. And guys who drive clapped out Ford utes with dodgy panel jobs, don't ask out girls driving red BMWs without hesitating."

"The car's a lease thing through my dad. It doesn't mean I'm rich. Anyway, guys are shameless. It wouldn't matter if they rode bicycles, if they thought they had a chance."

"I'm from the bush. We are honest, straight forward, trustworthy and true. Like boy scouts."

"Ha! What rot. Guys are guys. Always out for what they can get."

Seeing that Anne was starting to soften, Miles switched his line of attack.

"Anyway, I tried to ring you last week."

"Rubbish!"

"It's not!"

"'tis."

"I called!"

"I know you never called."

"All I got was a 'this number is no longer in service' message."

That stopped her cold. She had opened her mouth to snap at him but instead said, "When did you call."

"Think it was Thursday."

"Well, you take your time about calling - I changed my numbers, after I gave you a big chance to call and you blew it because you think I'm a rich bitch."

Miles had become very interested in the conversation. "I'm from the bush – we have to think about these things."

"Hah!"

"Anyway, what was wrong with the number?"

"Allen – he sued me and my aunt, and Jake and Tomasina, and you. It was all just sooo embarrassing, after you all helped me. Then he still wanted to go out with me. I couldn't believe it."

"He wanted half a million dollars from dirt poor me. I asked some lawyers I know and, when they stopped laughing, told me to throw it away. They said, he'd be after the insurance coverage on the house."

She nodded. "Tomasina told me that."

"As part of that grossly misrepresented conversation?"

"Hah!" she said, but smiled slightly. The storm had passed and Miles thought he could see sunny weather ahead.

"What did you do?"

"Gave it to dad's lawyers. They said to forget about it."

"Well..," he stood up still rubbing his head.

"Are you okay?"

"Planning a walk along the beach to recover. Does the super-rich city girl want to walk along the beach with the dirt-poor country guy? There is a kiosk at the end of the beach. I probably have a few coins for ice creams." The ex-schoolies had gone on to university or jobs and it was morning; the beach would be quiet.

She smiled again: "I don't know any super rich girls, and I should get back to the office."

"They won't miss you for half an hour. How long were you going to spend yelling at me, anyway?"

"Not long, I guess. I don't know how long it takes to yell at people who deserve it."

"Add twenty minutes onto that time and tell 'em at work you stopped to help a couple of homeless people on the streets."

"I'm not rich and horrible."

"Okay, condescend to walk with me for half an hour and we can point out super rich, horrible people. Then we'll see how they're different."

She raised one eyebrow, considering the proposition. "How will we know if they're rich?"

"I was hoping you'd tell me - maybe they'll be driving Porsches."

When Miles returned to the office later that morning, by the front stairs, with Anne's new phone number on a scrap of paper in his pocket, he was a very different man from the furious reporter that had left by the back. He even nodded cheerily at Kelly, who was momentarily surprised at the change in mood. Then she remembered the girl she had directed down the back stairs just after Miles had gone, and thought that it was about time.

CHAPTER TWENTY-TWO

Martin Towers did not try to return to the Koala Bay Bugle. Miles took what revenge he could by making sure that the Telegraph's news editor knew that Towers had stolen the story and had never been at the incident. That senior editorial personage pointed out that it was hardly the Telegraph's problem if the Bugle Group could not keep its stories under wraps until publication, but Towers' byline did not appear in any of the major papers for a long time after that. The other major result from the incident was that for weeks afterwards Miles kept seeing stories in various media about renewed faction fighting in the state Labor party. A Labor party official also rang him to check, off the record, whether Barry McKinnon had made the threat described and, by the by, what was the involvement of Martin Towers? Miles set him straight.

He would have made sure that his fellow reporters knew all about incident but before he even thought to pick up a phone the story had flashed all around the Bugle group of its own accord, with the details being exaggerated to the point of Miles pushing Towers all the way downstairs. Apart from head shaking and frowns from the women reporters about the use of violence in the office the general feeling among the oppressed journalists of the Bugle Group was that Miles had struck a blow for their side, with the incident adding weight to the general opinion that Miles was an "operator".

As for the consultant himself, he tried visiting the other Bugle offices as if nothing had happened, but was treated warily. Certainly no one made the mistake of showing him their lead stories. When he asked to see stories he was shown items about sports star of the month, missing war medals, local kids suffering from cancer, brawls over rubbish collection days, attempts to preserve disused railway stations and vandals tearing down soccer goal posts. What could he say about those stories? Towers looked at them blankly. He tried speaking to the subs at South Forest but they soon worked out that he knew nothing about subbing or production, and had no idea about the pressures under which they worked. Then the health of Tom, the senior reporter on the South Forest paper and Jake's immediate senior, took a turn for the worse. The doctors told him to retire. By that time Jake was quite capable of doing the job if given some assistance but Justin, who had taken Martin to the pub every time he showed his nose at South Forest, had the bright idea of putting in the consultant as a relief senior reporter to show the other reporters in the group how it was all done. After some hesitation, an assurance that it was only temporary and that he need only worry about "big" stories, Towers decided he would rise to the challenge. He thought it might be good for a few amusing stories for his colleagues when he got back to a "real" newspaper. No-one bothered to tell Jake, who only found out about the appointment to his own newspaper when Towers started sitting at Tom's desk. After two days he rang Miles to ask why his friend had not pushed the consultant harder.

"Don't reckon it's even registered with this guy that I'm on the same paper," Jake said. "He thinks that paper fills itself. Reckon I can get him to the top of the stairs here and give him a shove?"

"Been done. Its passe," said Miles. "You think up your own way of getting rid of the bastard."

"Hmm! What about those big rolls of paper the printers use." (The rolls stood waist high and could only be moved with a specially adapted fork lift truck.) "Lure him out there; get the printers to push a stack on him and send for the hearse."

"Maaaate, those rolls cost money. Don't damage 'em. Why not try lecturing him in philosophy? If that doesn't get rid of him then nothing will."

"Could try telling him about Derrida, the French deconstruction guy. Even philosophers describe him as 'subtle', so no one else has a hope in hell of understanding him. I'll give him a shot."

"What's Towers doing anyway, if he's not writing stories?" asked Miles.

"Fucked if I know. Looking for big stories I think."

"Good luck in South Forest."

Despite Jake's best efforts, Towers was able to cause Miles yet more trouble. After two days the consultant "found" a story about faction fighting on McCarrs council. The senior reporter on the McCarrs paper tried telling the consultant that his big story was a minor dispute about parking on the main street of McCarrs CBD, and barely worth reporting, but his objections did not register. Towers insisted that two pages be cleared of ads for a host of stories on this monster scoop. He succeeded in filling both of them plus the front page and, to Miles' disgust, a cut down version of the main story appeared in his own paper. All that nonsense triggered a steam of calls and letters to Justin who finally reacted by taking Towers out for drinks one day and not bringing him back. Jake was left to fill the paper without any help.

For Miles, the affairs of both the group political journalist and the editorial consultant would have completed his disillusionment with the Bugle Group if he had not already been fully disillusioned. He knew that he should move on, but where? Having slaved away for a year and a bit his CV had improved, and he had a few stories of interest to attach to it. But now he was reluctant to leave Sydney as that would mean leaving Anne. They had started going out, with her insisting that they do things on the cheap, and riding determinedly in his Orange utility.

To keep up with all these delights and still take a step up professionally, the *Newcastle Herald* was a good bet, being close enough to northern Sydney for him to continue to see Anne and play football. The editors on the Newcastle paper said they would keep him in mind but they were not hiring yet. What about a radio station in Newcastle? Miles also tried the metro media outlets, more in hope than expectation. He put his CV out to the papers, all the magazines and wire services and followed up with phone calls. In other words, he did the rounds, but with little success. The fortunes of the news media in general were still down and the supply of journalists well up.

In all of this the Koala Bay Tower Complex went through the final round of approvals, with one of the last hurdles being an evening meeting convened by council to consult with residents over last minute changes to the complex. Miles felt obliged to attend, which meant extra time for no thanks and no reward - requests to be paid for overtime were futile - and had little to show for his efforts except for one incident.

Only a handful of residents bothered to attend, mostly retirees with time on their hands, plus the odd activist still hoping that the project could be stopped. Miles took in the state of the meeting at a glance but had to stay to the end when the convener asked for questions. The one question was a query about when the project would start. Miles was walking out when he met the city manager, Michaels, going in.

"Just checking up on the meeting, Miles," he said. "No quotes today." Then he dropped his voice. "Miles have you been going through your mail recently?"

"You mean the ordinary mail? If I get any. Why?"

"Just keep looking out for your mail," he said and walked on.

The next morning a plain white envelope arrived in the mail. Inside was a copy of the council planning report for the foreshore development. Miles knew it was the planning report because he had done a story on it when it had been issued by council. It had given approval for the monstrous building. So what else was new? Clipped to the front was a note, reading

"Read and ring me – BM".

So why was Michaels sending him a copy of the planning report which he already had? thought Miles. He flipped over a few pages, puzzled, glanced at the conclusion and his eyes widened. He read the passage again, then re-read it, then closed his eyes for a moment, shook his head, and read it again. The conclusion was different. The development could not be allowed to go above six storeys, not 11 as proposed. The first report said 11 was permissible. Miles looked back through the report. What had changed? After a few minutes hunting he found it. Two long paragraphs in the main body of the report he had, which were not in the report issued by council, cited an old council regulation forbidding development within a set distance of the beach to be higher than six storeys. The developers could have 11 if they sited the project further back from the beach, but not 11 on the allotted site. They had to stick with six, unless council changed the regulations. Council could vote to change its own regulations, said the report, but state government laws concerning the foreshore had also changed since council had passed the bylaw. Councils were free to administer existing bylaws, but changes to bylaws concerning foreshore developments, such as the one under discussion, had to be referred to various government departments including, crucially, the Department of Environment and Conservation. Any one of those bodies could delay or even reject the changes.

How had the report come to be altered?

"Miles, been expecting your call," said Michaels, when the reporter rang. "It has occurred to me you haven't seen my own little place. Modest compared with your father's stud but it has its moments."

"Sure," said Miles taking the hint. "Sounds great. Is it possible to do it tonight?"

"Miles, you're an impatient young man, no one else has what you've got. Saturday will do. Have lunch. Then you can go off to your girl."

There is nothing worse than having a potential block-buster page one story and then having to sit on it, while sources got around to telling you vital pieces of information. To make things worse, there was simply no way the story would go into the paper for the following Tuesday. He had to get a formal response from council and then fight with the company lawyers, and who knew how that would work out?

He was there on the dot of 12. It was a sizable piece of land about an hour's drive north and west from Koala Bay CBD, but hardly large enough for a proper stud. Coming out to greet his guest, Michaels could see the high countryman's eye gauging the size of the place and quickly pointed out that the horses could be run on public land down the road. Apart from the space, Miles could find little to criticise in the city manager's property, right from the horse's accommodation through to an almost adequate sprint racing track, and the three horses actually in residence at the time. One was a promising young thoroughbred mare who came over to the paddock rail to inspect the newcomer. Expecting to meet horses, Miles had wrapped up a few sugar lumps in his pocket. He gave one to the mare, who visibly warmed to the stranger.

"Misty Bay here could do with a bit more exercise,"

said Michaels. "Care to take him over a few jumps?" Michaels had a few small jumps set out in his extended backyard on which he was teaching his grandchildren to jump horses.

"Is that okay?"

"Sure, go ahead."

Miles adjusted the stirrups to his height, mounted and swung Misty Bay to the miniature jumping course. The horse and rider team sailed over the obstacles at an easy canter almost, it seemed, without breaking stride.

"You are from Snowy country," Michaels said when the pair returned.

"Born to the saddle," said Miles then swung off the horse. "He's a heap different from the horses they've got at the riding stable."

"You can stay on a while longer. Misty Bay could do with a bit more exercise."

Miles smiled and shook his head, a little sadly, Michaels thought.

"No. Thanks but no. I like Misty too much already. If I stay on I'll get the urge to go back home. I'm out now…" Misty Bay nudged Miles in the hope of another sugar cube, which she got, "and I'm going to stay out."

They talked about Misty Bay while they took her to the stable, rubbed her down and put her in a stall. By then Miles had ran out of sugar cubes, so he gave the horse one last, regretful pat on the snout and followed Michaels inside. He did not get a sit down lunch; Miles did not see any of Michaels' wife or family. Instead he got sandwiches on the back porch, where they could have a quiet, off the record chat.

"Didn't anyone spot the problem with approving 11 storeys," Miles asked.

"Outside the planning staff? No, the by law is old and obscure. I didn't realise it was there until I saw the original report and went searching for it, and I've been city manager for five years. It'd come out if anyone challenged approval, but no one's going to do that."

"But what happens if they started building it, and someone finds out about this bylaw?"

"Once the building's started it's hard to stop it or not ask the courts for an exemption. Maybe they can keep on building; certainly they can sue council. I'd have to ask our own lawyers what would happen. But the regulation mightn't have come to light until after the building is finished, or not even then, as council just don't want to know about any problems with it."

"I see.. so this was the doing of the planner.. Jon Watkins." Watkins was the head of the planning department.

"Don't know, Miles," said Michaels firmly. "Maybe it was changed somehow after he saw it but I doubt it. For something this important he'd know what the report had said, and have consulted all the bylaws."

"Must've been a lot of money involved?" Michaels, who had been looking out over his property, glanced sideways at Miles and nodded. "Guess so."

"Any idea, how much?"

Michaels shook his head in mild irritation at the question. "Only way to find out is to start asking questions and he'd know someone had given me a copy of the original report. What I want to know is why the born fool didn't hunt out all copies on his computer, and the backups on the system drives but he didn't and someone found the original – I won't say who. Now that the original is about to become public, he's for it. The police will be called; corruption investigators will have a field day. I'll have to testify. I'll have to prove I didn't know about this. Half of my staff will be called to the stand; there'll be articles in the media."

"Sounds messy."

"Miles," said Michaels turning to fix the reporter with a stare, "it's very, bloody messy. I don't want to do it. I would do a great deal to avoid doing it."

"But you've given the report to me."

"Yes, I've given it to you. Any complaints?"

"Not likely, but why give it to me? Why not report it to the Mayor or council?"

"Like any council manager I am, of course, the loyal servant of the Lovett Bay council but, as a good servant, I know when to shield my masters from temptation. They're all in favor of the project, and they may make an improper request of me. If we try to pretend the report hasn't been altered, we'd become just as guilty as Jon and he could keep on doing it. Start offering his services. Maybe he's already been doing it. Then he'll get caught doing something else and they'll come asking questions of the city manager who allowed him to keep operating. No thanks. I'm too close to retirement."

"On the other hand, if the report should happen to fall into the hands of the media which then writes about it – well, there you are. I'm not labelled as a whistleblower; and council won't be tempted to shove it under the carpet. They'll be forced to follow procedures - there'll be no silliness' or, heaven help us, breaches of the Local

Government Act. And if the Local Government Act is breeched then you never know where you are, do you?"

As he sat there in the sun on Michaels's stud, Miles was not thinking of the story he had to write - it was not that difficult - he was thinking that the story would not be popular with a lot of people.

"So are you in favour of the project?" he asked Michaels.

"'Course I'm in favour of the project. Just what Koala Bay needs, some sort of landmark. Pity we now all have to follow procedure but there 'tis. We follow procedure. Ring me during the week and tell me about this report you've been handed. I shall be suitably horrified, check the regulation and inform the mayor. We'll work up a public comment, confirming its existence and saying that we have started an investigation. We'll tell the developers the bad news and then crucify Jon."

They were silent for a moment.

"I like Jon," said Miles. He had met the planner once.

"I like him too and he has a young family, but he's been naughty. I just hope it's not too bad in his section… Good town planners are hard to come by."

The next week Miles went through hoops as he had been instructed. The story had literally been dropped in his lap but he still had to do a lot of work on it, including getting comments from all parties. He officially contacted council and, in short order, he had both the mayor and Councilor Coustas on the phone cross-questioning him about the report. Then the council came back with an official comment, confirming the existence of the overlooked regulation, that approvals for the project had been withdrawn and that town planner Jon Watkins had been stood down pending further investigation. The developer Graeme Clark rang him before he could ring Clark. The developer had long been disgusted over Miles' refusal to act as unpaid publicist for the project, and now that disgust had developed into hatred.

"You're a disgrace!" he said, the moment Miles picked up the phone.

"Sorry?"

"You heard me. Everyone's in favour of this project; everyone except a bunch of half-arsed Greenies. Who cares about this fucked bylaw."

"Well sure, Mr. Clark, but I didn't make it a bylaw. All I'm saying is that it's there."

"Bullshit! You're a parasite. A good for nothing low life that wants to throw muck."

"You are entitled to your opinion of me, Mr. Clark," said Miles, thinking that when the police came for Clark – the developer had almost certainly bribed Jon Watkins - he would take great pleasure in writing about it. "But I'm interested in any printable comment you have to make about this. Development approvals have been withdrawn and the project has to be redesigned for six storeys, before it can go ahead. What do you intend doing now?"

"I'll tell you what my comment is," said Graeme, almost snarling into the phone. "My comment is that if you print this you'll be in disgrace – you'll be disgraced in all of Koala Bay."

With that he hung up.

His friends took the news of his declared disgrace lightly.

"You're socially ruined aren't you," said Anne, laughter in her voice. "I don't know if I can go out with anyone who's in disgrace in Koala Bay. What will my friends think?"

"Your friends don't know where it is?"

"I can point it out to them on a map."

Jake had his own tale of woe.

"I was disgraced once in all of the philosophy department after a particularly nasty incident involving a professor's bar fridge."

"Sounds grim. Was it you?"

"Nah, nah! I wus framed. I'm sure it was the post doc, but I was blamed because they found an empty can of VB under my desk. I ask you, what philosophy student doesn't have an empty can of beer under his desk?"

One immediate result of the story about the report was to land him straight back in Justin's office with Eve and this time just the female lawyer, Ms. Moore.

"You're becoming a fixture here, Miles," said Justin, with some semblance of bon homie. He wanted to put on a show for the lawyers. Miles did his best to smile but he was thinking of the time that the lawyers had killed his, as it turned out, completely accurate report on Werribee and Wilson.

"Whatever happened to Werribee and whatsit?" asked Justin, as if he had been reading Miles' thoughts.

"Closed up shop and gone. They weren't much interesting in telling me where."

"Funny about that," said Justin.

"Yeah, funny," said Miles, smiling, trying to show that he too could exchange banter.

"Look the story is just completely unusable," said Ms Moore, interrupting all this camaraderie and shaking her head. "We can't write 'Council town planner Jon Watson could not be contacted for comment.

"Why the hell not?" asked Justin.

"Because its implying he wrote these various reports."

"He did."

"How do we know that?"

"He's head planner and the report has his name on it," snapped Miles.

"Hmm! Well, what about this opening sentence, 'An overlooked council regulation concerning buildings on the foreshore omitted from the original council planning report has derailed the $30 million foreshore club development.'

"So what the fuck's the problem," said Justin.

"Well, we're saying the project won't go ahead."

"So? Council's already said they're going to can it."

"But it's a big project and this is just a.. just a local paper."

"We're too small to write the truth?" said Miles, deciding that he hated this woman. She had been tolerable over the Werribee and Wilson story, even ringing him to tell him not to worry, but now she was being deliberately obstructive.

"Well, yes," she spread her hands. "I mean, too small to write the truth when it's this damaging. I know you guys want to be a great big watch dog just like the

Herald or the Telegraph but you guys are more like.. like.."

"Like lap dogs?" inquired Miles, a dangerous edge to his voice.

The lawyer missed the edge entirely and smiled, glad that her listener had grasped his point. "Yes, that's it a lap dog."

"A poodle then?"

She smiled again, although more nervously. "Well, you can be whatever animal you want..."

"So what's behind this?" snapped Justin. "You haven't called us poodles before. Lawyers don't insult clients unless there's a reason.

Her smile faded. "Well, we've had a letter from a firm Clark and Hart, threatening us with substantial legal action if there is any matter arising in the story."

"Sounds like you have a problem there," said Justin.

"Mr. Clark is a very well-known lawyer."

"He'll be even better known," said Justin, "when the Independent Commission Against Corruption starts to look at this."

"He is very respected."

"ICAC spends a lot of time talking to respected guys, just like the police fraud squad. At their headquarters, I'm told, there's one line for ordinary people and another for respected people. They say the respected person's line is longer."

"I don't think you've taking this with the seriousness that it should be taken."

"I'm taking it very fucking seriously."

"We could be sued."

"More work for you in fighting it."

"We can't run with the story as it is," she wailed wringing her hands.

"Why the hell not. We have the original draft report and Council's confirmed that there is a problem. They've even rescinded approvals for the project, which the paper has to report. I dunno if the Bugle Group is a lap dog, but even lap dogs bark occasionally, especially when a fucking huge story drops right on top of 'em."

"But I just can't authorise it as it is."

Justin sighed. "Well, what do you need to do, to minimise damage. What will make it easier for you to defend. We can't not run it, and that's flat."

The lawyer thought about that for a moment. "Well, cut it back to talking just about the original report and a different report which has – what – 'come into the hands of the Bugle'. Cut out mentions of altering or doctoring, and just stick to the statement put out by council."

"Got that Eve?" asked Justin. Eve marked her copy of the story with a red pen. Miles looked on sourly at his beautiful story being tampered with. "Now I can't see a problem with the rest. So if that idiot senior partner of yours.."

"Mr. Bosworth?"

"That's the lunatic. If he interferes tell him that I said get fucked it runs. If Jim Charles tries to stick in his ore, tell him I said 'get fucked it runs'."

"What happens if Ros calls?" said Eve. "Sometimes she does."

Miles had not known this and it was an indication of how unimportant Ros was, that even Eve had not thought to mention the calls.

Justin's face showed his contempt of the subject

raised. "Oh that's different. Ros can drop dead in a fucking ditch."

"Amen," said Miles.

Much later, when the excrement had indeed hit the fan and several different kinds of law enforcement officials had descended on Lovett Bay Council, Miles looked at his CV again, wondering if there was any way he could modify the achievements section. He typed in 'Disgraced in all of Koala Bay'. It seemed to fit.

CHAPTER TWENTY-THREE

Down near the tall towers of Sydney where serious reporters roam, the senior editor of a weekly magazine was in a conference to decide who would fill a junior vacancy in the news room. Bodies were needed to do the work. The occasional terror to her staff, she had become silver-haired in media service. She was now gazing out over the newsroom, head resting on one hand, wondering if she would have been better off preening herself as editor-in-chief of a women's magazine group, as an earnest subordinate droned on.

"Now for the junior positions," the subordinate said, "there is Samuel, who has a double degree in law and economics, a writing award from the literature board, and is a junior consultant at the Reserve Bank. We couldn't hire him at anything less than a J6."

"Yeah, yeah!" said the editor, putting her head on her hand, "a writing award, right!" At the table, besides herself and the subordinate, was a women assistant editor to something and the magazine's deputy editor whom, she strongly suspected, was doodling in his notebook. The deputy was gazing intently through his enormous, round glasses at the notebook, propped up on the stack of printouts from the week's final conference, and making careful strokes in it with a pencil. What could interest the man so?

"Then there is Brittany who has a doctorate in race relations, and a gold medal in women's pistol shooting."

"In pistol shooting?" said the editor, without raising her head from her hand. "That's different. Has she shot anyone important?"

"Um, no, no, just targets. She's a vegetarian."

"Vegan," corrected the assistant editor, as if that was an important distinction for a journalist.

"If she'd shot someone important, she could have written about it. As it is, it doesn't count," said the editor.

"We are trying to broaden the skills of the staff," said the assistant editor.

"To include pistol shooting? The way most of staff feel about me I don't care for that skill. All the newsroom's in range. Anyway, what does this women, or any of those two gifts to journalism know about getting stories?"

"They can be trained in that," said the junior.

"Pig's arse they can," said the editor. "These academics get on staff and want to write reviews on bloody art house films from Iran. The blockbuster films don't get a look in, because they're too low brow. Can I get reviews of any of the Spiderman films in? No! What I get is reviews on films about AIDS-infected tribes people in Somalia who are misunderstood but noble, or rave reviews about alternate theatre pieces that no one understands; articles that are primers for frigging gender studies. No wonder people are playing video games instead of racing to the newsstand to get our magazine.

We're being killed by celebrity rags printing rehashed stories from Hollywood press agents, and the academics we hire want to write columns telling our readers that they are a load of uneducated wankers, because they rush to the newsstands to get magazines with rehashed stories from Hollywood press agents." The editor was warming to her theme, while the assistant editor and subordinate looked on helplessly. "Then there are the political writers; what political writers don't know is almost everything, especially if they've got double degrees and .."

"So who else was there?" said the deputy loudly, looking up from his notebook.

The editor stopped herself in full flight. "Was I raving again?" she asked of the deputy.

"The latest Spiderman was good," he said tactfully, and went back to his doodling.

"And the last one is this suburban journo," said the subordinate, putting a CV on top of the others in front of him, and frowning, "who lists as one of his achievements as being 'disgraced in all of Koala Bay'."

"Oh that guy," said the assistant editor doubtfully. "You put him in?"

The subordinate had in fact included Miles's CV at the last moment in order to make her favoured candidate, the vegan shootist, look better. She had even mentioned the achievement of being disgraced as she was sure that would sink his application. It did not.

The editor lifted her head from her hand at the mention of Miles' achievement; the deputy also looked up.

"I was disgraced in Kiama once," said the deputy.

"Oh please," said the editor, "not another story about being found passed out, face down in your own vomit in the pub car park then getting up to write a front-page story. I still haven't recovered from the one about the two bottles of red wine and the Walkley award."

"It wasn't a pub it was a casino."

"Big difference."

"My mates said that beer w'd make the pokies work better," he told the assistant, who make the mistake of catching the deputy's eye.

"So disgraced in Koala Bay?" said the editor, cutting off her deputy. "That's sad. How did he come to be disgraced up there?"

The junior flicked through a couple of pages. "He wrote a story revealing the existence of regulation that stopped a big development on the foreshore. The developer told him he was disgraced."

"I think I remember that story." The editor looked at the deputy. "They were going to build some monstrosity on the beach, but found a regulation preventing it just before work was going to start. Didn't the council there know about their own regulations?"

"It had been forgotten," said the deputy, make twin quotation marks in the air when he came to the word forgotten. "Everyone was for it, but now there's a big inquest."

"I'm sure there is. Should keep the courts busy for years." The editor was amused. "No wonder he was declared disgraced - and he broke this story?"

"Yeah, it was the suburban up there originally," said the deputy. "Wasn't there also something about lawyers up there?"

By way of answer the subordinate reluctantly held up a page from the CV which was a copy of the Werribee and Wilson story.

"Dear dear, naughty lawyers," said the editor leaning over to glance at the story's first few paragraphs. "Reads well enough. Could be the subs have knocked it into shape. I seem to remember that story also got in the dailies, as part of something bigger. We looked at it too, but didn't run anything. If we hire him maybe he'd get stories? Now wouldn't that be a nice change."

"Hang on," said the deputy, "now I remember, I think this is the same bloke who shoved Martin Towers down some stairs for stealing stories."

"That was him?" said the editor, who had heard the story, "well the poor lamb has been busy up there hasn't he."

"Should've shoved harder," muttered the deputy.

"But it's just the Bugle Group," wailed the assistant. "He just a suburban journo who came from the country…" The assistant stopped abruptly, because the editor had whirled round to unleash one of her full-voltage, high-beam stares that had reduced junior editors to gibbering wrecks and cracked glass at 20 paces, or so newsroom legend had it. The assistant hastily assessed her conduct and realised what she had done wrong. "I mean.. well, you were on suburbans too boss.."

"And in the country. Three years reporting in Mudgee and two years looking for stories in Parramatta, thank you very much. Have any of these academically trained yobs – he waved a hand in the direction of the news room – tried looking for stories in Mudgee. I think not. That settles it." She rounded on the subordinate:

"is he in one of those Bugle single or double reporter papers?"

"It's just him, sounds like," said the subordinate, surprised at the turn of events.

"He's just got an Ag Science degree at Albury!" protested the assistant.

"No degree in the arts? Good. He probably doesn't want to write film reviews. He's not on staff and already he's gone up in my estimation. If he can do one of those Bugle Group single reporter papers for a year and break stories he can do anything we've got." She switched sights to her deputy. "Get this guy in. If he arrives sober and appears to be in his right mind then hire him on a J4. After the Bugle Group rates of pay he'll think he's a millionaire." She shifted back to the assistant. "Tell the writing award person to come back when I'm drunk and the shootist can go fuck herself. Oh yes, and this Bugle guy," she targeted the deputy again, "if we hire this guy it's on the condition that he has to get himself disgraced in all of Australia. I won't have any of reporters disgraced in just one part of Sydney, we're a national magazine."

"But we can't have this guy!" protested the deputy, who had been handed Miles' CV.

"And why not pray?"

"He plays AFL."

The editor rolled her eyes. "It could be worse," she snapped, "he could support Canterbury." She departed abruptly for her own office.

"There's nothing wrong with the Bulldogs," said the deputy to the assistant. The assistant rolled her eyes.

The meeting was over.

Two weeks later near the end of another busy day, Miles dropped into South Forest headquarters carrying an unsealed envelope containing his short resignation letter. He waved at the journalists on the reporter's side of the room, which included Jake, and nodded at the subs – he would mingle in a moment. Then he found that Bronwyn was not at her usual perch guarding the entrance to Justin's office. As he approached, the door opened and a small man with a fringe of white hair, wearing a tie but no coat, came out of the office.

"You must be one of the reporters," he said, stepping away from the door. "Jim Charles." He offered his hand.

"Oh you're Mr. Charles," said Miles, shaking the chief executive's hand. "I'm Miles Black."

The older man's eyes were briefly round with astonishment, "Oh you're Miles Black."

"The same."

"Heard a lot about you." He said, looking down and shuffling his feet.

"I've no doubt," said Miles, cheerfully. "And now I can tell you it's all true."

"It is?" Charles looked up in surprise.

"Uh huh! But listen Mr. Charles, did you know we don't have email up there and we can't get IT support to return our calls."

"Um no." Mr. Charles was surprised by the sudden turn in conversation. "Why don't they return your calls?"

"Because we're not part of the network they're contracted for."

".. not part of..," Charles was clearly astonished. "How is that so?"

"Your sister bought the computers, had them installed and won't pay for IT support. We're not on the same network as everyone else."

"Oh! No one's told me anything about this. How long has this been going on?"

"Since last year?"

The chief executive seemed stunned. "And no-one said anything?"

"We complained to everyone we could think of. No result."

"I see. I will look into this immediately, and try to get a technician there tomorrow. We must have all our people on the company email system."

"We'd really appreciate it."

"Perhaps not all my sister said about you is true Miles," said Charles, offering his hand again as a way of saying goodbye.

"Nah! I'm really worse then she says."

His business with Mr. Charles complete, Miles pushed open the door to Justin's office to find the editor in chief sitting at his desk, staring into space.

"You don't have another bloody scoop do you?" he asked sourly, when Justin realised the reporter was there. By way of reply Miles offered him the unsealed envelope, meaning for him to take it. Justin looked at it but did not bother to reach for it. He knew perfectly well what the envelope contained. It had happened often enough.

"Always knew you'd go," he said sourly. "Chuck it in the in tray." He indicated the near empty tray in the right hand corner of the desk which Miles had noticed in his first interview. "Have you put in any personal abuse." Miles shook his head. "Two weeks from Friday alright? I wouldn't want to keep you from your new employment niche too long."

"Two weeks is fine."

"You know, the reason I never bother to give pay rises is that people like you shoot through no matter how much extra we pay." Miles opened his mouth to retort that at least the Bugle Group could treat its reporters like human beings, but shut it again without saying anything. Something told him that Justin was not interested in being lectured, yet again, about journalist's rights. He dropped the envelope into the indicated tray, and then noticed the tray on the other side of Justin's desk piled high with papers. On the top page of that pile he could just make out the word 'resume'.

"I've found Angela," Miles said.

"Yeah?" Justin was now more interested in the conversation. "Where's she gone?"

"Singapore."

"Singapore? How do you know she's there?"

"She's on TV. I saw her when I passed a shop selling entertainment systems, presenting a cable TV news bulletin in English, from Singapore. She's just bright enough to read the auto queue, she's had her teeth capped and she smiled at the end. They must have told her to smile. She looks good."

"Was this Steve person there?"

"On the show? No, he's selling ads for the station."

"Suddenly you know all this?"

"I rang up the station and asked for a guy called Steve connected to Angela, saying I'd met him at a party. They said he was in a meeting, but if it was about advertising there were other people I could talk to."

"Sounds like they didn't get much money from that scam?"

"They got some but must've run through it. Told it often happens with fraudsters; they run though it just as quickly as they make it."

Miles did not tell his boss that he also intended to curry a little favour with his police contacts by informing them of the whereabouts of Steven Gerard Coombes.

"You didn't think much of her, did you?"

"Angela? There was nothing to think about. As a reporter she was hopeless."

"Hmm! So where are you going?" Miles told him and for an instant, a split second, Justin's eyes flashed with what Miles supposed was a look of envy. Then the look was gone and the editor in chief seemed bleaker and older. "It's better to be on the way up, Miles," he said after a moment, "than on the way down. Take it from me. At least you get to be on a real publication for a change."

"Whadda you mean?" said Miles indignantly. "I am on a 'real' publication, I turned it into a real newspaper. Why don't you make an effort to make sure it stays that way?"

Justin was startled at the response, but before he could think of a retort Miles walked out, leaving the editor in chief to his dusty souvenirs. He would tell Eve the news, then the others. Then he would debate the existence of beer with Jake but only a little, as he was also going to meet Anne to celebrate. There were no windows in the South Forest news room but outside, he knew, the day was bright.

AFTERWORD

I doubt if there are now many newsrooms on the give-away suburban newspapers quite as lonely as that of the Koala Bay Bugle. I was in such a newsroom in Melbourne's Eastern suburbs in the 1980s, but that was before the patchwork of tiny councils – each council area being serviced by its own newspaper - were all swept up into much larger organisations. My understanding is that the tiny publications I worked on back then have all long since also been merged into larger publications.

When I wrote this book some years back I switched the action to Sydney, replacing the Ku-ring-gai Chase national park close to when I live in Hornsby with suburbia, and using place names from there for my localities. I send no apology to the park's many supporters for this fictional desecration. They'll just have to deal with it.

Reviewing the book now, eight years after putting it on the shelf (it got a second reading with one major publisher) I realized that technology and trends in newspapers have moved on quite a way. However, essentially the background is 1980s Melbourne suburban reporting shifted to Sydney, with some high-tech additions, such as mentions of web sites, email, mobile phones and social media – the inventions which have been slowly killing off traditional newspapers. Readers can make of that mish-mash what they will.

As for the events and characters some, and I emphasise some, of what I wrote is heavily fictionalized echoes of people and events that I encountered. In particular, I never knew anyone like Justin, Ros, Angela or Martin Towers, worked anywhere that was quite so dismissive of its journalist staff as the Bugle Group, or where an administrative assistant like Bronwyn would be allowed to meddle in editorial matters. Instead, I hope, the tale reflects the frustration which journalists do often feel with management, rightly or wrongly. Also, it should show that they kept on reporting independently despite, seemingly, every man and women's hand raised against them.

Below are some notes for non-Australian readers of this e-book.

Bogan – Anne calls Miles a bogan – a term unknown outside Australia and New Zealand. A translation may be crass working class. For Americans a translation may be white trash, but this seems harsh. My daughter, a trained, experienced bogun spotter, tells me that a barefoot, tattooed pregnant women who is smoking may be considered bogan. The definition is flexible, however, and Anne was simply teasing Miles. There are proud boguns, and I would not dream of contesting their right to be proud.

Christmas – this occurs during the Australian summer, so the Christmas-New Year period and the weeks after it are the natural holiday time in Australia, hence the two week break for the hard-working journalists on The Bugle Group.

Councils – there are three tiers of government in Australia, Federal and state governments and then local councils. Most government services are provided by the states. Local governments concern themselves with roads, rates, refuse and urban planning.

Factions – the Labor party is loosely organized into three factions – center, left and right - which rub along, more or less. As part of that co-existence they do deals with one another in which they trade off which faction's candidate gets what position in the party or which Labor seat. The factions are not everything. Independents still get spots. But there are those who say that they matter too much.

Football – football codes split along state lines in Australia. In the South and West the dominant football code is Australian rules. In the North and East, notably in the states of Queensland and New South Wales, which includes Sydney, it is rugby league. Arguably Australian rules is more widespread, but both codes are played everywhere as is soccer, which is gaining coverage, and rugby union.

Kiwi – an Australian term for a New Zealander. Quite a lot of them in Australia in general and journalism in particular.

Ute – utility vehicle. Think American pick-up truck but with an extended space at the back and room for just two in the driver's cab.

Walkley award – Australian Pulitzer Prize

Mark Lawson worked as a journalist for 38 years, the bulk of that time on the finance daily, The Australian Financial Review. He has previously written two non-fiction books. He lives in Sydney with his family.

Printed in the United States
By Bookmasters